SUNSHINE WAKES UP GRUMPY

A SMALL-TOWN ROMANCE WITH COFFEE, KIDS AND COMPLICATED FEELINGS.

SABLE BURNS

Lumora Press

To request permission for use beyond brief excerpts or review purposes, please contact:

hello@lumorapress.com

Thank you for supporting authors, original storytelling, and the creative process.

www.LumoraPress.com | hello@lumorapress.com

ISBN: 978-0-9828108-6-6 (ePub)

ISBN: 978-0-9828108-9-7 (Paperback)

Formerly published as "Brewing Truth" (ISBN: 9780982810859)

Edition 2.2

SUNSHINE WAKES UP GRUMPY

For my father,
Louie Edward Barta, II—
who taught me that real love is sacred, practical, and shown
through good coffee, a slice of apple pie, and a sense of humor.

ONE
BLACKOUT COFFEE

MAX

THERE ARE a few things in life I take seriously: my kids, my farm, and my coffee.

I'd throw "my sanity" in there, but that ship sailed when Oliver, my son, built a homemade trebuchet and accidentally launched a pumpkin through the barn roof.

I need caffeine before dealing with the latest adventure in single parenthood, which is why I'm standing in line at Perk Up, the only coffee shop in Willow Creek.

Willow Creek is small-town Pennsylvania at its finest. The kind of place where everyone knows your name, your family history, and what brand of butter you buy. Willow Creek isn't the kind of place you move to for excitement. It's the kind of place you settle in because you want quiet mornings, neighbors who know your name, and a Main Street that looks like something out of a Hallmark movie, if Hallmark had more farm trucks and fewer people randomly falling in love at Christmas.

It's a day's drive from the nearest city, surrounded by farmland, rolling hills, and woods that turn postcard-perfect in the fall. The town square is a collection of mom-and-pop stores, including this café, a hardware store that still sells nails by the pound, and a grocery store where the owner will absolutely judge your snack purchases.

I live ten miles out, where cell service is optional and the rooster does not care if it's the weekend. But the sunrise over my fields is mandatory viewing.

My farm's small by corporate standards, but plenty for me: organic vegetables, pasture-raised livestock, a greenhouse I built myself, and an ever-growing list of repairs. I'd rather be there, but I dropped the kids at school, and my tractor parts won't pick themselves up. And if I don't get coffee first, I will absolutely regret it.

That's where this morning takes a turn.

"Morning, Max! Want to try our seasonal special—Cinnamon Honey Lavender Delight?"

The barista grins at me like this is the day I break my streak of ordering black coffee.

I blink. "That's a lot of flavors for one cup."

"It's like a hug in a mug."

"I don't need a hug. Just the usual. Black. No sugar. No nonsense."

A soft, amused snort comes from directly behind me.

"Wow," a woman says. "That's tragic."

I turn slightly and find myself facing someone I definitely would've remembered meeting before.

She's standing too close, because of course she is—it's a small-town coffee shop, and personal space is more of a concept than a practice here. She's got hazel eyes sharp enough to slice through nonsense, dark hair pulled into a high ponytail, and the general air of someone who gets what she wants. Dressed in a designer-fitted blazer over dark jeans and boots, she looks like she belongs somewhere important —like a city or a high-powered meeting—not here.

And then it clicks.

Elle Sinclair.

Editor of *The Willow Gazette,* the town's small but surprisingly fierce newspaper. I don't read it often, but I've seen her name on opinion pieces that make the local government sweat. I know of her, but I don't know her personally.

Yet here she is, standing way too close, eavesdropping on my coffee order.

"My experience is waking up," I tell her. "Not drinking a melted Yankee Candle."

Her lips twitch. "That's an uninspired way to start the day."

"I own a farm. My days start with roosters and whatever my son's broken in the last 24 hours. This is survival, not art."

"Hmm," she hums, clearly unimpressed. "I'll have the seasonal special with an extra shot, please."

The barista beams at her, and I swear the cash register dings in approval. "A woman of taste!"

"Debatable," I mutter.

"You say that now, but one sip and you'll be rethinking your entire life."

I let out a low laugh. "Highly unlikely."

We move to the side to wait for our drinks. Normally, I'd take mine and leave, but for some reason the barista is still making it. Maybe I look extra tired today. Maybe she's adding an extra shot out of pity. Either way, I wait.

Elle glances at me. "You always this grumpy before coffee?"

"I prefer focused."

"That's just grumpy with a thesaurus."

I shake my head, fighting a smile.

She tilts her head slightly. "Do I know you?"

"Probably not."

"You look familiar."

I shrug. "I've been here a while."

"Oh," she muses. "That's right. You're the mysterious farmer raising two kids out in the middle of nowhere."

I raise a brow. "Mysterious?"

"Well, I don't think you have any social-media presence, and that makes you an enigma in this day and age."

I snort. "Trust me, I'm not interesting enough for social media."

"People say that, and then you find out they've had a secret past as a pirate or an underground poker champion."

"I'm neither of those things."

"Shame."

The lights flicker.

Darkness.

A collective groan rolls through the café. Looking around, I realize it is only me, Elle, and an older man in the corner muttering complaints about the power grid. The sound of the espresso machine dramatically dying in the kitchen signals just how much of a problem we've been thrown into.

Elle shifts beside me. "Well, this is unfortunate."

"You sound amused."

"I am. Something about standing in a coffee shop without power is ironic."

"Yeah, real knee-slapper."

The glow of the streetlights barely filters in, casting us both in shadows and dim gold reflections. It's weirdly intimate for two people who just met, but somehow I don't mind.

"So," she muses, "what's the protocol for a power outage in a small town? Someone call the mayor? Summon a town meeting?"

"No, we just panic and start looting."

She laughs, genuine and warm. "Good to know."

I shift, oddly aware that it's just the two of us talking in the dark, our voices the only thing filling the space.

"Let me guess," she says. "Your farm prepared you for this."

"I wouldn't say prepared. More like... resigned."

She chuckles. "Ever milk a cow by flashlight?"

"Last week, actually."

"I was kidding."

"I wasn't."

Another pause. "Well, I suddenly feel like my life is missing adventure."

I snort. "Yes, nothing screams 'adventure' like a pitch-black barn and an annoyed dairy cow."

She leans against the counter, intrigued. "Tell me more."

"I don't know. This is top-secret farmer intel."

"I swear I won't leak it to the press."

"You are the press, aren't you?"

"But I won't leak it."

The shadows and dim gold reflections give us cover to risk a real connection.

My eyes move up to look at her. She is already looking at me.

Our eyes lock, and in a breath, something passes between us.

She smiles.

I smile, but I don't look away.

"Beautiful." I realize that thought escaped through my lips. "Ah, the sunrise this morning—I caught it just as the geese took off from the field, their underwings reflecting the brilliant colors of the emerging sun as they banked. Did you see it?"

"Not over your field. Sounds like another adventure I've missed."

The lights suddenly surge back on, cutting the moment in half. The barista cheers from the kitchen, and Elle pretends she's not disappointed.

We both turn back to the counter, where our drinks are finally ready.

I reach for mine.

She reaches for hers.

I take a sip. My soul leaves my body.

"What in fresh hell—" I cough, gripping the counter for support.

Elle laughs way too hard.

She grins, raising her cup to her lips. "You're over-reacting."

Then she takes a sip of what should've been mine. Her entire face convulses in betrayal.

I shove the cup toward her. "Take it back. Take it back right now."

"Max." She chokes. "This isn't coffee. This is punishment."

"Right back at you."

We switch cups, still suffering.

"Okay," she concedes, "maybe our coffee tastes are too different for us to be friends."

"Who said we were going to be friends?"

She arches a brow. "Oh, we're going to be something."

As she strides out, I sip my reclaimed coffee, watching her go.

Interesting. So that's Elle Sinclair.

That was unexpected.

TWO
THE LIBRARY BOARD GAMES

ELLE

THERE'S one universal truth in small towns: if the mayor calls you, you pick up.

Because if you don't, they'll find you—at the grocery store, at the post office, mid-latte at Perk Up, or worse, during a town event where they can guilt you in front of witnesses.

That's why, when my phone buzzes with Mayor Hank Calloway's name, I consider yeeting it into the nearest corn-field. Instead, I sigh and answer.

"Elle Sinclair."

"Elle!" Mayor Calloway's voice booms through the receiver like he's announcing a high-school football game. "Hope I didn't catch you at a bad time."

I glance at my laptop screen, where a half-finished article on pothole-repair politics is taunting me.

"Not at all," I say, lying like a professional. "What's up?"

"Well, we've got an open seat on the Library Board, and I immediately thought of you."

I pause. "I'm sorry, why?"

"Because you're a pillar of the community and believe in literacy."

I narrow my eyes. "And?"

"...And I still have a seat to fill."

Ah. There it is.

"Mayor, I'm flattered, but—"

"Elle, the Library Board needs someone who understands books and isn't afraid to speak her mind."

Well. He's got me there.

As the editor of *The Willow Gazette,* I spend my life advocating for funding public institutions, free speech, and the radical idea that libraries should have books people actually want to read.

I chew my lip, seconds from caving.

"Who else is on the Board?" I ask.

"Oh, you'll love them! Great group. Also, Max Donovan just agreed to join."

...Wait.

Max? As in black-coffee-no-nonsense Max? The grumpy farmer I spent an alarmingly enjoyable morning verbally sparring with?

I lean back in my chair. "Max said yes?"

"Yep! Just talked to him this morning."

Now, I don't know Max well, but nothing about our caffeine-fueled, blackout-induced banter suggested he was the volunteering type.

This feels suspicious.

"Fine," I say, because curiosity is my greatest weakness. "I'm in."

"Fantastic! First meeting's at six."

"Tonight?"

"You know how it is, Elle. No time like the present!"

The plot reveals itself, I've been trapped.

THE WILLOW CREEK Library Board meets in a conference room straight out of a government procedural drama. The walls are off-white in the way that suggests they used to be white but lost the will to live. The chairs are a crime against lumbar support. There's a large oak table in the center, covered in stacks of paper, coffee rings, and at least two pairs of forgotten reading glasses.

It smells like books, cleaning agents, and bureaucracy.

I step inside and scan the table.

The faces are exactly who I expected: Mrs. Edna Thompson, the head librarian with a death glare that could melt steel. Her glasses hang around her neck on a beaded chain with pineapples, coconuts, and pink-flamingo bead accents. Ed Mulligan, the retired school principal who still treats everyone like a delinquent teenager. His shirt's breast pocket holds a pocket protector with several pens clipped inside. Janine Moore, who runs the bakery and only volunteers for things so she can "accidentally" promote her pastries. She wears a white baker's jacket, and her hair is pulled back into a ponytail.

And then there's Max Donovan.

Sitting across the table, arms crossed, looking exactly as enthused as I feel.

He's in a dark Henley and worn jeans, his sleeves pushed up just enough to be distracting. His reddish hair's still a little messy, like he was either in a rush or just gave up halfway through fixing it.

His eyes meet mine.

There's a half-second pause before he says, deadpan, "Oh. It's you."

I flash a toothy grin. "Surprise!"

His lips twitch like he's fighting a very reluctant smile.

Before we can get any deeper into our unspoken war of sarcasm, Mayor Calloway claps his hands. "Let's get started! Sorry, but the gavel is missing."

"Thank God for little blessings," Mrs. Thompson mumbles.

"And what did that mean, Edna?" Mayor Calloway asks.

"Just that you love to pound on things, Hank. Since you were a little child. The only reason you run for office is because you get to pound your gavel. It's noisy."

"Edna, if I find you purposefully misplaced the gavel, we'll have words. Not kind words."

"Oh, get over yourself, Hank. I used to change your diapers, so watch your tone with me."

Chairs scrape on the floor as we all sit at the table.

Mayor Calloway huffs and turns back to the rest of us.

"I call to order the Willow Creek Library Board meeting." I notice Max glance at his phone—a message. He smiles, then taps the thumbs-up and puts the phone facedown on the table. Shallow applause brings my attention back to the meeting. The others are looking at me and Max with *I-feel-your-pain* smiles, clapping.

"Can I ask a question?" Max leans forward.

"Go ahead."

"Does the library carry young-adult fantasy novels, like

this series all the kids are crazy about—Ver-die-on," Max stumbles over the name.

"*Veridion Chronicles?* It's like very-dion — say it fast, with the emphasis on the di in *dion*." I assist.

"Thanks. *Veridion Chronicles?* My children love them, and they seem to have good core values."

"Yes, we have them, along with the months-long waiting list. The third book will be released in two or three months, and there's already a waiting list. I don't judge what our young people are reading. That series is on so many lists, we felt obligated to add it to our collection." Mrs. Thompson shares her disapproving look.

"Well, if they're that popular, shouldn't we get more copies—digital or paper? I mean, reading is a skill best learned by doing, so if the kids want to read, we should encourage it, shouldn't we?" Max's face shifts like he realizes the deadpan expressions are just tolerating his interruption because we're new.

"Collection concerns will be addressed at the next meeting, or I'm sure Mrs. Thompson will be happy to show you our collection policy. Tonight we have an agenda, so let's get to it. Old business, reports, ready?" Mayor Calloway nods to Mrs. Thompson, who has papers in front of her.

After covering so many of these tedious meetings for the *Gazette,* what am I thinking, agreeing to this? Oh yes— my fellow sufferer, Max. I enjoy our banter.

"So," Mrs. Thompson says, adjusting her reading glasses like she's about to deliver a verdict, "the question at hand: should we add a coffee and/or snack bar to the library?"

Janine Moore, our pastry chef, beams. "I think it's a wonderful idea! Imagine, books and freshly baked pastries

—a perfect pairing! And the town already has a discounted account at my bakery."

"Libraries aren't cafés. They're places of learning," Ed Mulligan grunts.

Max shifts in his chair. "Can I ask the obvious question?"

Mayor Calloway gestures. "Go ahead."

"Why is this a debate?" Max asks. "People drink coffee while they read. Seems logical."

Mrs. Thompson zeroes in on him like a hawk. "You believe in logic?"

"Only before my first cup of coffee."

I cough to cover a laugh.

Ed squints. "You'd support this... frivolous addition?"

Max shrugs. "If it makes people use the library more, sure."

Janine practically vibrates with enthusiasm. "Exactly! We could hold book clubs, poetry readings—"

"—open-mic nights," I add.

Max shoots me a look. "Oh, great. Now you're getting ideas."

I grin. "Terrifying, isn't it?"

Ed leans forward. "What about the maintenance costs? People can be filthy. Ask any principal. The library doesn't clean itself. How would allowing food and drinks affect the building?"

I roll my eyes. Leave it to Ed. I open my mouth to respond, but Max shoots me a look—a flicker of amusement in his eyes—and I know he's thinking the same thing. I stifle a laugh.

"We wouldn't allow them to have food or drinks all over

the library, Ed. Just designated areas, like the coffee bar. A few tables and chairs. Maybe a library book," I add.

"They'd better not get those library books messy. I won't have that," Mrs. Thompson warns. "You don't know what we have to do to get them into our collection."

"Edna, I think we all understand the stellar job you do in managing our fine collection. But today's people have health reasons for drinking often, even if it's just water. I'm sure the town can adjust the library budget to help cover any damage by adding the coffee bar." Mayor Calloway adds, "We just put a coffee kiosk in the lobby of our new city-government center. It's the wave of the future, Edna."

"Oh? Then why couldn't the town increase the library budget when I was asking to update our technology section and periodicals? That was important—it supports our young people in getting good jobs."

"A solid academic curriculum is what it takes for our young people to get good jobs. This vocational nonsense— A.I., digital media, theatre, cooking—I say we need to restore a good classical curriculum. That I can support." Ed leans back from the table.

"I know I'm new, but aren't we getting off-topic? Ambiguous emotional sentiment won't get us to a good decision," I offer.

Mrs. Thompson sighs. "Right. We need facts, not feelings."

"How about we do a trial run—a pop-up coffee shop for a weekend," Max offers.

"Good idea. All those opposed? Passed." Mayor Calloway taps the table.

Ed folds his arms. "Fine. But if this turns into a circus—"

"Oh, Ed," I say, beaming. "I promise to personally ensure maximum circus levels."

Max shakes his head. "That might be the most honest thing you've ever said."

Mayor Calloway taps the table again. "Great! Max and Elle, you'll organize it."

We both freeze.

I turn to Max. "This was a trap."

His expression is pained. "I hate that you're right."

I lean back, arms crossed. "You gonna quit?"

His jaw tightens. "Nope."

"Good," I say, grinning wide. "Because this is going to be fun."

Max exhales slowly, like he's already regretting every decision that led him here.

I grab my phone. "We should set up our first planning session. Got your calendar?"

Max exhales slowly, rubbing a hand across his forehead. "Fine," he says, but his voice doesn't quite carry the enthusiasm.

We quickly find the date and swap numbers.

Having his contact info feels better than it should.

THREE
LAVENDER AND LAUGHS

MAX

I HAVE SURVIVED FIRES, floods, and a rogue bull named Diesel who once decided a fence was merely a suggestion.

But I may not survive Elle Sinclair.

"Okay, listen," Elle says, leaning over the library's battered conference table like she's about to command a covert military operation. The brass buttons on her tailored blazer catch the afternoon light, and the subtle scent of whatever expensive perfume she wears drifts across the table. It's something warm, a little sharp; kind of like her. I catch myself inhaling it, a completely inappropriate reaction to a business meeting.

"We need a game plan for the pop-up café," she says, tapping a pen against a pristine leather notebook.

I lean back in my chair, if it can even be called that. The library conference room furniture looks like it was last replaced when rotary phones were still cutting-edge technology.

"I have a plan," I reply, crossing my arms.

She arches an eyebrow. "You do?"

"Yes. Step one: Serve coffee. Step two: Don't make it complicated. Step three: Avoid disasters."

She stares at me like I just said I milk cows for fun. (Which, to be fair, I do. But she doesn't need to know that.)

"That's not a plan," she says. "That's an outline written by a caveman."

I shrug. "I like efficiency."

She lets out a dramatic sigh, adjusting her blazer sleeves. The motion exposes a sliver of skin at her wrist, and for a split second, I catch myself watching it. It's a small thing, too small to mean anything, but my brain decides to catalog it anyway.

"Max, you may be good at farm things—"

"Gee, thanks."

"—but an event like this needs flair, pizzazz." She makes an unnecessary hand flourish.

"This is a library," I deadpan. "Not Broadway."

She smiles, unfazed. "Oh, trust me, I know. You still have to whisper here, which makes threatening people less effective."

That gets me. I chuckle, shaking my head.

She tilts her head, assessing me. "Huh."

I frown. "What?"

"I didn't think you had an actual laugh."

I narrow my eyes. "What did you think I had?"

"A low, gravelly grunt of disapproval."

I roll my eyes. "I'm not a damn bull."

She grins. "Are you sure? Because I feel like you've got some territorial energy."

I cross my arms. "And you have instigator energy."

"Oh, absolutely."

Before I can figure out why I find that oddly attractive, Janine, the town's pastry queen and shameless marketer, arrives. "I made samples!"

A box of perfect-looking scones lands between us. Lavender honey, if the smell is any indication.

Elle claps her hands. "Oh, this is excellent. We need high-quality pastries to make the café pop."

I eye the scones like they're highly suspect.

Elle notices. "What?"

"I don't trust anything purple," I say.

Janine gasps like I just insulted her grandmother. "Max Donovan, I will have you know that lavender is an elite flavor."

Elle nods far too seriously. "It's sophisticated. Cultured."

"It's soap."

Elle sighs like I'm a lost cause. "Just try one."

"Fine." I grab a scone, take a bite... and instantly regret everything. She didn't freeze her butter, so they're dense.

Elle watches, waiting.

"Well?" she prompts.

I chew slowly, because one: my pride won't let me admit defeat, and two: this is not food. This is punishment.

"It's... complex," I say diplomatically.

Janine beams. "See? Sophisticated!"

Elle leans forward slightly, grinning. The movement brings her closer, and I catch a flash of something amused, almost playful behind her hazel eyes.

"Want a glass of milk to wash down all that culture?" she teases.

I scowl. "I'd rather eat dirt."

She laughs, and damn it, it's a good laugh: bright, unrestrained, the kind that hits unexpectedly and makes you want to hear it again.

I clear my throat. Get a grip, Donovan. We are not here to flirt. Focus.

Elle straightens, getting back to business mode. "Okay, so we need a location. The library lobby isn't big enough for seating."

I gesture towards the window. "So we set up outside."

"Like... an outdoor café?"

I shrug. "Weather permitting, yeah."

She taps a pen against her chin, thinking. "That could work. It makes the event more visible."

"And gives people a reason to accidentally wander over and spend money."

Janine grins. "That's the kind of capitalism I like!"

Elle jots something down in her immaculate leather notebook, looking annoyingly competent.

"Alright," she says. "Next: menu. Coffee is a given, but we need variety."

"We already have coffee," I say. "The end."

Elle scoffs. "Max, not everyone drinks plain black coffee."

"They should."

"They don't."

We have a standoff.

I narrow my eyes. "No pumpkin spice."

Elle's lips twitch. "Fine. But we're doing seasonal options."

I exhale, deeply regretting my life choices.

Janine, meanwhile, writes down an entire dessert menu.

Elle leans in. "Last thing. We need a gimmick."

I frown. "Why?"

"Because this is a small town, and people need a reason to talk about things."

"I was thinking 'good coffee' might be a strong enough reason."

"You're adorable," she says dryly. "We need a hook. Something to draw people in."

I cross my arms. "Like what?"

Elle taps her chin. "What if we hold an open-mic night?"

I freeze. "No."

"Why not?"

"Because public speaking is a nightmare."

Her grin turns positively wicked. "Max... do you have stage fright?"

"I don't have stage fright. I just have common sense."

She lights up like she's just won the lottery. "Oh, I love this."

"I hate you."

"No, you don't."

We stare each other down, but I know I've lost.

"Fine," I say through gritted teeth. "But if this turns into a disaster, I'm blaming you."

Elle leans back, smug as hell. "Noted."

I exhale and cross my arms, finding it hard to accept. "We're really doing an open-mic night."

Elle grins like she's just won a bet I didn't know we were making. "Absolutely."

I rub my jaw, stalling for time. "Fine. But if we're doing this, we need a theme."

Her eyes spark with amusement. "Oh? And here I thought you didn't believe in gimmicks."

"I don't," I say flatly. "But I believe in controlling disasters before they happen."

She taps her pen against her chin, thinking. "How about *Literary Legends*? People can read excerpts from famous works or even original pieces."

"Sounds dangerously close to homework."

Elle rolls her eyes. "It's a library, Max. Education is kind of the whole point."

"No pleasure reading at your house, then. Got it. People actually have to show up for this to work—not just the town's three existing poetry lovers."

"You're really underestimating the number of retired English teachers in this town."

"You're overestimating their enthusiasm for reading out loud."

She sighs dramatically. "Okay, fine. What's your idea, then?"

I lean back in my chair, pretending to think. "What about *Bad Book Night*? People bring in the worst book they've ever read and do a dramatic reading of the worst passages."

Elle gasps. "That is... incredible."

I blink. "Wait. Really?"

"Yes! Imagine it! People dramatically reciting terrible dialogue, tragic plot twists. It would be hilarious."

I wasn't actually serious, but now she's fully invested, her eyes practically glowing with excitement.

"We could give an award for the worst excerpt," she

continues, flipping open her notebook. "Like, *Best Worst Metaphor*. Or *Most Ridiculous Plot Twist*."

I chuckle. "You really want to organize an event where people just roast books in public?"

"As long as we're not burning them." She shrugs. "I'm a journalist. Exposing bad writing is my love language."

I shake my head, grinning despite myself. "I have a feeling this is going to cause actual fights."

"That's the best part," she says, too gleefully.

I give her a long, appraising look. "You're way more chaotic than I originally thought."

She winks. "Stick around, farmer. I'm full of surprises."

And for the first time all afternoon, I believe her.

The meeting finally ends, and as we leave the library, Elle walks beside me.

"So," she says. "On a scale of one to 'This was a terrible mistake,' how much do you regret agreeing to this?"

I grunt. "I need a drink."

She grins. "Coffee?"

"Whiskey." I turn my head and look at her.

She laughs, shaking her head. "Oh, you're going to have so much fun."

Her great laugh sends my eyes to her lips. "Doubt it."

She stops walking, tilting her head. "You know, Max, for a guy who claims to hate fun, you seem very determined to argue with me about everything."

"You make it easy."

Her eyes spark with something unreadable, something charged.

For one brief second, I wonder what would happen if I kissed her just to shut her up.

And then I remember this is Elle Sinclair, and that thought is dangerous.

Instead, I shove my hands in my pockets and nod toward the café. "Come on. I need coffee before I do something stupid."

She grins. "Like admit I'm right?"

I groan. "Like agree to this entire thing."

We head to Perk Up, and I already know this pop-up café is going to be absolute chaos. Damn it. But she's right; it's going to be fun.

FOUR
BALANCING BUTTER AND BANTER

MAX

HERE'S a short list of things I enjoy in life: a quiet morning on the farm, coffee in hand, watching the sunrise over my fields. The simple predictability of raising animals and growing things; plants don't lie, and cows don't play mind games. Time with my kids; listening to Oliver ramble about his newest tech project or watching Lily's sketches evolve from doodles to something incredible.

Nowhere on that list is Elle Sinclair, and yet, here I am, sitting across from her in a café, watching her critique a pastry like she's judging a five-star restaurant. I take a slow sip of my black coffee, watching her with mild amusement.

She breaks off a piece of croissant, tilting her head slightly as she chews. "This one is flakier. Good structure. But maybe a little too buttery."

"Too buttery? It's a croissant. That's like saying water is too wet."

She waves a dismissive hand. "Balance, Max. It's all about balance."

I smile. "This is the third bakery we've hit today. At this rate, my entire routine is thrown off. Do I need to start tracking croissant consumption on my farm ledger?"

She snorts, setting down her coffee. "That might be wise. You wouldn't want the cows thinking you've abandoned your strict, no-nonsense schedule for a life of luxury pastry tours."

I shake my head, grinning despite myself. "Pretty sure they'd be more upset if I showed up smelling like a scone instead of hay."

This is her idea, a 'research trip' for the pop-up café, testing the best places in the area for inspiration. I agree, though I'm still not entirely sure why. Maybe I'm curious. Maybe I like the challenge. Maybe I just want to spend more time with her.

Elle moves with purpose, even when she's doing something as simple as reaching for her coffee. There's a fluidity to her movements, a confidence. But it's not just that; she's sharp. Quick-witted. Smart as hell.

I knew her name before I met her.

Her articles in *The Willow Gazette* aren't puff pieces about fall festivals or town hall meetings. She's tackled real issues: unbiased, well-researched pieces on local government spending, small business struggles, and the complicated politics of land development. They rival articles in the mainstream financial papers, if not in breadth of topic, certainly in depth and understanding of the issues at play.

She sees the connectedness of it all. If the farmer can't plant or has a bad harvest, then the grocer doesn't have food to sell. Or has higher costs from importing it from other regions, meaning prices are up and fewer full baskets at the checkout. In my prior life, I learned quickly that business—well, life really—is a kinetic sculpture, or a line of standing dominoes waiting for a tap. And she's right, it is all about balance.

It's one of the things that intrigued me before I even met her.

And now I'm sitting across from her, watching her analyze a scone like it holds the secrets of the universe.

She leans forward, resting her elbow on the table. "So, grumpy farmer, tell me, what do you think of the scone?"

I glance down at the perfectly normal scone in front of me. "Tastes fine."

Her eyes narrow. "Fine?"

I take another bite, chewing slowly just to irritate her. "Yep. You know. Like food."

She gasps dramatically. "Oh, this is tragic." She shakes her head, clearly appalled. "Max, you are wasting this experience."

I raise an eyebrow. "You know, I've eaten actual dirt before. This is already a step up."

Elle bursts out laughing. It's genuine, unguarded, and entirely too pretty.

I like that I made her laugh.

And that realization hits hard, getting my attention.

I shake my head, fighting a smile. "I don't think I've ever met someone so emotionally invested in baked goods."

Elle picks up her latte, stirring it with unnecessary flair. "That's because you lack refinement."

"Sweetheart, I raise livestock for a living. My job is literally rolling up my sleeves and getting dirty."

She sighs, reaching for her latte. "You are a lost cause."

I lean back in my chair, studying her. She's beautiful. That much is obvious. But it's more than that. It's the way she holds herself, the way she speaks with absolute certainty, the way her eyes light up when she's debating something she cares about.

I glance at her left hand. No ring.

Which raises a question: How the hell is she single?

Because if we were together, I wouldn't let her go so easily.

That thought comes out of nowhere, and I shake it off.

Her gaze flickers briefly to my hands, which admittedly are rougher, calloused from years of work. I don't miss the way her eyes linger for half a second longer than necessary before she looks away.

Interesting.

I grin. "See something you like?"

Elle blinks, then scoffs, recovering quickly. "Just wondering if you ever use lotion. Or if you believe that's also too 'refined' for you."

I chuckle, shaking my head. "Nice save."

She sips her latte, avoiding eye contact.

Yeah. That wasn't nothing.

"You never answered my question," I say, refocusing.

She arches a brow. "Which one?"

"Why'd you drag me on this pastry tour?"

She hesitates, tapping a finger against her cup. "Honestly?"

"That'd be nice."

She sighs, then shrugs. "I needed a break."

I tilt my head. "From what?"

She waves a hand. "The office. The news cycle. The

mayor calling me every time he wants a 'narrative' spun in his favor."

I purse my lips. "So, instead of taking a normal break, you decided to torment me with pastries?"

She grins. "Yes."

I chuckle, shaking my head. "Figures."

She watches me for a moment, something curious flickering in her expression. Then, she props her chin on her hand. "Why'd you agree to come?"

The question catches me off guard.

I could say it's for research. I could say it's because she wouldn't shut up about it.

But the truth?

"I don't know," I admit.

Her lips part slightly, like she wasn't expecting that answer.

For a moment, just a moment, the air between us shifts.

Then, she straightens, brushing it off with a smile. "Well, I'm glad you did. Otherwise, you'd still be living your sad, flavorless existence."

I scoff. "You act like I survive on boiled potatoes and despair."

She tilts her head. "Do you?"

I laugh. Actually laugh. "No. But I'd rather eat that than some of the stuff you forced me to try today."

She gasps. "I will not apologize for expanding your horizons."

I shake my head, still grinning. "So, what's next? Another café?"

Elle checks her watch. "Actually, we're done."

I blink. "Wait. No fifth bakery?"

She grins. "I have to leave some mystery in our relationship."

I choke on my coffee.

She laughs, completely unfazed. "Relax, Max. It's just a figure of speech."

I eye her suspiciously. "Sure it is."

We step outside, and a sharp autumn breeze hits, sending a strand of her dark hair flying across her cheek. She tucks it behind her ear, glancing up at me.

For a second, just a second, something shifts.

The banter fades, replaced by something quieter. More aware. I don't know who looks away first, but it happens fast. My heart skips a beat.

Elle clears her throat. "Well, I should get going."

"Yeah. Me too."

She hesitates. "Same time tomorrow?"

I blink. "What?"

"For the pop-up prep. At the library."

The pop-up. Right. "Yeah. See you then."

She flashes one last smile before walking off, and I watch her go, hands in my pockets, feeling…something.

Something that long ago was put away.

But that doesn't mean it's not there.

I exhale, shake my head, and head to my truck, wondering what the hell I just got myself into.

Later, over dinner, I decide to test the waters.

Oliver picks up his plate with one hand, his phone with the other. "Can I be excused?"

"What? No." I set my fork down. "I want to talk to you and your sister."

He sighs dramatically and drops back into his chair. "Fine."

Lily watches me curiously, still chewing.

"How was school? Anything new?"

A perfectly synchronized, "Fine," from both of them.

Right. Should've seen that coming.

I try another angle. "You know I'm on the Willow Creek Library Board, right? They're planning a coffeehouse-style event. I expect you both to be there."

Oliver squints at me. "Mandatory?"

"Absolutely."

Lily smiles. "Translation: expect is mandatory."

I ignore that. "I've been working on it with Elle Sinclair, the newspaper editor. You know who I mean?"

Another synchronized response. "Uh-huh."

Good enough. "Well...she and I are becoming friends. I wanted to see how you two felt about that."

Lily hesitates. "Friends are good."

Oliver, more direct. "Friends how? Like hanging out? Or something more?"

I take a breath. "Not sure yet. But I wanted to check in with you both before I invite her out. Outside of committee meetings."

They exchange a look. A full sibling telepathic conversation I'm not privy to.

Lily is the first to speak. "Would she be, like...our stepmom?"

I huff a quiet laugh. "Let's not get ahead of ourselves. I haven't even asked her out yet. A lot of steps happen before it gets to that point."

Might as well use this as a teachable moment.

"Relationships have stages. It's different for everyone, but you can't skip steps just because someone's pushing you into something, or because your body wants something your emotions aren't ready for. If you don't build it right, there's no fixing it." I glance at Oliver. "Even *Romeo and Juliet* would've broken up if they had rushed things."

He snorts. "Yeah. They rushed things and died."

"Exactly." I smile. "Point is, heartbreak isn't just about loss. It's about rushing into something before it's solid. I want you both to be careful with that. Promise me?"

Lily nods. "Promise."

Oliver exhales, but nods too. "Promise."

I study them both for a second. They've been through enough loss already. They deserve something steady.

"So... thoughts on me asking Elle to lunch?" I keep my voice casual, but they know me too well.

Two head shakes. No objections.

"Good. Thanks for the input." I push back my chair. "Lily, you're on cleanup. Oliver, trash cans to the road. Pickup's in the morning."

"Mandatory?" Oliver deadpans.

"What do you think?"

He groans but stands.

Lily just grins.

FIVE
ONE VERY REAL DATE

ELLE

I AM A RATIONAL PERSON. A logical, organized, plan-everything-three-steps-ahead kind of woman.

Which is why it's annoying that Max Donovan, grumpy farmer and current unshakable presence in my life, has made his way into my thought process without my permission.

And, apparently, my schedule.

Because despite my best efforts, I keep finding reasons to see him. Or maybe he keeps finding me. Either way, I haven't decided if that's a good thing or a potentially catastrophic, very attractive, blue-eyed problem.

But I'm not thinking about that. Nope. I have more pressing matters to deal with.

Like the buzzing phone on my desk.

I brace myself before answering. "Toma."

"Elle! *Mon étoile!* My most talented, most infuriating client!"

I rub my temple. "We're starting strong today, I see."

"I must." He sighs, full of exaggerated suffering. "Because I know you are avoiding me."

"I am not avoiding you."

"You are not responding to my emails. What is the difference?"

"Semantics."

"Do not semantics me! There is a book launching, Elle! And I, your devoted agent, need to know if you will finally make an appearance."

I exhale. "You already know my answer."

A beat of silence.

"You cannot hide forever, *mon ange*."

I don't respond.

Because we've had this conversation many times. Because Toma has been patient, understanding, strategic, but also persistent.

Because four years ago, I did one fan event.

And someone, a fully grown man in an actual suit of armor, decided I was his *Seraphine Valis*, the heroine of my books. And then handcuffed us together.

It took five security guards to separate us.

Five.

That's when I stopped making public appearances.

Toma, sensing my wall of silence, sighs. "I know, Elle. But it has been years."

"I know."

"The books are bigger than ever. The readers adore you."

"I know."

"There will be security. A controlled environment."

"I know."

He pauses. Then, softer, "Do you want to stay hidden forever?"

That hits differently.

I close my eyes. "I don't know."

Because I miss it. I miss seeing the impact. I miss hearing from readers.

I miss the good parts.

But I don't know if I'll ever feel safe enough to go back.

Toma lets out a breath. "You do not have to decide now. But promise me you will think about it."

I hesitate. "I will think about it."

It's not a no. It's not a yes.

It's a step.

"Good." He brightens. "Now, I must go. Your publisher is breathing down my neck, and I prefer my head attached to my body. But call me. And, Elle?"

"Yeah?"

"Do not lock yourself away from the world."

I don't promise anything. We both know better.

Toma changes tactics. "I know. Come into the city and meet me Saturday," he says casually, as if he didn't just drop a trap in my lap.

I snort. "No."

A gasp. "Elle! Why so fast?"

"I have plans."

A long, intrigued silence.

Then Toma's voice turns absolutely predatory. "Plans?"

I should have lied.

I should have said laundry or taxes or staring into the abyss with a bottle of wine.

But no. I had to hesitate.

"Elle," he purrs, smelling blood. "Do tell."

I backpedal. "It's nothing."

"Lies."

"It's not a big deal."

"I will determine that. Is it romantic?"

I rub my temple. "Toma."

A sharp inhale. Then, gasping, dramatic, and overjoyed:
"You have a date."

"Goodbye, Toma."

"ELLE. YOU CANNOT—"

Click.

I drop my phone onto my desk and groan at the ceiling.

The moment I hang up with Toma, I immediately call
Elliot.

Because if anyone can ground me after a conversation
like that, it's my twin brother.

He picks up after two rings. "Let me guess. Business or
emotional crisis?"

I exhale. "Both?"

He laughs. "That's the Elle I know."

"I hate that you're smug about it."

"You hate that I'm right."

...Fair.

"Okay, listen," I say, shifting gears. "You needed me for
something?"

"Yeah. It's a legal thing. Minor, but I need your signature
on a shareholder document for *Green Agricultural*. Something about restructuring one of our European supply
chains. Shouldn't take more than ten minutes."

"Send it over. I'll review and sign it today."

"Thanks." He pauses. "You know, sometimes I forget
you're still technically a part of the family business."

I smile. "I like to keep you on your toes."

"Well, if you're so involved, maybe you can start showing up to board meetings."

I fake gasp. "Me? Sit in a room with a bunch of executives talking about grain export policies?"

"Perish the thought."

We laugh, but there's warmth in it.

"Hey, what's happening with the foundation we discussed? Have you taken any action yet?" I ask, aware my ideas find the back burner too often.

"It's a good idea. Dad and I talked about it last week. I'm working on it, but it's not a high priority right now." He pauses. "I understand you have another royalty payment coming, and you want it before the end of the year."

He softens. "Dad's working with the attorneys to see how *Green Agricultural* can support the foundation. Be patient."

He adds, "We'll need someone not named Sinclair to sit on the board, so put your thinking hat on."

I chew my lip. "Hey, speaking of the family business... I may have met someone."

Elliot goes silent. "Hold on. What?"

"I might be seeing someone."

A pause. "Who is he?"

"...An organic farmer."

A longer pause. "An organic farmer?"

"Yes."

"You don't even like dirt."

"I respect dirt."

Elliot laughs. "What's his name?"

"Max Donovan."

Elliot hums. "Donovan. That sounds... familiar."

"He uses *Green Agricultural's* products."

"Oh, so he's a loyal customer." He chuckles. "Mom and Dad will be thrilled."

I roll my eyes. "Let's not get ahead of ourselves."

"Fine. I'll let you pretend you're not completely intrigued by him."

"I hate you."

"You love me."

"Goodbye."

"Call me after the date."

I hang up before he can gloat any further.

That night, my phone buzzes.

The name on the screen makes me nervous. A text from Max.

Max: *Still on for tomorrow?*

I smile.

Elle: *Depends. Do I get to pick dessert?*

Max: *I'll even let you critique it.*

I chuckle. He's getting to know me.

Elle: *Now we're talking.*

Max: *Seven o'clock. I'll pick you up.*

I hesitate.

Because this is real now.

No library board meetings, no excuses to "accidentally" run into each other.

Just a date. With Max. I exhale. Smile.

Elle: Looking forward to it.

And for the first time in a long time, I actually mean it.

I'M LAUGHING. As in real, unexpected laughter. The kind that sneaks up on you and leaves you feeling exposed.

Max sits across from me, looking entirely too pleased

with himself, arms stretched along the back of the booth, looking like he belongs here. Which is dangerous. Because I shouldn't be deriving this much pleasure from this.

"See?" he says, grining. "I told you I was funny."

I shake my head, still grinning. "No, you said I just didn't notice you were funny before. I still don't know if this is intentional or if you just have really bad luck with phrasing."

Max takes a slow sip of his coffee, eyes on me, completely unbothered. "Maybe both."

I roll my eyes. "I'll take that as a yes."

Our plates are mostly empty, a few stray crumbs from our shared pastries the only evidence that we've been sitting here for over an hour. It's been easy to talk, like we have a natural connection.

It starts when Max tells me about his kids; Lily's latest negotiation tactics and Oliver's near-lethal drone-delivery experiments. And I laugh. Hard.

"She's scary persuasive," he admits.

"How so?" I ask, intrigued.

"She got me to agree to a dog."

I gasp dramatically. "You have a dog?"

"Storm."

"Oh, that's an excellent name."

Max sighs, shaking his head. "Yeah, well, it's short for Brainstorm, because Lily said she and Oliver 'brain-stormed' the idea to convince me."

I completely lose it.

And now, here we are, comfortable, relaxed, and talking about what it would be like if we were actually dating.

Max tilts his head. "So, hypothetically..."

I raise an eyebrow. "Oh, this is going to be good."

He grins. "If we were actually together, would you be able to handle it?"

I blink. "Handle what?"

"Me." He leans forward slightly. "Two kids. A dog. A full farm. The whole 'grumpy but ruggedly handsome' thing." His eyes meet mine.

"You added that last part yourself."

He shrugs. "Doesn't make it less true."

I take a sip of my coffee, pretending to consider. "Well, I do like your kids."

His smile fades slightly, replaced by something softer. "Yeah?"

"They're funny. Smart. I'd like to get to know them better."

He watches me for a moment, too carefully. "That's... a dangerous thing to say."

I tilt my head. "Why?"

"Because they'd love you."

Something flutters in my chest. Something I wasn't expecting.

I break eye contact, tapping my fingers against my cup. "Well, good thing this is hypothetical, then."

Max doesn't respond right away, but I can feel him still watching me.

Or is it someone else?

SIX

UNMASKING ELLE

ELLE

A SHADOW LOOMS over our table. I feel it before I
see it—the weight of someone watching too intently. I
glance up, and my stomach drops.

Max follows my gaze, taking in this spectacle of a man.
His eyebrows slowly rise. "Uh. What the hell?"

He stands beside the booth in full fantasy cosplay. Dark
tunic, armored vest, a dramatic cloak billowing slightly
from the movement of the café door closing behind him.

I know him. And then I see it. *Oh God, no.* A broadsword
strapped to his back. *Oh no. Oh no, no, no.*

Eric Harris. Or, as he insists, Maldric. I thought he was
still in a treatment facility. Clearly, I was wrong.

Maldric lowers to one knee. "Seraphine," he says, his
voice trembling with emotion. "I have finally found you."

Max blinks. "Did he just—?"

"Shh!" I say, my eyes flashing a warning.

Eric's eyes burn with devotion. "I have walked through shadow, through fire, through endless nights to find you." He places a fist to his chest. "And now, at last, we are together." His eyes are starting to get glassy.

Max leans slightly toward me. "Is this normal for you?"

"No," I hiss. "Shut up."

Maldric reaches for my hand. Memories of Indianapolis flash before my eyes. I see the handcuffs. I pull my hand back. I don't want him to take my hand. Learned that lesson, thank you.

We were at a conference in Indianapolis. I was drinking a *Hobbit's Harvest* in the lobby bar when he approached me, declared his devotion, then handcuffed us together. When security came, he demonstrated his mad swordsmanship skills—while I was still handcuffed to him. It took five officers to finally subdue him. *Five.* That was four years ago. I truly thought he was still getting the help he needed.

"Maldric, how did you escape the Realm of Shadows? Has Aldric Dorne followed you here? Do you need to hide?" I think playing along might buy me some time.

"Yes, they are fast upon my heels. Save me, Sera, please —my friend, my love." He grabs my hand, kisses it, then I pull it away.

"As you can see, we are not alone. I am no longer free to go with you, Maldric. So you should go, now, before Aldric comes." My mind is working on multiple levels, playing out scenarios. None of them seem good.

Maldric narrows his eyes at Max. "You," he says darkly, "are in my way."

Max looks completely unfazed. "Can't say I've heard that one before."

I need to de-escalate this fast.

I glance at the nearest server. "Is Lawrence coming?"

The server hesitates, confused. "Uh?"

"Can you call him? Please?" I see the moment she gets it —Lawrence, as in Sheriff Lawrence. The server nods and walks away, phone in hand.

Eric doesn't notice. He's too busy glaring at Max.

Max leans forward, elbows on the table. "You ever consider therapy, buddy?"

"Shh!" I say again, my eyes flashing another warning.

Then my phone signals a FaceTime call. It's my manager, Toma Hector. He's not a native English speaker, so he uses FaceTime. I aim for the decline button but hit the green one instead. *Damn.*

"Elle, Elle? It's Toma, are you there?"

"Hey, hold on." I lay the phone down on the table, because I notice Maldric reaching back for that broadsword. *No, not again.*

Eric shakes his head. "You don't understand. She's pretending. They made her pretend."

Oh, hell no.

Max stands up, his posture shifting completely. I know that look—the look of a man about to handle a problem.

"Max, we'll ..." I'm too late.

Without breaking eye contact with Eric, he reaches over, takes my hand in his, and laces our fingers together.

"She's not pretending," Max says, voice calm, steady, and devastatingly firm.

Eric blinks. "What?" His broadsword slides back into its sheath.

Max squeezes my hand. "She's engaged." He then kisses my hand. "To me. Last week."

The entire café goes dead silent. Eric stares at me, completely wrecked.

I force a smile. "It's true. To eh, him—Max. Well, I'm sorry Mal..."

Sheriff Lawrence walks through the door, his hand on his sidearm, wearing protective gear. He walks up to Maldric—or maybe Eric Harris by now—and cuffs him. The deflated fan no longer seems large.

Just then I hear an air horn blaring from my phone's speaker. *Oh no, Toma!* I pick up the phone.

"Toma, are you still there? I'm sorry, a little busy here. Toma?"

The phone just shows the ceiling and the edge of a bookcase. I end the call.

Max and I lock eyes. So many questions swirl in his blue eyes. Ones I know I need to answer.

Then the whispers at the other tables filter through to us. I look around; several people are on their phones, texting or talking. The Willow Creek gossip vine is buzzing tonight. I have to sit for a moment.

Max sits down, looks at me, then reaches across the table and lays his hand over mine. "How are you doing?" Then he adds, "Fiancée."

"Oh, Fiancé—actually, I'm confused, exhausted, and ... and I know you must have questions about what just happened. And I have answers, I want to talk about it, but is there somewhere more private than here?"

Max looks around the café. There are still those who steal a glance in our direction, though the whispers are not as loud.

"Of course. I'm sure we can find somewhere. Are you ready to go, or are you expecting someone else?"

"I wasn't expecting him."

"We can talk tomorrow, coffee at Perk Up, then we can go sit in the park. You are looking very tired."

"Yes, to coffee tomorrow. But as a journalist I know things change with time. I really want to at least get started tonight. Please. Take me home; we can talk there."

THIRTY MINUTES later I'm bundled in a fleece wrap, sitting on a metal chair in Max's barn. He stands before me offering a mug of something steaming.

"Here, it will help you feel better."

"What is it?" I look up at him.

"You either trust me or you don't. If you don't, then we need to call off the engagement and go our separate ways, don't you think, fiancée?" Max smiles.

I take the mug and sniff. It has overtones of cinnamon and anise with maybe some rum. The aroma starts to melt my anxiety, and I relax into the moment. The drink mixes with the sweet smell of hay and wood, with only a faint whiff of the animals. The wind outside is dinging the rope against the flagpole, and the large old Charter Oak leaves sound like applause just outside the door. Something about this space is relaxing, secure, and very homey.

It's Max's place. This is Max's peace.

Sitting opposite me on a stool, Max watches me get comfortable with my surroundings. A lantern hangs on a support beam, giving a warm glow that mixes with the light filtering in through the high window from the utility light outside. The lighting gives Max a warm glow, accentuating his dark red hair and making his blue eyes softer. I realize, probably too late, that he's handsome. Not just handsome, but annoyingly so—and warm, and good. My fingers tighten around the mug. *Damn it.*

"Thank you." I clear my throat. "For bringing me here, sharing this with me. And for earlier."

His expression doesn't shift. He just watches me—like he's waiting. Like he's patient.

My chest starts to build a pressure. Just don't cry. Instead, it releases through my lips. I force out a chuckle. "Okay. Big confession time."

One of his brows lifts. "Yeah?"

"Max, I want to tell you something. It's been my secret ever since I moved to Willow Creek." I take a deep breath. "But after tonight, you deserve to know the truth. About me. About ... why we're engaged now."

Max doesn't react immediately. He just studies me, his face unreadable. I press on.

"At the first Library Board meeting you asked about *The Veridion Chronicles*; you said your kids are fans."

He nods slightly.

"Well," I continue, tapping the side of my mug, "they're mine. I wrote them. Under the pen name Liane Cillser—an anagram. I've written other books too, but those ... those are the ones people care about."

Max's face shifts slowly. His brows knit together, his eyes narrowing slightly, like he's trying to piece together a puzzle that suddenly makes sense.

"What happened tonight—that's the reason you keep that a secret."

"Yes, but I was raised to be a private person. My family founded Green Agricultural. Elliot, my twin brother, is CEO now. My parents stepped down almost ten years ago.

But it is still very much a family international business. We've fought to keep it private, to avoid going public. Thank God."

Max leans back, rubbing his jaw. His gaze flicks up to the rafters, processing.

"So if I understand you, your family is behind Green Agricultural. So you were raised in wealth and privilege."

"Yes."

"Since your brother took the CEO spot, that allowed you to become a writer-journalist, not concerned about income, therefore chasing whatever story you want."

"Mostly yes."

"Your creative side is released in young-adult fantasy books that are hugely successful."

"Also yes."

"The downside is over-enthusiastic cosplaying fans wanting you to save them."

"Unfortunately, yes." I chuckle.

Max looks at me. "And you appear as a small-town editor who likes to drink atrociously sweet coffee. Is that about right?"

I sigh. "Pretty much."

But I'm laughing now, the tension breaking just enough to breathe again. Max grins—just a flicker, there and gone, but enough to make my chest squeeze.

"I was concerned tonight because Eric Harris first approached me in Indianapolis at Comic-Con about four years ago. He has mad swordsmanship skills. No fatalities, but a couple of security guards were hospitalized. I asked that he be put in a treatment facility in lieu of pressing charges. I just thought he needed help. Maybe he can't be helped." I look at Max over the rim of the mug. "Thanks for stepping up, my gallant knight."

"I should be a king at least."

"Veridion doesn't have kings and queens. *Lumea*—The Power of Truth—keeps people in line. If you're honest, truthful to yourself and others, you keep your power, which is life. If not, well ..." I shrug my shoulders.

"Really, that's what my children have been so obsessed with? Seeking truth."

"Seems so."

"I guess I have some reading to do."

"I'm surprised you haven't. You're a good father, Max. I see it. You're present in their lives."

I don't expect the way his face softens—the way something shifts in the air between us. The non-physical space lessens.

"They are certainly going to love you." And for some reason, that gets me. The warmth spreads through my chest, all the way to my fingertips. I glance down at my mug, willing my expression not to give me away.

The light outside the window goes dark. I hear a motor stop with a grind. The shadows shift. Only the lantern on the support beam illuminates the space around us.

"See, I really do milk cows in the dark some days. I should go restart the generator. If you need facilities, there is a bathroom at the end of this hallway on the left. That's where my office is. It's on a backup power system. Let's meet there—it will be warmer and more comfortable." He hands me his mug, then takes the lantern from the post and hands it to me.

"Refill these for us?" he says, his voice so casual. "My turn—I need to tell you something."

We're not done here. This night isn't over yet.

THE BATHROOM IS ACTUALLY A BATHROOM—VERY nice and smelling of lavender.

The attractive and expensive tile lines the walls and ceiling. It is spotless; the shower, sink, toilet, and urinal gleam. I wash my hands—the hot water is immediate. Organic-cotton hand towels are rolled up in a basket or tossed in a laundry bin. The space speaks volumes about Max—and that I shouldn't invite him into my space unless the maid has just left. I'm not a cleaner.

The office is just as orderly and clean. Functional, efficient, and comfortable seems to be his design plan. More than an office, it is a studio apartment with a business office. The kitchen area is large enough for a farmhand-size table; a microwave and a speed oven (microwave and convection combined) are stacked on the wall near a line of small appliances. As I refill our mugs, the lights come back to full strength, followed by a chorus of beeps as equipment returns to ready mode. I settle on a futon sofa, one leg tucked under me, facing the space I left for him.

As I wait, my thoughts review the night's events. There is something about Max like no other. It is a feeling—no, a knowing—that we belong together. His declaration earlier carries a truth I can't quite comprehend. We've been speaking for only a few weeks, yet I've just revealed myself to this man who should seem a stranger but is quite the opposite.

He is comfortable; being with him is comfortable. He is attractive—*oh so attractive.* That power outage at Perk Up woke up parts of me I thought had given up on partnership

—and developed into a want as we disagreed about coffees and pastries. *Max is the delight in my otherwise bland days.* There, I've admitted it.

My heart starts to pulse, then the door to the office opens. It's Max. He's here.

SEVEN
INSTINCT AND INTIMACY

MAX

I'VE HAD my fair share of strange nights. I've dodged bar fights, put out literal and figurative fires, and once had a woman sneak into my hotel room in Dubai, claiming we were "destined lovers in every lifetime."

But this? This is new.

Two hours ago, I was sitting across from Elle Sinclair, actually enjoying myself, thinking about how effortless it is to talk to her. And then some fully grown man in a cape and a sword drops to one knee beside our table.

At first, I think it's a prank. Some kind of elaborate town joke I missed. Maybe a bachelor party gone rogue. Then I make the mistake of looking at Elle. She's not laughing. She's pale, frozen, like someone just walked over her grave. That's when my stomach tightens. That's when I know this isn't a joke. This is real. And I have no idea what the hell is happening.

I watch the guy, Maldric, apparently, with the same

slow, measured patience I used to have during contentious negotiations when dealing with unstable situations. The guy is too intense. Too fixated. And Elle? She's trying to control the situation. Trying to talk him down without setting him off. She even leans into the act, playing along just enough to keep things from spiraling. Which means this isn't the first time she's dealt with him. The weight of that realization hits hard. She's dealt with this before. And she's scared.

That's when I know. I have to end this. Because I've been here before. I've seen what happens when obsession turns toxic. When people convince themselves of a narrative so deep they refuse to let it go. And I'm not about to let that happen to Elle.

So I do the only thing that makes sense. I grab Elle's hand, squeeze it, and say, "She's engaged. To me."

The reaction is instant. Maldric freezes. His face shatters. And for a second, just a second, I almost feel bad for the guy. But then I remember the crazed devotion in his eyes, the way he called Elle "Sera" like he had some claim over her. And I know I made the right call. Because his fixation is broken now.

And Elle? Elle lifts her chin, squares her shoulders, and says, "It's true." And with two words, I'm engaged. In front of at least fifteen witnesses.

I reset the fuse, walk over to the generator, and press the start lever. It jumps to life. I wait, watching it hum, buying myself a second to think.

I like her. I thought that would be complicated. Maybe it won't be. Elle comes from a world I know too well, one I walked away from, for many of the same reasons she doesn't advertise it. But you never really walk away, do you?

You just shove it in a closet and pretend it's not there. But it informs every choice you make. I sigh.

The generator huffs like it is going to stop again. I give it a kick, and it returns to humming.

The engagement? It was instinct. A snap decision. But now? Now it's a problem. Because it didn't feel like a lie. And that's what's screwing me up the most. I replay the moment over and over; the way Elle looked at me, the way she trusted me to step in, the way I like the way it feels to stand between her and something that scared her. I liked it too much. And that's not good. Or is it? No, I don't do this. I don't get involved. For years, I've had one simple rule: keep my life contained. Keep things easy. No complications. And Elle? Elle is the definition of a complication. But here's the thing. For the first time in a long time, I don't think I mind.

She's waiting for me in my office. That feels right. She's here, on the farm. Would it be so bad if this wasn't fake?

I close my eyes, exhaling slowly. And then I see it. Lily, laughing with Elle over breakfast. Oliver telling her about his latest invention. Elle, sitting on the porch, barefoot, curled up in my sweater, reading one of her books. My home, full again. Not just with the kids. Not just with responsibility. But with someone who makes it feel like more.

And I realize something. I'm not just protecting Elle from some obsessive fan. I'm protecting myself from the truth. And that truth is simple. I like this. I like her. And maybe, just maybe, I don't want to be alone anymore.

If I mean this, then I've got to come clean and share my secret.

.   .   .

ELLE IS SITTING on the futon sofa, one leg tucked under her, facing the space she left for me. She has the throw over her lap. I feel a pull to her, a connection. She looks settled here. Like she belongs. I want more of this, more of walking into this space and finding her here, ready to "figure things out" together.

I sit down, and she tosses the blanket over my lap. "Your turn. What do you want to share with me?"

"Before the farm, I had my own financial firm. I managed billions in European markets. The work was cutthroat, strategic, intense. I loved it." Her eyes flicker with recognition. I take a breath. "I had an obsessed fan... there was a woman. A high-net-worth acquaintance who convinced herself we were 'destined.'" I exhale. "Even though I was married."

Elle's brows pull together.

"She'd pose as my wife to get through the hotel reception, and plant herself in my room. Worse, she showed up at my business meeting and caused all kinds of havoc. When I resisted, she eventually created a scandal carried by the gossip rags, especially in Europe where most of my clients were. As you can guess, even the hint of scandal caused clients to back away. Who could blame them, I wouldn't trust the management of millions, billions of euros, to someone without the highest ethical and moral reputation.

"This drama caused chaos, and more drama, and lies to manage the drama. It became insane to me. I loved the world of finance, but the drama was pulling me away from it."

"So you left," Elle says softly.

"I was spinning down my business when my wife was

killed in an auto accident. So, I became a single parent to a
seven-year-old and ten-year-old. I sold every trace of that
life, and we moved here to start recovery from the loss,
heartbreak, and grief. We all made it through. Thank God."

I turn to look at Elle, "So now I'm just a single dad,
grumpy organic farmer who drinks lots of black coffee. I
don't share our former life, and I've asked the kids not to
either. So, there is my secret."

"I'm sorry for the loss. Thank you for telling me. I won't
tell, on my journalist oath." She moves to sit closer to me.
She lays her palm on top of the back of my hand, sliding
her long narrow fingers between my tanned bulky ones.
The contact of her skin is comforting and electrifying at the
same time. I can smell her fragrance—like floral or the sea,
fresh.

My body responds as the space between us is heavy
with something. Turning my head to look at her, I meet her
lips inches away. Our eyes see the other, our breaths
become purposeful, and without thinking my lips join hers,
and a spark of knowing, of connection passes between us.
She parts her lips, so I push deeper, as my arms surround
her body, pulling her slender frame into my chest. I hear
her moan, a release of that something between us. I
respond in kind.

"Elle," I whisper.

Suddenly, I'm falling, with her in my arms, as we lay
down on the sofa, our bodies pressing together. My groin
feels like it is on fire, growing and rising to fulfill desire.

My hand is caressing Elle's breast, then moves to find its
way under her blouse. Sensitive fingertips feel the lace of
her bra. I savor the touch of the silky bumps and valleys of
the lace. It's been too long since my fingertips felt such

insane stimulation as they move over her heaving mounds, which are begging my attention. She bites my lower lip, followed by her lips parting, accepting my tongue. She is fire. She can consume me, my flaws, my past, making me whole again.

My hand is pushing the lace out of my way. I leave her neck and move my mouth to find her nipples, standing firm on the beautiful full mounds of pink pleasure. My tongue licks them, my teeth tease them, and she lets out a moan. I discover I like making her moan.

She pulls at my shirt. Reluctantly, I move to allow it to be removed, then I fully remove hers, gasping at the mercy I'm being given, to find this sensation again. She is beautiful. Her hands rub the hair on my chest, then a finger traces down to my pants. She looks up at me, we're in a haze of want and new discovery. I lower myself and the contact of our bare chests sends sparks through us both.

"God, that feels good," I whisper.

"Oh, Max," she cries.

Her leg wraps around my hip, pulling my groin into hers, and lightning strikes. I want. She wants. My tongue returns to her breast, her glorious breast. Licking. Sucking. Biting. I want her, all of her. But I do as I have told Oliver to do; I pause, pull back, and look down at this angelic woman.

"Elle, do we stop? Are you alright? What do you want? I need your permission here."

Her eyes are glassy, red rimming them, as she whispers, "I want you, Max. I want you, now."

I swallow. Hard. I start to lower myself to kiss her again.

"But maybe we are rushing this, this wonderful thing." I sigh. Push back slightly. She reaches up and touches my lips with her fingers, then caresses my jaw. Her touch feels so natural. "I want to do this right. Because I want it to last."

She watches me, something warm and knowing in her gaze. The conversation I had with my children flashes through my mind. How I asked them to promise not to rush a relationship, to skip steps, rush stages—certainly not because your body wants. I chuckle at the realization.

Then I pull myself back, sitting on the sofa. She reaches for her clothes, but my hand flies to her arm, pausing her motion.

"Just one last look, please. You're beautiful. Enticing. Sexy." Then I add, "I promise to be less grumpy." She laughs a laugh that sends joy throughout the room, and through to my soul. And damn, I like making this woman laugh.

She stands up, pushes her bosoms together, and leans into my face. I inhale the scent of her. Then she starts moving her body as if to be a model, or rather a temptress, now knowing the power she has over me, an embarrassed laugh accompanying her antics. I find her play stimulating, but I agree, we need to move a little slower. To be sure. Have a solid foundation.

"Okay, okay, enough. Here, put your clothes back on, you she-devil." I lean in and kiss her lightly. "Thank you."

Hugging her clothes to her chest, Elle steps into the bathroom, and I slide my shirt back on and adjust myself. I also adjust to this change between us.

A few minutes later, she steps out, fresh-faced, her chin faintly reddened. I smile. "Remind me to shave more often," I murmur. She rolls her eyes, but I catch the small smile she tries to hide.

Then reality settles back in.

"So," I say, leaning against my desk. "What do we do about this engagement? Stick with it, or print a retraction in the morning paper?" My voice is lighter than I feel.

Elle crosses her arms, tilting her head. "I don't think you realize what that means."

I raise a brow. "Enlighten me."

"My agent heard it," she says. "Which means he probably already has headlines running in entertainment news sites. He's supposed to keep my pen name separate from my real identity, but... he also loves a dramatic reveal. If this spins too far, we could both end up in the middle of a media circus." She meets my gaze. "Are you, and your kids, ready for that?" Elle's concern is obvious in her eyes.

"Well, we have to be. The alternative is that some cosplaying fan accosts a local small-town editor. That won't play. Fishy. Our lives will be examined, and that risks more than just your pen name." Elle hesitates. I step closer, keeping my tone even. "Elle, we like each other. That much is obvious. And right now? This feels truer than most facts about my life. I'm not saying we make it real. Not yet." I pause, then add, "But I wouldn't mind seeing where this goes."

Something flickers in her expression. "People saw you last night declaring you were engaged to the small-town editor. Won't they connect the dots and figure out I'm also the author?" Elle's eyes flash up as she engages her creative mind to analyze the issue.

"Do they know the author is a woman? Why couldn't it be either of us, or neither of us? A shell game," I offer. She walks over to the futon and sits, legs tucked neatly beneath her. I want to sit next to her, feel her energy, but I know better. Instead, I pull a chair opposite her; just enough space to be smart about this.

It's interesting to watch her as she gets into creative problem-solving mode. Her head shakes, like answering her own internal question, then she gets excited, chasing another idea until her head shakes again. I notice her hands are moving as well, clearly moving pieces of the problem around in her mental solving board. I really need to read her books; her world-building skills must be awesome.

Finally, she speaks. "We spin it." I raise a brow. She turns to me, animated now. "I run the usual engagement announcement in the *Gazette*. Then we pick up the news service story about the fantasy author's engagement."

My mind catches up. "Two separate stories."

She nods. "Two separate stories."

I lean forward. "And if people start connecting dots?"

"I can send an email to the virtual press agent Toma uses with details about the fantasy author Liane Cillser's engagement. Once I shape that engagement, then our local story stays local and unconnected. I'll run a really small story about Eric Harris, a confused cosplay fan, coming up to us, the paper editor and a local farmer."

She smiles at me, sending warmth to my chest. I study her. She's not just smart. She's fast. And something about that is wildly attractive. Not that I'm saying that out loud.

"Think it'll work?" I ask.

Elle grins, a little too pleased with herself. "Tricky, but doable." She's impossible. And I like her anyway.

. . .

IT'S ALMOST midnight when we walk out of the barn, the cool night air swirling around us, the sound of dried crops rustling in the field. In the distance, I hear a dog bark and wonder if it is Storm. The light in Lily's bedroom is shining, making the house look warmer.

I take Elle home. We say good-night at her door.

"So is this typical for a first date with you?" She laughs, a beautiful laugh that is warm. I do like her laugh.

As I drive back to my farm, so many thoughts play in my mind against the night-clad, headlight-illuminated, narrow two-lane roads. I catch the twin beacons of a raccoon as it looks into the truck headlights. Frozen. I slow down. Enough that it regains awareness and scurries off into the dark.

"Just have to pray I do the same."

If our plan shifts.

If our backgrounds are exposed.

If.

I remind myself that backup plans are good, but trusting the first plan is better. I pull into the driveway, check on the kids, turn out the lights they left on.

Finally, I sit on my bed. She's on my mind. So, against my better judgment, I pick up my phone.

Max: *Let's Perk Up together in the morning.*

Elle: *Can't. Gazette goes to bed by noon. I have articles to write. Day after?*

I smile.

Max: *Look forward to reading. Tuesday am. 'Night.*

Elle: *'Night, farmer.*

I chuckle. Set the phone down. Then close my eyes. And for the first time in a long time, I sleep easy.

EIGHT
THE ENGAGEMENT EDITION

ELLE

IT'S a puzzle that just got really involved.

Newspapers aren't really about the news. It's about advertising, with just enough journalism thrown in to keep people flipping pages and seeing those ads.

As editor of The Willow Gazette, I have to juggle editorial duties, layout, and production prep, all while making sure we don't run out of money or piss off the wrong people. If I had my way, newspapers, print or digital, would be news first, ads second. Hard-hitting investigative journalism. Thoughtful human interest stories. Limited, carefully crafted editorials.

But I don't get my way.

Instead, ad sales determine how many pages we print. If there aren't enough ad buys for the week, there isn't enough space for the stories people claim they care about. So before I touch a single article, I pull up the layout software and check the weekly ad placements. Subtracting those gives me the number of news inches I have left to fill.

Once I have my number, I start the puzzle: balancing required content like government announcements and legal notices (which we can't skip unless we want angry phone calls) with the stories people actually read, like community updates, local sports, and human interest pieces. Then there are the vital statistics—births, deaths, engagements, and marriages—which people only care about if their names are in them.

If I can't fit everything, I can add four pages—a single sheet folded in half. If I do that, then I have to make sure I have enough ads to support the additional four pages. The publisher won't publish for long if the paper doesn't make a profit, at least a slim one.

A puzzle.

Alphabetizing the vital statistics, I measure how many inches. Too much for the space I have.

I have to get the engagements in, including mine, which is at the end of the list. And I need to make sure of the newswire article about our favorite teen fantasy author. I'd almost break even with the ad buy I currently have, so technically, I should call the publisher and let the decision be his.

Books, even successful series, need to be advertised, don't they?

I text Toma's assistant and ask him to please place an ad order before the hour strikes, a full page, about the upcoming book.

Okay, it's a cheat I've used before, but I can't wait to announce Max and my engagement, nor miss the buzz about the fantasy author's news.

I'd draw the publisher's attention if I use too many house ads, usually promoting a public service message so he can take it as a donation to a nonprofit.

Ten minutes later, I have a new, just-under-the-wire ad buy for a whole page. This should leave about two pages to fill.

Ninety minutes until this paper goes to bed.

I've written an article, with the help of an AI chatbot due to my time crunch, about the effects of teen fantasy novels on the mental health of teens and young adults. I quoted Mrs. Thompson from the library and a mental health professional from an interview I found online.

A news item about the cosplaying fan who came up to me Saturday night.

My engagement announcement tucked down the list with the "S" names.

And picked up the wire story on the fantasy author's engagement.

With the full-page ad about the fantasy author's next book, the issue looks like it is a themed edition advertiser, which is exactly what it is supposed to look like.

At 11:50 a.m., the phone rings.

It is Mayor Calloway with a last-minute announcement about a water main break, and the town square will be closed for two days starting tomorrow afternoon for repairs.

Of course Mayor Calloway asks I get that in tomorrow's edition. But before we hang up, he asks me about some gossip he heard at Sunday service.

"I heard you were the person this strange fan had come up to, is that accurate?"

"Yes, I was having dinner with Max Donovan Saturday night, when this young man in costume came up to me, claiming I was his savior or something. Sheriff Lawrence took him away."

"Oh, that's right, I heard you're engaged to Max Donovan. And to think I'm responsible. I tapped you both for the Library Board. Not such a bad thing now, is it?"

"No, I mean, yes, Max and I are engaged. It happened fast. We haven't been ring shopping yet." I write "get ring" on my to-do list. "Maybe being in our forties we move faster through relationship stages. Experience has to count for something, right?"

He laughed. "Well, I wish you both the very best. I'll keep an eye out for my invitation to the wedding. I don't imagine you've set a date."

"No, just announcing it in tomorrow's edition. Which has to be sent to the printers after I make your last-minute addition. So I have to run, the clock is ticking."

"Yes, yes, of course. Thank you, Elle. And congrats, I'm thrilled. See you later at the library."

"What?" He had hung up.

I totally forgot.

I grab my phone and send Max a quick reminder text.

Elle: *Library Board meeting at 3:30. Last one before the pop-up. Don't be late.*

A moment later, my phone buzzes with his reply.

Max: *Wouldn't dream of it, fiancée.*

I stare at the word.

My stomach flips; whether from dread or something else, I'm not willing to unpack right now.

Instead, I square my shoulders, exhale, and at 12:08 p.m., I hit submit.

The Tuesday edition of The Willow Gazette is now published.

The great spin has started.

I need coffee. Preferably Irish.

By the time I reach the Willow Creek Library Board meeting, I am running on fumes, a slightly expired protein bar, and sheer willpower.

I step into the stale, fluorescent-lit conference room, expecting the usual suspects in their usual seats. Instead, I find... Mrs. Thompson. Alone.

She sits at the long oak table, arms crossed, giving me a look that could melt steel.

I freeze. "Did I—?"

"You're on time," she interrupts, voice as sharp as her reading glasses.

I glance at the clock. 3:32 p.m. Okay, technically two minutes late, but this is a record for me.

I clear my throat. "And... where's everyone else?"

"Water main break," she says flatly. "Mayor Calloway is at the town square overseeing repairs. Ed Mulligan and Janine Moore got stuck in the detour traffic. Which means, for now, it's just you and me."

Well. This is awkward.

I take my seat across from her, placing my notebook and tablet on the table. "I assume we're still discussing the pop-up?"

She nods once, steepling her fingers. "Yes. And I have concerns."

Shocking.

Mrs. Thompson always has concerns.

Before I can ask what her particular concerns are today, the door swings open.

And in walks Mayor Calloway.

Followed by Max.

I blink.

Max looks a little too pleased with himself. I narrow my eyes. "You're late."

"Traffic," he says smoothly, dropping into the chair beside me. "You're lucky I made it at all."

"Lucky?" I arch a brow. "For me? Or for you?"

His mouth quirks, like he's fighting a smile. "Both."

Janine Moore hurries in, wearing a business suit and makeup, her hair down and low pumps. The change in her appearance is startling. She is an attractive woman. Janine nods and slips into her seat.

"What, no scones today?" my stomach prompts me to ask.

"No, sorry. You've ordered, so I didn't think we needed samples." She seems a little emotional. "Don't worry about the pop-up, I'll be sure to get them done by Wednesday."

Before I can respond, the mayor claps his hands together. Ed Mulligan, clearly frustrated by the delay, moves his chair with a little too much force and plops down, imitating one of the teens he would have had sitting outside his office.

"Now that we're all here," he says, beaming, "let's get started. And first, congratulations are in order!"

Oh, no.

I feel all the eyes in the room turn toward me and Max.

"Max and Elle, engaged!" Mayor Calloway practically cheers. "And to think, it all started right here, in this very room!"

Max chuckles under his breath. "I don't remember signing up for a meet-cute, but sure."

I shoot him a look before pasting on a smile. "Thank you, Mayor. It... happened fast."

Beside me, Max leans back in his chair, completely at ease. "Experience counts for something, right?"

I stab my pen into my notebook.

Mayor Calloway chuckles, then turns back to the table. "Alright, let's talk about the pop-up café event."

Ah, yes. The real reason we're here.

I glance at Mrs. Thompson, who looks about as enthusiastic as someone about to get a root canal.

"The library," she begins, in the tone of a woman who has already lost too many battles, "is not a coffee shop."

Max tilts his head. "But people drink coffee while they read."

"Finally, a word of reason," Ed mumbles.

"The library," she repeats, slower this time, "is not a coffee shop."

I rub my temples. "It's a one-weekend pop-up. A test run. We're not replacing books with espresso machines."

Ed huffs. "This whole thing is a slippery noodle!"

I exhale. "A slippery slope to what, exactly?"

"First, coffee. Then what? Pastries? Lounge chairs? A live jazz trio?"

I blink. "That... actually sounds nice."

Max leans toward me, voice low. "Think we should mention the open mic night now, or let them recover first?"

I sigh. "Just rip off the Band-Aid."

He nods, sitting up straighter. "We're also adding an open mic night."

Silence. For several beats.

Then Mrs. Thompson sighs. "Of course you are."

Ed looks horrified. "And what, exactly, does that involve?"

Max shrugs. "People read poetry, share their writing,

perform spoken word. It encourages creativity and community engagement."

"It sounds like a riot," Mrs. Thompson deadpans.

Max doesn't miss a beat. "Not unless you serve wine."

Ed sputters like Max just suggested sacrificing a goat in the library.

Janine hums, eyeing Max. "My bakery is providing the pastries. At a discount, of course."

Mrs. Thompson looks one second away from resigning.

I clear my throat. "We're also recording the event."

Ed groans. "Of course you are."

Max leans back, unfazed. "Oliver, my son, is recording the open mic night. He'll get permission from readers, and the library can use it for promotional materials or an audio archive."

Ed shakes his head. "Children these days. Always with the technology."

Max raises a brow. "That technology is why we're getting young people involved in the library."

Mrs. Thompson sighs again, adjusting her reading glasses. "Fine. The event can move forward."

A beat.

"Unless," she adds, "it disrupts the library."

Max nods, sincere and respectful. "Wouldn't dream of it."

Ed grumbles something about "glorified coffeehouses," but no one listens.

Meeting adjourned.

As we step outside, Max falls into step beside me.

"You survived," he muses.

I sigh. "Barely."

He grins, then glances toward the parking lot. "I have

the kids with me. Thought we'd grab dinner at The Hayloft. You should come."

I blink. "With you and the kids?"

His grin softens, turning into something more sincere. "Yeah. Fiancée. It's time you meet them."

Then he takes my hand. Something warm flickers in my chest.

"Alright. But if I end up in a small-town parenting lecture, I'm ordering dessert first."

"Deal."

The narrative clicked. I'm having dinner with Max Donovan and his kids.

A piece of cake. Right?

NINE
TRIVIA FANTASY

ELLE

THE AROMA of wood smoke and roasting vegetables fills the air as we–Max, his two kids, Oliver and Lily, and me–walk into The Hayloft. The space, once a sprawling barn, has been transformed into a warm and inviting farm-to-table restaurant with exposed brick walls, reclaimed wood tables, and soft Edison bulb lighting.

"Hey Donovan crew! Your usual table's ready," Kim said, gesturing towards a cozy booth near the fireplace. "Trivia night's starting in an hour, so get ready to put your knowledge to the test!" She grins at Oliver, then flicks her gaze to me, curiosity sparking in her dark eyes.

Kim leans in to Oliver. "Is this her?"

Oliver nods.

Kim shakes her head and starts to walk away. Max stops her.

"Kim, I would like to introduce Elle Sinclair, maybe you

know her as *The Willow Gazette* editor. Elle and I recently got engaged, maybe Oliver told you."

"Congrats. Nice to meet you, Ms. Sinclair."

I correct softly. "Call me Elle, please. Nice to meet you as well. Lovely place, I haven't been here before. I will definitely be back."

"The Donovans are here at least once a week. I'm sure to see you again." Kim's gaze lingers on Oliver for half a second too long before she recovers. "Well, good timing. Trivia night starts in an hour. Get ready to prove your worth."

"Sounds like a plan. We'll need some fuel. What's good tonight?"

Kim gives him a look. "Max, you order the same thing every week."

"Yeah, but I like to hear my options."

Oliver exhales, like this is the single most embarrassing moment of his life. Lily, quiet but observant, just smiles.

Kim doesn't miss a beat. "Tonight's special is braised short ribs with rosemary mashed potatoes. But since I already know you're getting the burger, should I just put in the order?"

Max grins. "You're a mind reader."

Kim jots something down, then turns to me. "And you? First-timer special?"

I tilt my head. "And what's the first-timer special?"

She grins. "Whatever I feel like bringing you."

I half-smile. "Risky. I like it."

Max gives me a look. "You're not going to regret it."

I lift a shoulder. "I live dangerously."

Kim laughs. "Love the attitude. Be right back."

She disappears toward the kitchen, and Oliver exhales sharply, his entire body relaxing.

Max leans back. "Alright, so, since we're here, let's talk about the pop-up event at the library. I know you both will be there."

Oliver smirks, leaning back in his chair with an air of exaggerated wisdom. "In Max Donovan's Dictionary, 'know' is defined as mandatory."

I arch an amused brow. "Oh, there's a Max Donovan Dictionary? I need a copy."

"Give it time," Oliver replies, his tone smug. "You'll learn the translation. I'm working on an app that should be out soon."

Lily grins, doodling on her napkin. "I'm designing the logo."

Oliver nods solemnly. "We're calling it Max Trans-late-again."

Laughter ripples through the table.

I clap my hands together. "Because he is often late."

Max is unimpressed. "I'm a busy guy."

I give him a knowing smile. "We know. We all love you just as you are."

The kids exchange a glance, one of those silent sibling conversations that speak volumes. Then Lily picks up her pencil again, this time sketching me with Max, the beginnings of something thoughtful taking shape.

Oliver, however, shifts gears, tapping a finger against his drink. "Isn't the engagement kinda quick? I thought we weren't supposed to skip stages. Didn't you guys just start going out?"

Kim, who had just arrived at the table, redirects

smoothly. "Hey, Oliver, what did you get on our English test? I passed. You?"

Max leans slightly toward me, murmuring under his breath. "How'd I not see this before? They're totally crushing."

Oliver groans. "It was so unexpected. I can't wait until Mrs. Stone is back from maternity leave."

Kim sighs dramatically. "Me too. This sub actually expects us to do our homework." Her phone buzzes, and she glances at it. "Well, best of luck on the Fantasy Fiction Trivia tonight. Gotta get the door."

I watch her leave, then turn to Oliver with a teasing tilt of my head. "So, you and Kim have the same English class? She's pretty. Seems nice."

Oliver shrugs, but there's a telltale flush creeping up his neck. "Uh-huh. Pretty smart too. She's one of the few I can talk to."

Lily, ever the instigator, smiles as she continues sketching. "They sit together for lunch almost every day. Own it, bro. She's your girlfriend. Or you want her to be."

Oliver snaps his head toward her. "Lily! You promised. Snitch. Freshman snitch."

Lily giggles, entirely unrepentant. "Ollie's got a girlfriend. Ollie's got a girlfriend."

Max sets his drink down. "Stop. Now." He fixes his son with a look. "Ollie, is this true? You like this girl?"

Oliver shifts uncomfortably. "Dad, not so loud!" In a lower voice, "We can talk. Kim understands the power of emerging technologies in the modern marketplace."

Max blinks, then deadpans, "Who are you? My son or a technology analyst?"

I chuckle, shaking my head. "Apparently, an analyst."

Oliver crosses his arms. "You told me to read a lot. Industry journals, to stay abreast of trends."

I tilt my head, watching Lily work. "What are you doing over there? Can I see?"

Lily hunches over the placemat, eyes twinkling. "In a minute, not done. Ollie, keep your eyes on your half of the table, Mr. Brainy."

Oliver, eager for a distraction, turns to me. "You ever play trivia? We're here at least once a week. Dad says it's fun for our brains."

I hum, considering. "No, can't say I have a strong trivia background."

Oliver half-smiles. "That's okay. The theme is Fantasy Fiction, so you wouldn't know anything about it, like most older people."

I raise a slow, deliberate brow. "Oh, I know some about Fantasy Fiction. Try me."

Max leans back, amused. "This will be good."

Oliver scrolls through his phone, searching for a worthy question. "Okay. Let's see… something older, that you might have read. In J.R.R. Tolkien's *The Lord of the Rings*, what is the name of the sword Frodo Baggins receives from Bilbo?"

I barely pause. "Sting. Easy. Where's the challenge?"

Max snorts. "I knew that one. Make them harder, Ollie."

Oliver's eyes narrow as he ups the difficulty. "Who is the author of *A Song of Ice and Fire*, which was adapted into the *Game of Thrones* television show?"

I sip my drink before answering nonchalantly, "George R.R. Martin." I shoot Max a look. "We've met. Mutual admiration society."

Oliver's face scrunches as he scrolls for something trickier. "Alright, something current. In Liane Cillser's *The*

Veridion Chronicles, the world of Veridion is divided into five realms, each reflecting a core virtue of the Balance Accord. Name at least three."

Max looks at me, intrigued. "Really? I can't wait to read it now."

I grin. "Oh, this is current. I should know this... Realm of Clarity: Truth Seekers. Realm of Hearth: Protectors & Caretakers. And..." I tap my finger against my chin. "Oh! Realm of Embers: Warriors & Defenders. Gotta have warriors for that conflict to shine."

Oliver leans back, grudgingly impressed. "That's three. Good job."

I grin. "Realm of Tides: Artists & Visionaries. And Realm of Shadows: Outcasts & The Lost. Boom."

I throw my hands up in victory. "Who knows her Fantasy, yeah, yeah. Fiction, yeah, yeah."

Max chuckles, shaking his head. "Alright, you made your point." He looks to his son. "You walked right into that one, son."

Oliver stares at me in disbelief. "You've read *The Veridion Chronicles*?"

I wink. "Several times. So, I hear you're a fan."

Lily chimes in, still focused on her drawing. "Oh, I am. I just finished book one. I wouldn't mind visiting the Realm of Tides."

I nod approvingly. "That makes sense. Bet you'd enjoy that. Are you finished with the drawing? Can I see?"

Lily hesitates, then hands it over. "It's not that good, but you can have it if you want."

I study the sketch. "Oh, I want. Very much. This is wonderful, Lily. Thank you. I'm framing it."

Max looks over my shoulder, nodding. "Great job, honey."

Lily beams. "When I look at you with my dad, it's like you're twin flames, burning together. So that's what I tried to show, by the flames behind you. I think you and my dad are more than just friends."

Oliver groans. "They're engaged, Lil. Pay attention."

I say softly. "Friends first. But yes, we're engaged, your dad and I."

Max clears his throat. "Did they talk about it at school today? Any problems?" He glances at me before adding, "Whole truth?"

I shake my head slightly.

Max exhales. "Well, that's what everyone thinks. We like each other, but like we talked about before, you shouldn't skip stages when building a relationship. I didn't mean to tell everyone in Blecker's Saturday night that we were engaged. But I did. For good reason. And... it felt right."

Max looks at me and we lock eyes for a moment, a smile reflected on the other's face.

I turn to the kids. "You'll see an announcement in the paper tomorrow. And your dad will get me a ring. But the truth is, we're getting to know each other. We won't be setting a date anytime soon. Is that okay with you guys?"

Long silence.

Then Lily pipes up, hopeful. "Can you braid hair? Dad sucks at it."

Max sighs. "Thanks, Lil. But... it's true, I do."

I grin. "I don't think I'd suck at it. Would love to braid your hair sometime, Lily."

Oliver glances at the trivia host setting up at the front of the restaurant and straightens. "Trivia is about to start. I'll get our scorecards." As he stands, he turns toward the counter. "Kim, give me four. Dad's got his girlfriend with us."

Kim Ho smiles as she hands Oliver the scorecards. "Here." Then to me, "Elle, have we met before? You look familiar."

I smile warmly. "I don't know. Don't think so."

Max leans back, his arm resting on the back of the booth. "Kim's parents, Chris and Belle Ho are customers of mine. They buy organic produce, a little dairy." He scans the room briefly. "Your parents are here tonight? I'd like to introduce Elle to them."

Kim nods. "Yeah, somewhere. I'll let them know to stop by."

I tilt my head, "Kim, can you join us for a bit?"

Kim glances at the host stand. "Until someone comes to the front, sure." Oliver moves over making room for Kim to slide in next to him.

I ask her, "Are you a fan of *The Veridion Chronicles*, like Lily and Oliver?"

Kim's eyes brighten instantly. "Of course. You could call me a mega-fan. I've been to all the fan events since the first book five years ago." She elbows Oliver lightly. "Ollie, you've got to come with me to the next one. Book Three is out in two months; I'm talking Christmas presents. But that means by spring, fan events will start." She grins, then lowers her voice as if sharing a sacred phrase. "Your power is in your truth."

Without missing a beat, Oliver echoes back, "Your power is in your truth."

Their shared enthusiasm makes me chuckle, but before

she can comment, the server appears with our food, setting down plates in front of us.

Oliver picks up the ketchup bottle. "Kim, you want ketchup or hot sauce?" He pours some on the fries.

Kim reaches for a fry from his plate, completely unfazed. "Ketchup."

Oliver raises an eyebrow but doesn't protest as she takes another.

Max watches the exchange, then turns to me, lowering his voice. "Who is this kid, and what happened to my son?"

I suppress a smile. "Love makes fools of us all. At least he's doing this in front of you and not when you're not looking."

Max exhales, shaking his head as if resigning himself to some inevitable reality. Then, without overthinking it, he slides his hand into mine, lacing our fingers together under the table.

I blink at the unexpected contact. It feels comforting.

Max leans in slightly, his voice quiet but deliberate. "Just for show. People are watching."

My lips curve, but I try to make my gaze soft as I squeeze his hand back. "Right. Honesty Donovan." I lift our joined hands slightly, letting the warmth of his touch linger. "But I'm not complaining."

THE TRIVIA HOST taps the mic, clearing his throat. "Alright, everyone, time for the final round. It's neck and neck between the Donovans and the Wrights. This one's for the win."

He pauses dramatically before reading the question.

"For the sudden death point, correctly answer: What

type of creature is Falkor in Michael Ende's *The Never-Ending Story*?"

Oliver leans forward, confident. "That's easy. Dragon." He shoots his hand up.

My eyes widen, and I shake my head. "No, that's wrong."

Oliver frowns, turning to me just as the host calls, "For the answer, Donovan table."

"Luckdragon!" I yell. "A luckdragon!"

Oliver stares at me, confused. "Drag... what?"

The trivia host nods. "Right. The Donovans win!"

Our table erupts in cheers.

Max grins, clapping Oliver on the back. "We won."

Lily pumps her fist. "Good job!"

I shake my head with a playful smirk. "Close call."

Oliver exhales, relieved. "Good save, Elle. I almost lost that."

Max nudges his shoulder. "Team effort."

I lift my glass slightly in a toast. "We played as a team. *E pluribus unum*."

Oliver studies me for a second before nodding, his expression softening. "Well, welcome to the Donovan team, Elle."

I meet his gaze and smile. "Thank you, Oliver."

Max squeezes my hand under the table, his voice low but sure. "Like I said," he murmurs, "a match made in heaven."

TEN
HIDDEN MESSAGES

MAX

MORNINGS AT PERK UP are as predictable as my coffee order: black, no sugar, no nonsense.

The usual crowd hums around us—early risers getting their caffeine fix, a few retirees in a heated discussion about municipal parking, and the ever-watchful Mrs. Thompson, our town head librarian, casually keeping tabs on Elle and me from across the room.

Elle, completely unbothered, takes a slow sip of her abomination of a latte—something caramel, something vanilla, something that definitely doesn't belong in coffee. She sets it down with a satisfied sigh and grins at me.

I know that grin. That's the I'm-about-to-do-something grin.

She slides a book across the table.

I glance down. *The Veridion Chronicles: The Choice. Book One.*

I raise a brow. "You're giving me homework?"

"No, I'm giving you a collector's item."

I flip it open, running my fingers over the title page. "You realize I could just go buy one, right? I can afford it."

She sighs, exasperated. "Yes, but why would you do that when I'm literally handing you one?"

I lean back in my chair, pretending to consider. "Because how often do you get to buy a bestseller written by someone you know from an actual bookstore? It's an experience, Sinclair. I want the experience."

She blinks. "You want to stand in line behind a teenager with neon hair buying twelve copies for their fan club? You want to deal with a clerk asking if you've read the entire series yet?"

"Exactly."

She snorts. "You are ridiculous."

I grin. "Possibly. But I'm still going to buy it."

She rolls her eyes and pushes the book toward me again. "Fine. But this one is special. Open the cover."

I do. Looks normal enough.

Then she pulls something from her bag and slides it across the table: a tiny UV flashlight.

I arch a brow. "Please tell me this doesn't reveal a secret map to a treasure buried under your office."

"Nope. Better."

I click on the light and sweep it over the inside cover. And there it is.

Max—sometimes the best secrets are hidden in plain sight. Just like us.

I stare at the words. My throat tightens; my eyes mist. I look at her, feeling it hit hard.

Focus, Max. Focus on the truth of this moment. Elle.

Elle watches me, her usual smile softer now. "See?"

I clear my throat, dragging my thumb across the message like I can somehow feel it. "Damn. Now I have to get you a really nice ring, because I don't know how to top this gesture."

She grins, leaning in slightly. "Well, good thing I have high standards."

Damn the town gossip mill. I lean over the table, cup her jaw with my hand, and kiss her. "Thank you. A treasure indeed," I whisper.

As I reclaim my chair, I see her eyes misting now, too.

"Let me thank you in private. Meet me in my office tonight."

"Always. It's our standing date, though. I'm growing fond of your office, Max." Elle wets her lips with her tongue.

Before I can respond, Tony Holsolm strolls over, wiping his hands on a rag. He looks concerned.

"So," he starts, crossing his arms, "should I be worried about this coffee thing you two are running at the library?"

Elle and I exchange a glance.

"The pop-up?" I ask. "I mean, technically, it's just a one-time event to test demand."

Tony gestures around his café. "Demand? I open at 6:30 a.m., and I still have people standing at the door before I turn the lights on. And now you're introducing them to a competing coffee option?"

Elle shakes her head. "Not competing. Complementary. And the library doesn't open until nine."

Tony narrows his eyes.

"Okay, fine," she amends. "Maybe slightly competing. But the library café is still hypothetical. The Board hasn't committed to making it permanent."

Tony scratches his chin. "Hmm."

I watch him carefully, my brain kicking into gear. There's opportunity here.

I lean forward. "Tony, if this pop-up proves there's strong demand for an evening café in town, you could be the one to capitalize on it."

He blinks. "What do you mean?"

"Well, think about it." I gesture around Perk Up. "You close at 2:30 p.m. right now, but what if you extended your hours, even just a couple of nights a week? We're talking open-mic nights, live readings, maybe a space for the local writers' group to meet. You'd have built-in customers. If the Library Board drags their feet or ultimately says no to making the café permanent, you'd already be the obvious alternative."

Tony frowns, but I can see the wheels turning.

Elle tilts her head. "It's not a bad idea. You could start small—maybe a test run, see what the demand looks like?"

Tony exhales. "It is something to think about. Especially if Oliver's podcast gets people talking."

Elle nods. "Exactly. And you'd already have a built-in event schedule with what we're doing at the library."

Tony points a finger at me. "Didn't you once mention you used to do business consulting?"

I take a sip of my coffee. "Once upon a time."

He studies me for a moment, then nods. "Alright. I'll keep an eye on how your pop-up does. If there's interest, we'll talk."

I tip my cup in a silent salute. "Looking forward to it."

Tony mutters something about damn good ideas sneaking up on him before he's had his second coffee and heads back to the counter.

Elle watches him go, then turns to me, an amused glint in her eye. "So... you just casually lay the groundwork for expanding small businesses over breakfast?"

I shrug. "It's a hobby."

She leans in slightly, her voice softer. "That was impressive."

I hold her gaze. "Yeah?"

She nods, tapping her fingers against the book still sitting between us. "I knew you were more than just a grumpy farmer."

I grin. "And I knew you were more than just a small-town newspaper editor."

Her eyes flicker with something unreadable before she shakes her head with a small laugh. "You know, if you had bought that book, you wouldn't have found my message."

"True." I pull the book to me. "Guess I'll have to settle for this copy after all."

Elle arches a brow. "Giving up on the 'experience' already?"

I grin. "Oh no, I still want the experience. I'm just going to buy Book Two instead."

She groans, laughing as she takes a sip of her coffee. "You are impossible."

"Yep," I say, completely unapologetic. "And you're stuck with me now."

She leans back in her chair, shaking her head. "Yeah. I guess I am."

And for the first time, the weight of those words doesn't feel like a lie.

It feels... exactly right.

. . .

I TELL myself I'll only read a chapter.

Just one.

I have a farm to run, kids to raise, and a fake engagement to keep from feeling too real. I don't have time to be pulled into some elaborate fantasy world.

And yet, an hour later, I'm sitting on my couch, legs stretched out, coffee cold on the table, completely gone.

I knew Elle was successful, but I hadn't realized just how successful until now. Her writing isn't just good; it's sharp, immersive—the kind of storytelling that makes you forget reality exists at all.

The world of *The Veridion Chronicles* is built on one rule: truth. A society where magic, Lumea, isn't about wands or potions but about alignment with oneself. The more honest you are about your desires, your fears, your strengths, the stronger your power. But lies? Lies corrode it, weaken it, until you have nothing left but shadows.

I close the book for a moment, running my thumb along the cover.

Honesty equals strength.

If that's the case, then what the hell does that make me?

I shake my head and turn the page. Maybe Lumea wouldn't even light up for me. Maybe I'd have been exiled to the Realm of Shadows before I stepped foot into that world.

But then I think about Elle.

She built this. This entire world where truth literally shapes reality. A world where you have to be honest with yourself, or you'll lose everything.

And I start to wonder... is that what she's doing here, with me?

Is she testing how much of the truth she can stand?

Because I've seen the way she watches me when she thinks I'm not paying attention. The way she slips in under my guard with a well-placed joke, a teasing remark. The way she lights up when my kids actually talk to her, engage with her.

And I know Elle's been living in her own kind of exile.

She built a fortress of fiction, just like I built a fortress of routine.

I stare down at the book in my hands and realize something strange.

I want to live in this world. Not just *The Veridion Chronicles*. I want to live in a place where truth actually means something. Where speaking it doesn't tear you apart but makes you stronger.

I think about Lily, my daughter, growing up without a strong female figure. She's independent, sure, but she's just thirteen. She still asks me to braid her hair, and I try, but she always ends up having to redo it. I picture Elle sitting with her, hands working gently, voice soft as she explains something about one of her fantasy worlds. Or the real one. Maybe they're talking about art, maybe about life. Either way, it's easy to imagine—too easy.

I blink, shaking the thought away.

Then my mind shifts to Oliver.

Oliver, who is teetering on the edge of something that looks a lot like first love.

I've seen the way he looks at Kim Ho when he thinks no one is watching. I've seen the uncertainty—the way he's trying to figure out what comes next, how to bridge that space between childhood and whatever comes after.

And I know, sooner or later, he's going to leave.

Maybe not tomorrow, maybe not next year. But the countdown has started.

The thought knots something deep in my chest.

Because if Oliver leaves, and then Lily grows up and moves on, what does that leave me with?

An empty house. A stack of memories and not much else.

I exhale and close the book, setting it on my chest.

For the first time, I let myself imagine it—really imagine it.

Elle, in this house. Not just as a visitor, not just as a temporary arrangement, but as something real.

I picture her at the kitchen table, arguing with me over whether coffee should taste like actual coffee or a dessert experiment gone wrong. I picture her laughing at one of my dad jokes while pretending not to. I picture her stealing my flannel shirts just to mess with me, rolling up the sleeves because they're too big.

I picture her here, in the everyday moments. Not just the grand gestures.

I rub a hand over my face, forcing a slow breath.

This isn't just about Elle needing cover from the press.

It isn't just about keeping people from digging into my past.

It's about the fact that for the first time in a long time, I can actually see a future that doesn't feel like a compromise.

Because Elle gets it.

She knows what it's like to build something from nothing. She knows what it's like to live under the weight of expectations and still carve out something meaningful. She knows what it is to be a self-sufficient, independent woman, while thriving with a partner.

And maybe... just maybe... I could be that for her, too.

I glance at the book again—at the world she created.

A world built on truth.

Maybe it's time I start living like I belong in it.

MY PHONE BUZZES JUST as I'm finishing up evening chores. The name on the screen makes me half-smile.

Elle Sinclair.

I wipe my hands on a rag and answer. "Let me guess—you need me to bail you out of some elaborate lie you spun for the Gazette?"

"Not today," she says, amusement clear in her voice. "Though I appreciate knowing that's an option."

I lean against the fence, watching the sunset bleed orange across the fields. "So, what's up?"

"I was wondering if I could take Lily shopping and out to dinner on Thursday."

I blink. "She voluntarily agreed to shopping?"

Elle laughs. "She agreed when I told her it included art supplies. She's got her art lesson that afternoon, so I figured I could pick her up after."

I rub the back of my neck, glancing toward the house. "You know she'll probably come home with half the store."

"Would that be a problem?"

I shake my head, even though she can't see it. "Nah. She could do worse for an addiction."

Her voice softens. "She's a talented kid, Max."

"Yeah," I murmur, watching the house lights flick on. "She is."

There's a small pause before she speaks again. "So, it's a yes?"

I exhale. "Yeah. But just warning you, she's going to make you look at every single sketchpad and brush set before she decides."

"Max," Elle deadpans, "do you think I got to be a best-selling fantasy author without extreme patience?"

I chuckle. "Alright. Just make sure she eats real food at some point."

"I will. But define real food?"

I narrow my eyes. "Elle."

She laughs. "Fine, fine. No cake for dinner. You're such a responsible father."

I roll my eyes. "You're just realizing this now?"

"Oh, I knew. Just didn't want to encourage the grumpy-farmer ego too much."

"Appreciate your restraint," I deadpan.

We wrap up the call, and I pocket my phone, heading inside where my kids are already at the table.

It's a little surreal, seeing them sitting there, shoveling food into their mouths like they haven't eaten in weeks.

I clear my throat. "Alright. We need to talk."

Oliver doesn't look up from his plate. "That sounds ominous."

Lily tilts her head. "Did we do something?"

"No," I say, taking my seat. "Just... wanted to check in. About Elle."

Oliver finally looks up, brow furrowed. "What about her?"

I exhale. "Look, I know this whole engagement thing

happened fast. And I wanted to make sure you two are okay with it. With her."

Lily shrugs. "She's nice. And she actually listens when I talk about art."

Oliver spears a piece of chicken with his fork. "And she makes you less grumpy."

I pause. "Less grumpy?"

"Yeah," he says, smirking slightly. "You smile more. You joke more. It's weird."

Lily nods. "But a good weird."

I glance between them, something warm settling in my chest. "So... you're okay with all of this?"

Oliver shrugs. "We just want you to be happy, Dad."

I clear my throat, not sure what to do with the sudden emotional punch to the gut. "Right. Good. Thanks."

Lily, ever perceptive, narrows her eyes. "You like her, don't you?"

I pause. "I mean... yeah. She's smart. Funny. Sharp as hell."

Oliver grins. "And hot."

I glare at him. "Finish your dinner."

He chuckles, but obeys.

A beat passes before I switch gears. "Speaking of liking people... Oliver, what's going on with Kim?"

Oliver chokes on his water. "Dad!"

Lily, delighted, claps her hands. "Oh! This is so fun."

Oliver shoots her a shut-up look before turning back to me. "Nothing's going on."

I raise a brow. "She seems nice. Smart. Funny. Sharp as hell."

Oliver groans. "You're impossible."

Lily grins. "And hot."

I snort. "Thanks for the callback."

Oliver glares at both of us. "We're friends. That's it."

I nod slowly. "Okay. But if it ever becomes more than that, I just want you to know... relationships aren't about finding the perfect person. They're about being the right person."

Oliver frowns. "What does that mean?"

"It means you need to know yourself before you can know if someone's the right fit for you. And you for them."

He stares at his plate, expression unreadable. "And what if you don't know yet?"

I exhale. "Then take your time. Figure it out. No rush."

Oliver doesn't say anything, but I see the wheels turning.

Lily, ever the wildcard, picks up her fork and announces, "Mom's happy about Elle."

I blink. "What?"

She chews, then shrugs. "I just feel it."

Oliver shifts. "Lily, you can't just—"

"I can," she insists. "And I do. She likes Elle. I like Elle."

The room falls silent.

I swallow, something pushing in my throat. "Thanks, honey."

Lily smiles. "You're welcome."

We finish dinner, and as I clear the plates, I realize something.

For the first time in a long time, the future doesn't feel so uncertain.

It feels... possible.

And maybe, just maybe, Elle Sinclair is the reason why.

ELEVEN
BEACHSIDE PROPOSALS

ELLE

BY NOW, Max's barn office is as familiar as my own at *The Willow Gazette*. It's become a place where our fake engagement somehow feels more real than anything outside these walls. Where we're becoming partners in "figuring things out," supporting one another, or just enjoying being in each other's physical energy. Max's energy is peaceful, protective, and oh, so sexy.

I throw my purse down at his desk, pull out my iPad, and go join my companion.

Max is already on the sofa, his feet up on a chair. Seeing him there with my book in his lap seems odd to me—but good. He must be lost in the pages because he doesn't acknowledge I've arrived. I'm not sure what to make of that. Truthfully, I'm a little jealous of the hold my words have on him.

So I clear my throat loudly and speak. "You know, it's a

little nerve-wracking watching someone read my work like it's a car manual."

I kick off my shoes and drop into the chair across from him.

He wry smiles, flipping a page. "I don't know. Pacing is solid. World-building's tight. Might have potential."

I gasp, clutching my chest. "Oh, you did not just say 'might have potential.'"

His lips twitch. "What? I'm still forming my critical opinion."

"Unbelievable," I huff, nestling my feet under his leg. "And to think, I actually liked you."

He grins. "Don't worry. I like you enough to keep reading."

I roll my eyes, but before I can fire back, my iPad vibrates. I glance at the screen and groan.

Liane Cillser's Mystery Fiancé Identified as 'Maxwell'; Rumors of Romantic Getaway in St. John's!

"Oh, for the love of coffee." I wonder where the name Maxwell came from. Is this unraveling? My press release only cited the sighting in St. John's. Toma doesn't know his name, so how—who?

"What now?" Max frowns.

I turn the iPad toward him. "Apparently, we were seen on a beach in St. John's."

His eyebrows rise as he leans in to read. "Huh. Not gonna lie, Elle, I would've remembered a romantic beach vacation."

I sigh dramatically. "I knew I should've taken more selfies on our trip. You, me, the crashing waves—"

Max cuts in smoothly. "Holding hands under the moonlight. That little seafood shack we found where you insisted I try the coconut shrimp."

"Oh, and don't forget, those damn seagulls kept trying to steal your scone." I muse.

"That was a battle, Sinclair. They came at me like they had a personal vendetta."

"Maybe they knew you don't appreciate delicate flavors."

His eyes narrow playfully. "Or maybe you bribed them."

I press a hand to my chest. "How dare you accuse me."

"Oh, don't even pretend," he says, shaking his head. "I saw the way you tossed that last piece of croissant straight toward them."

I gasp. "That was an accident."

"Uh-huh. Sure." He leans forward, laughing. "And on that very same beach, if I recall, is where I gave you this ring." He takes my hand, pulling me onto the sofa next to him.

I blink at him, catching the way his blue eyes spark with amusement.

"Oh?" I arch a brow, playing along. "You proposed to me there?"

Max nods slowly, voice dropping to something danger-ously smooth. "Right there, with the waves at our feet, the sunset behind us, a stray dog watching from the dunes..."

"A stray dog?" I bite my lip, fighting laughter.

He nods solemnly. "Very majestic. Wise beyond his years. Probably officiated weddings in a past life."

I shake my head, grinning. "Okay, and then what?"

Max lifts my hand, slipping a small diamond ring onto my finger. The gold band and the single, clear diamond catch the light. "I looked into your eyes, said, 'Elle Sinclair, you are the only woman I've ever met who can make sarcasm sound like a love language, and I'd be an absolute idiot not to make this real.'"

Something tightens in my chest, but I push past it with humor. "And then?"

I study the ring. It's a simple diamond solitaire—the cut classic, the setting understated. Not billionaire level, not even remotely flashy, but exactly what an organic farmer with a practical mindset would buy. The diamond, though small, sparkles with an inner fire.

Max grins. "Then we had really bad piña coladas at that tourist bar and spent half the night debating if a flamingo could beat a seagull in a fight."

I snort. "I still say the flamingo would win."

"Sinclair, it's only got one leg."

"It has range."

Max just shakes his head, laughing. "This is ridiculous."

I grin, tucking my hair behind my ear. "But admit it—you love it."

His expression softens just slightly. "Yeah. I do. Is it acceptable?"

Before I can answer, my iPad buzzes again. This time, it's a video call from Elliot.

"Oh, hell," I mutter.

Max frowns. "What's wrong?"

"My brother." I sigh.

I hit accept, and Elliot Sinclair appears—immaculately put together, looking as if he were born suspicious.

"Elle," he greets, eyes sharp. "You've been busy."

I force a bright smile. "Elliot! What a lovely unannounced interrogation."

He raises a brow. "Imagine my surprise when I hear that my sister—or her pen name—is engaged. I did a little online searching to find your newspaper with a little vital-statistics notice that you, as my sister, who last told me she had a date, are now engaged to Max Donovan. Quite a first date, Sis."

I clear my throat. "Life comes at you fast."

Elliot studies Max for a beat. "And this must be the mystery farmer. Your fiancé."

Max leans forward, nodding. "Yeah, eh—hello. Max Donovan. Nice to meet you."

Elliot tilts his head. "So. You grow vegetables."

Max shrugs. "And dairy cows. Used to grow businesses, too."

Elliot stills. "Businesses?"

Max nods. "I started in hedge funds, expanded into private equity and venture capital. Specialized in strategic relationships and growth—especially with innovation."

I watch as Elliot's entire demeanor shifts.

"Really," he says, intrigued.

Max nods. "Worked in the industry for years. Left when it stopped aligning with what I stand for. And life shifted."

Elliot steeples his fingers. "Interesting. I was actually calling Elle about a business expansion for *Green Agricultural*. But if you have a background in private equity, maybe you should be the one I'm talking to."

Max lifts a brow. "You looking at innovation partners?"

Elliot nods. "Independent suppliers. Long-term growth. We're evaluating new agricultural technology investments for sustainable expansion."

Max leans back, considering. "Could be mutually beneficial."

Elliot grins. "Then maybe I should visit your farm this spring."

Max nods. "You'd be welcome anytime."

The truth sharpens. My brother and my fake fiancé are now business networking. And I have no idea how we got here.

As they keep talking, I lean back, watching them.

They fit. Max isn't intimidated by Elliot's sharp business mind. Elliot isn't dismissing Max as just a farmer. Somehow, their worlds have collided, and seamlessly at that.

And so have ours.

I look at my ring.

This started as strategic fiction. But now? I'm not so sure.

Max ends the call and glances at me, smug. "Well, that went well."

I shake my head, exhaling. "You are impossible."

He grins. "Yeah. But you love it."

Damn it. I just might.

Max is still grinning at me like he just won something when my iPad buzzes again.

I sigh dramatically. "What now? Another fan sighting? Maybe this time we were spotted on a gondola in Venice?"

He grins. "I'd like to think we'd at least be in France. You seem like a Paris type."

I scoff, swiping to check the message. "Oh, please. You'd hate Paris. The traffic, the small coffees, the electric cars—"

"Okay, yeah. That's a hard no."

I chuckle, but my attention shifts as I read the actual text. "Oh. Pastries."

Max raises an eyebrow. "That sounds dangerous when you say it like that."

I turn the screen toward him. "Janine just texted. The order will be ready for pickup tomorrow by noon."

He scans the message and nods. "Alright, I'll pick it up."

I tilt my head. "You volunteered suspiciously fast. You're not trying to sabotage the pastries again, are you?"

Max narrows his eyes. "That lavender scone was an attack on my taste buds, and I stand by that."

I half-smile. "You sound traumatized."

"I am."

I chuckle and lay my tablet on the table, stretching my arms over my head. "Alright, with that settled, I officially declare this strategy session complete."

Max leans back, watching me. "Big day at the paper tomorrow?"

I sigh at the thought of what tomorrow will be. "Putting the Gazette to bed. It's always chaos on deadline day."

He raises an eyebrow. "You make it sound violent."

"Oh, it is," I say, grinning. "Last-minute article rewrites. Ad placements shifting because a local business forgets to send over their payment. And my personal favorite: the mayor calling at the eleventh hour to remind me about some boring city-ordinance update that absolutely no one cares about."

Max chuckles. "Sounds thrilling."

"Oh, it's a rush," I say dramatically. "Nothing like the sheer panic of realizing you have exactly ten minutes to fill six column inches with something that isn't pure nonsense."

He smirks. "And yet, you thrive on it."

"I do not thrive. I survive with flair."

Max shakes his head, amused.

I exhale, stretching my legs out and tapping my fingers on the armrest.

Max glances at me. "Still sure about it?"

I blink, caught off guard.

Am I?

The truth is, I stopped questioning this whole thing weeks ago. Somewhere between library board debates, open-mic scheming, and pretend beachside proposals, it became too easy.

Too... right.

I look down at the ring, small but solid on my finger. "Yeah," I say finally, quieter this time. "I am."

Max watches me, something unreadable flickering in his expression. "Good."

A silence settles.

I clear my throat. "Well, I should go before I start hallucinating punctuation errors in my sleep."

Max, closing down the office, walks me to the door. We stroll down the hallway toward the main barn doors. We fall in step together; then he hooks my arm and pulls me close. Before I say anything, his lips press into mine, his body into my body. The kiss is more than just our lips—it's our beings. My back relaxes against his strong arms, and it feels incredibly good. The moment is electric, leaving us breathless.

We steady each other, our eyes locked, before we continue together.

Before I know it, we're standing at my car. He opens my door, and I get in. Then he leans on it before closing.

"You want me to bring you anything from the bakery tomorrow?"

I pause, tapping my chin. "I don't know... think they have revenge scones?"

Max groans. "I swear, Elle."

"See you tomorrow, fiancé."

"Looking forward to it, fiancée."

TWELVE
FEDERAL MUFFINS

MAX

THERE ARE a lot of things I expect to see when I pull up to pick up the pastry order for the library pop-up. A sleep-deprived baker covered in flour? Sure. A "Be Back in 10 Minutes" sign? Annoying, but possible. An actual FBI seizure notice slapped across the door? Not even on my list of nightmares. I put the truck in park and just stare at the sign, waiting for my brain to catch up.

THIS PROPERTY HAS BEEN SEIZED BY THE FEDERAL BUREAU OF INVESTIGATION. ALL OPERATIONS HALTED UNTIL FURTHER NOTICE.

I blink. Well. That escalated quickly. I scan the area, half-expecting a tactical team in black suits to storm out carrying trays of confiscated croissants, but the place looks eerily still. Janine Moore's bakery. Library Board member, pastry enthusiast, and, apparently, covert criminal mastermind? Fantastic.

I rub my jaw, trying to process. The bakery is supposed

to have our full order: scones, muffins, those ridiculously bougie lavender pastries Elle made me try. All the essentials for the pop-up café event. Janine sent a text late last night. I'm literally here to pick them up. And now? Now the FBI has the muffins.

I sigh, step out of the truck, and walk up to the door. It's locked, obviously. I plant my hands on my hips, scanning the building like I'm going to miraculously find a secret underground black-market pastry tunnel. What the hell is this place doing? Laundering money through artisanal bread sales? Smuggling illicit goods in sourdough loaves? Running an underground donut fight club?

I cup my hands to the glass and lean in. Maybe our order is still on the counter, waiting to be picked up. But what I see stops me cold. The bakery racks are stripped bare and left half-loaded, trays jammed in at odd angles or hanging crooked in their rails. One tray lies on the floor; another dangles as if it was shoved in mid-shift and forgotten. The display cases are wide open and empty, doors gaping like mouths in shock. The countertop is scattered with flour smudges and paper scraps. The checkout screen is missing, its cords hanging down like snapped tendons. And yet, the Shriners' donation box still stands next to the register. Untouched. Like a relic that refused to fall.

It looks like someone pulled the place apart in a hurry and didn't care about the mess they left behind—fast, clinical extraction. It's like looking at a crime scene, the aftermath of a theft. But it's more than that. It's a business—someone's livelihood—ripped apart. The sheer, violent disregard for everything built here—the systems, the effort, the reputation—makes my jaw ache. This isn't just a failure; it's an obliteration. And it's a gut punch to witness.

Then I see it: one cracked, pumpkin-shaped sugar cookie on the floor, taking cover under the front counter. Like it tried to hide and almost made it. As business failures go, it's apparent this one was fast and violent.

I pull out my phone and snap a picture of the FBI notice. Elle is never going to believe this. A cold breeze tugs at the paper, and I take several more shots. Then I fire off a text:

Max: *Slight issue with the pastries.*

Max: *By slight, I mean the bakery is closed.*

Max: *By closed, I mean the FBI shut it down.*

Max: *I think our muffins are in federal custody.*

I stare at my phone. No response. I sigh, drag a hand through my hair. This is going to ruin Elle's entire deadline day. And somehow, I just know she's going to blame me personally for the tragic loss of baked goods. Fantastic.

I get back in the truck, pull out of the empty lot, and head toward *The Willow Gazette*, preparing for a very interesting conversation.

THE WILLOW GAZETTE office is exactly what I expect—controlled chaos, heavy on the chaos. Stacks of paper teeter on desks, phones ring from every direction, and the printer in the back sounds like it's considering an early retirement. A young reporter, wild-eyed and caffeine-fueled, types like they're physically wrestling a deadline into submission.

And in the middle of it all, Elle Sinclair. She stands behind her desk, hair twisted up in a messy bun, flipping through a proof like she's single-handedly responsible for the fate of journalism itself.

I don't bother knocking. That ship sailed weeks ago. I drop into the chair across from her desk, lean forward, and clear my throat. "We have a problem."

Without looking up, she flips another page. "Is it an actual problem or a Max problem?"

I prop my arms on the desk. "That depends. Do you consider the FBI shutting down our bakery a Max problem?"

Her pen stops mid-edit. Slowly, like she's bracing for impact, she lifts her head. Her eyes zero in on me. "I'm sorry, what?"

I slide my phone across the desk, the FBI seizure notice glowing on the screen like a beacon of bureaucratic doom.

Elle blinks. Then blinks again. Then slowly sets her pen down. She exhales. "What... why... how is this my life?"

I smile. "Great question. Shall we unpack it?"

Her glare could start a fire. "What exactly did they do?"

I shrug. "Well, they seized things. That's their whole deal. What those things were, I don't know. But considering they've locked the place up, I'm gonna go ahead and say the muffins are in federal custody."

Elle leans back, staring at the ceiling like she's having an out-of-body experience. "So, we have no pastries for the pop-up?"

"Correct."

"And there's no way to get more in time?"

"Well," I say, dragging out the word, "not from a bakery that isn't currently under investigation for what I assume is some kind of high-stakes croissant crime."

Elle groans and lets her head drop onto the desk.

I drum my fingers on the surface. "So, I take it that means the pop-up is canceled?"

She lifts her head just enough to glare at me. "Oh, I don't know, Max. Do you know a local underground pastry ring that can supply us with seventy scones and an undetermined amount of gluten-based hope by tomorrow?"

I grin. "You really need to start writing crime fiction. 'Underground Pastry Ring' sounds like a bestseller."

Her groan is pure agony. "So now, on top of the pop-up being in jeopardy, I have a front-page story about the bakery closing. Janine Moore's bakery. A Library Board member's bakery." She drags a hand down her face. "And I have two hours before deadline."

I blink. Oh. That's bad.

She glares at me. "You couldn't have waited until after our noon deadline to tell me this?"

I hold up a hand. "Would you have preferred I let you find out when half the town started calling for a comment?"

She mutters something under her breath. Then, as if she's just realizing something, she grabs her phone. "Where's Janine?"

"I have no idea," I say. "No one was there. No staff, no cops, no rogue FBI agents sneaking out with trays of confiscated French crullers. Place was locked up tight."

Elle dials, presses the phone to her ear, waits. And wait. Then lets out a frustrated sigh and drops the phone onto her desk. "Voicemail. Great."

She exhales slowly, processing. "Does the mayor know?"

"Would you like me to inform him," I ask, "or do you want to catch him off guard with an ambush call in fifteen minutes?"

"Ambush," she says, drumming her fingers. "Definitely ambush."

"Smart."

"This is a mess."

"Yup."

I sigh, leaning back. "Alright, fine. So the pop-up's off. It happens."

She shakes her head, exasperated. "We did so much work for this."

"I know," I say. "And I was just starting to mentally prepare for another round of lavender scones."

That earns me a sharp look. "You hated the lavender scones."

I smile. "And yet, I suffered in silence."

Elle scoffs. "That is a bold-faced lie, Max Donovan. You dramatically gagged after the first bite."

I tilt my head. "Did I? That doesn't sound like me."

She points an accusing finger. "You literally said, and I quote, 'This tastes like a soap factory exploded in my mouth.'"

"...Fair point."

She sighs again, crossing her arms. "I guess I'll have to write a cancellation notice."

I watch her as I contemplate a solution. The disappointment is written on her face, just below the stress of deadline day. There is an answer. I need to save this for her.

She drops her head into her hands. "The pop-up was supposed to be a win. A feel-good event."

"So we don't cancel," I say.

She peeks at me through her fingers. "Oh?"

"We make our own pastries."

Elle lets out a sharp laugh. "Oh, sure. Let's just whip up seventy scones in our spare time. That sounds totally doable."

"I can make them."

Her head snaps up. "Make what?"

"The pastries." I stretch my arms. "You know, if you really want to salvage this thing. I could make them."

Elle stares at me like I just suggested we construct an entire bakery from scratch in the next twenty-four hours. "Max. Do you even know how to bake?"

"Yes."

She waves a hand. "I mean, like, competently?"

I narrow my eyes. "You do realize I went to culinary school, right?"

Silence.

Elle leans forward, palms flat on the desk. "I'm sorry, you what?"

"I told you this," I say.

She shakes her head violently. "No. No, you absolutely did not tell me this."

I smile. "Huh. Thought I did."

She looks personally offended. "You're telling me that we hired a bakery—which, might I remind you, was just raided by the federal government—when you could've made them yourself?"

I shrug. "I wasn't particularly interested in making lavender soap-scones at the time."

She throws up her hands. "Unbelievable. This whole time you were secretly a trained chef and you just, what— let me think you were a basic farmer with a grudge against pastries?"

"I am a basic farmer," I say. "But with range."

Elle groans and drops back into her chair, staring at me like I'm an unsolvable puzzle. "Max. Culinary school. When?"

"Before finance," I say casually. "I liked it. Still do. But I wanted something more challenging, so I shifted to finance. Then that world... shifted. You know the rest."

She's still staring, blinking like her entire understanding of me just tilted.

"Elle," I say, amused. "You good?"

She points a finger. "You are, without a doubt, the most frustratingly layered human being I have ever met."

"Thank you."

She lets out a long exhale. "Fine. If you're actually serious about this, we need to get the ingredients tonight and bake all morning tomorrow."

"No problem."

"This is insane."

"Welcome to life with your fiancé."

She rubs her temples. "I cannot believe I have to update the paper to say 'homemade pastries by Max Donovan.'"

I lean back in my chair, very pleased with myself.

Then I half-smile. "Oh, and make sure you leave room for another headline."

Elle eyes me like she's already regretting asking. "What now?"

I flash a wicked grin. "Library Board Member Janine Moore: Pastry Queen or Criminal Mastermind?"

Elle groans. "I hate that that might actually be a real headline."

I nod, satisfied. "Glad we're on the same page."

THIRTEEN

BAKING POP-UPS

MAX

I CRACK an egg into the flour well, the motion easy, practiced, automatic. Baking is all about precision, but it's also about rhythm, knowing how the ingredients will behave, how the yeast will rise, how the dough will react to warmth. And right now, it's about Elle Sinclair standing two feet away, arms crossed, watching me like I just sprouted an extra head.

"So," she says, tilting her head, "do I call you Chef Max now?"

I smile, whisking the yeast into warm milk. "Only if you say it with reverence."

She scoffs. "You're enjoying this way too much."

I shrug. "I like working with my hands."

She blinks. Then, slowly, a smirk curves her lips. "Do you, now?" She crosses her arms over her chest, raising her bosom.

I pause in the middle of mixing and level her with a look. "Sinclair."

She grins but doesn't press further. Smart woman. Instead, she leans on the counter, watching as I measure flour into the bowl. "Alright, so talk me through this. What's happening in yeast magic land?"

I chuckle, shaking my head. "This is the part that matters. Yeast needs just the right conditions; warm liquid, not too hot, not too cold. Too much salt? Dead yeast. Too much sugar? It eats itself into a coma. It's a delicate balance."

Elle hums. "So, basically... yeast is dramatic."

I laugh. "Pretty much." I glance at her. "You know, you'd make a good yeast."

Her mouth drops open. "Excuse me?"

I smile, mixing the dough. "You require the perfect conditions to thrive."

She narrows her eyes. "And you require constant supervision."

I grin. "See? Balance."

She mutters something uncharitable under her breath, but I hear her suppressing a laugh.

I cover the bowl with a towel and nod toward the counter. "Alright. Dough's got to rest."

She raises a brow. "Like a nap?"

I grin. "Exactly. If you don't let it rest, it won't develop right."

She crosses her arms. "So, what do we do while the dough gets its beauty sleep?"

I roll up my sleeves. "We start another batch."

Elle's eyes widen. "Max, how many pastries are we making?"

I smile. "Enough to make the FBI regret stealing our first batch."

She groans. "I cannot believe that bakery was baking hot dough."

I laugh. "Guess their dough was cooking in more ways than one."

Elle snorts. "I swear, if we find out they were smuggling cash in cream puffs, I'm writing an exposé."

I reach for another mixing bowl. "I'd read it."

She watches as I measure flour again. "Okay, what's next?"

I hand her a cutting board and a knife. "You're on fruit duty. Chop those apples."

She eyes me suspiciously. "Can I be trusted with a knife?"

"Tough call. You're highly unpredictable."

She grins. "Fine. I know how to slice and dice... until it doesn't make sense anymore."

I pause, watching her. I already know she's been holding onto something. "I believe in you, Sinclair."

She rolls her eyes but starts slicing.

As we work, we talk, easy, comfortable, like we've done this a hundred times before.

"The water main still isn't fixed," Elle says, tossing apple slices into a bowl. "If it's not done soon, it might affect the event."

"Yeah, Calloway's pushing the whole small-town resilience angle, but we'll see."

She sighs. "Speaking of Calloway, did you hear he's telling everyone he's responsible for our engagement?"

I snort. "Oh, I heard. He's practically demanding an invite to the wedding."

Elle grins. "Well, I am glad we said yes to him."

I glance at her. "Yeah. Me too." And damn if that doesn't hit different now. For just a moment I think about what life would be like now if I hadn't said yes.

She stirs cinnamon into the apples. "Speaking of weddings... let's say this wasn't fake."

I raise a brow. "Let's say."

She glares, but her lips twitch. "Would we combine fortunes? Or keep them separate?"

I shrug. "Prenups aren't a bad idea. But it'd depend on us."

"And our attorneys... financial planners, families. Between us we have a small army invested in our lives." She throws more apple slices into the bowl with a bit of force. "Does that bother you?"

"Sometimes."

She turns to make her point, still holding the knife. "Does it ever bother you, all the people who we hire to manage our affairs, and then more professionals to oversee them? When did we start accepting the dishonesty, Max?"

"Not that long ago, really," I say, concentrating on measuring the salt and baking soda.

She starts slicing apples a little too aggressively. My attention moves to Elle. "Something on your mind?"

She snorts. "Oh, let's see. Yesterday, I had to completely rearrange the weekend edition just to fit in a breaking news story about a Library Board member's bakery being seized by the FBI. Today, people are reading it, and I'm getting texts, calls, and one lovely email about how I should be more 'discreet' with reporting federal investigations."

I let her vent. She's not done.

She swipes the knife through another apple. "Meanwhile, the mayor is still refusing to comment, the sheriff is 'handling the situation,' and Janine Moore is nowhere to be found."

I watch as she picks up another apple, cutting faster. "And the courthouse? Yeah. Turns out someone was trying to plant listening devices in the judges' chambers. And," she huffs a sharp breath, "I'll have to write a neutral, facts-only report about it while everyone else just pretends like this isn't insane."

I take the knife from her before she slices off a finger.

She scowls. "Give that back."

I set it down. "Nope."

"Max."

I turn to her, arms crossed. "Elle."

She clenches her jaw, breathing hard. And yeah, I see it now. She's not just angry. She's furious. Not just about Janine. Not just about the story. About the system. The corruption. The endless cycle of lies.

She presses her palms against the counter. "You know why I wrote Veridion?"

I nod. "Because truth is power."

She lets out a sharp laugh. "Yeah. But is it, Max?"

I hold her gaze. "I think so."

Her jaw tightens. "Then tell me why the hell lies still win."

I don't answer right away. Because I know what she's really saying. This isn't just about Janine. This is about her. She's spent years exposing other people's truths while keeping her own locked away.

I move closer, slow and deliberate, until I'm just inches away. "Tell me," I say quietly.

She exhales, looking away. "I just... I wanted to believe

that truth mattered. That if you put the facts out there, if you pushed people to be better—" She cuts herself off, fingers curling into the counter.

"You shouldn't be pushing, Elle. When someone pushes, we push back, we resist. Try adopting Scripps' slogan... 'Give light and the people will find their own way.' You do that in Veridion, so try it in this world too."

Her fingers relax on the counter. I take her hand in mine. She stills. I don't let go.

"You are right," I tell her. "Truth does matter. You printed it. People are reading it. They're talking. They're finding their way."

She shakes her head. "And what happens next? Nothing. The mayor will have his press conference, say a bunch of words that don't mean anything, and life goes on."

I squeeze her hand. "You don't actually believe that."

She lets out a slow, shuddering breath. "I don't know." Her eyes move to mine. "Thanks. We'll find out tomorrow morning at the press conference." She grabs another apple. "Can I have my knife back now? Please."

I put the knife on the counter. Taking a moment to examine her, I release her hand. "We need about ten cups of apples, mostly diced so they cook faster. Save a few slices for garnish." I step back to the batter I was mixing. "I plan on being at the library with the crew by 4:30 to set up. Oliver needs to test the equipment. I think Kim Ho will be with us, so we have another pair of hands."

"How are Kim and Oliver? Anything new?" She's chopping apples in a rhythm now.

"Not that I'm aware. I guess they must be officially a thing, item, whatever it is called these days."

"Talking. It's more than just hanging out or crushing.

It's when you're getting to know each other... with romantic intentions."

"So, we're talking, with engagement."

"No, we seem to be taking the stages out of order and two at a time. After you proposed, we zoomed through talking with our truth reveals in one night. Dating is occurring while we hang out for morning coffee, late-night check-ins, and library board schemes. The engagement is bonding with trivia and dough. I think we're about out of stages, eh, Donovan?"

The dough is ready to be kneaded. "Yep, fiancée, as far as I'm concerned that is what you are to me, for real. No more 'talking.'"

I can feel her working through it, deciding something. Then she meets my eyes. "Me too." And like that we commit to the truth that has been "us" all along. No more questions.

I put the mixing bowl down on the counter, throw out some flour, and slap the dough ball into the middle of it. "Your turn. We're going to be together, so I should teach you how this is done."

"Really? I haven't done this before, at least not successfully. So it was edible, I mean."

"That's why I'm teaching you. The dough is sticky, so dust your hands with flour. Then knead it."

She does, then starts rolling the dough, getting too much flour on it.

I move behind her. She stills when my hands close over hers, guiding them back to the dough. I guide her hands; push, fold, turn. I can smell her floral fragrance, feel her heat. My chest presses against her back as I lean in to meet her hands. We move together. Reluctantly, I pull back just a little once she has the movement, but I stay behind her, ready to adjust her hands again if necessary. I sense her nervousness.

We stand like that for a few moments.

"So, we discussed our finances. I don't have plans on leaving Willow Creek, not before Lily is through school here. This house is big enough, isn't it? You could set up a writing space here."

"Yes. I would like that."

"Good. So, what else?"

She exhales, thoughtful. "And... kids?"

I pause, my hands stilling over the dough. Then, carefully, I say, "I wouldn't mind more."

She is quiet. "I'm 41, Max."

I say softly in her ear, "And?"

She lets out a breath. "And... I don't know if I can."

I hold, speaking softly into her ear. "Then we don't. Or we try. Or we adopt. Doesn't change anything for me."

She swallows hard, fingers tightening on the dough. "Okay." Just one word. But it shifts something between us.

I clear my throat, nudging her. "And you? Any preference on wedding location?"

"City... Or the beach... Or something ridiculously romantic."

I chuckle as I lean over to see her face. "So, not Willow Creek?"

She wrinkles her nose. "You want the entire town at our wedding?"

I shake my head. "No. Just the ones who bet against us." I move back behind her.

Elle laughs, shaking her head. "You are terrible."

I grin. "You love it."

She huffs but doesn't deny it. And then I move my hands over hers. The chemistry becomes electric, palpable. She stills when my hands close over hers, guiding them back to the dough.

"This is the fun part," I murmur.

Her breath hitches.

I press just enough, guiding her movements; push, fold, turn.

She slowly exhales, "Max."

I lean in. "You're overthinking."

She swallows. "You said that last time."

I lower my voice. "And was I wrong?"

She shudders. I press her hands into the dough again, slower this time. She leans into me. We don't talk. We breathe. We move together. I turn her gently, just enough to meet her eyes. And then I kiss her.

It's not hurried. It's not playful. It's deep, slow, the kind that sinks into your bones and rearranges things. Elle's fingers curl into my shirt. My hands settle on her waist, pulling her closer. My chest starts to burn, moving to my stomach. Everything in the room shifts. This is real. And it is our truth. I start to calculate what would burn if we moved somewhere more comfortable, somewhere we could finally explore our physical connection. She is sending me every signal that it is time. We are ready.

BANG.

The kitchen door swings open. "Dad, the—"

Oliver's voice cuts off. I whip around just as both kids step inside. Lily stops dead, taking in the scene: Elle's flour-covered hands, my proximity, the obvious moment they just walked in on. She grins.

Oliver groans. "Oh God, are you guys doing it over baking?"

Elle makes a strangled noise and jerks away from me so fast she nearly face-plants into the counter.

Lily beams. "They totally were."

"Was not," Elle sputters, brushing off her apron aggressively.

Oliver crosses his arms. "Uh-huh. So you weren't making out over bread dough?"

Elle groans. "You know what? No one asked for your observations."

Lily giggles. "Ollie, we should leave them alone. I think we interrupted something."

Oliver snorts. "Nope. I refuse to be part of this."

I clear my throat, running a hand over my jaw. "Alright, alright. Everyone relax. Since you two are here, you may as well help."

Lily perks up immediately. "Oh! Can I shape the dough?"

Oliver frowns. "Why are we making our own pastries?"

Elle, still looking like she'd rather vanish into flour dust, answers, "Because the bakery we hired was shut down by the actual FBI."

Oliver blinks. "Wait, what?"

Lily gasps. "Oh my God, did they steal the muffins? Were they criminal bakers?"

Elle groans. "I swear, if that ends up in the school newspaper, I will sue."

Oliver grabs an apron, eyes the ingredients, and smiles. "So what's the plan? Are we just guessing?"

"Nope. I got this."

Elle mutters under her breath, "Oh, now he's confident."

Lily claps her hands. "Okay, I want to make cinnamon rolls!"

Elle blinks. "Are we equipped for that?"

"We can do it."

Lily beams. "Yay!"

Our moment shifts. It stops being about a pop-up disaster and turns into something better. Elle starts rolling out dough with Lily, both of them laughing as flour somehow ends up in Elle's hair. Oliver reluctantly takes charge of mixing icing, claiming that he's only participating because bad frosting is an abomination to humanity. I finish the scones and get them into the oven.

At some point, I step back, watching them, something warm settling in my chest. This is good. This is us. It may have started as a fake engagement in response to a threat that became a cover story, but we're through that now. This is something real, with Elle. She's laughing with my daughter, arguing playfully with my son, covered in flour like she's always been part of this family.

Lily nudges Elle. "You should come over for Sunday breakfast. Dad makes the best pancakes."

Elle glances at me, something soft in her expression. "Yeah?"

I nod.

She smiles. "Okay. Sunday breakfast it is."

We're not pretending anymore. We're something real. A family.

FOURTEEN
BURNING POP-UPS

MAX

THE LIBRARY SMELLS LIKE COFFEE, cinnamon, and success. The pastries are actually edible, the coffee is flowing, and there's a steady buzz of conversation filling the space. Something that the Library Board members are clearly uncomfortable with. But the town? The town is loving it.

I scan the room, catching sight of Oliver at his recording setup. Kim is with him, leaning in to check a mic cable, the two of them moving in perfect unison. Kim adjusting, Oliver responding instantly, like they've done this a hundred times before.

Elle nudges me. "They work together like they're one person."

I exhale. "I know."

She watches them for a moment, eyes soft. "You're worried."

"First anything is intense. I just don't want him to get... lost in it."

Elle tilts her head, thoughtful. "And if he's not lost? If this is just who they are together?"

I cross my arms, watching the way Kim nudges Oliver's hand away from a button and he just lets her, trusting her completely. "He's fifteen, Elle."

"For what, two more weeks? Two weeks until he gets his learner's permit. Two weeks he doesn't need your permission to work. Two more weeks, Max."

"Yes, two weeks he's still my boy. Maybe I should talk to him again."

She sighs. "Max, would you want him telling you how to handle our relationship?"

I glance at her.

She raises a brow. "Golden Rule, Donovan. Don't meddle unless you'd want meddling."

Damn it.

I huff out a breath. "I hate when you make a good point."

"I know."

Before I can respond, Mayor Calloway steps up to the small open mic we set up. He taps it, clearing his throat. "Alright, folks, hope you're all enjoying the coffee and pastries. Big thanks to our engaged couple, Max and Elle, for making this happen."

A smattering of applause follows, and I catch Elle's eye, watching her fight a grin.

"Since we have a microphone," Calloway continues, "we figured we'd do a little something special. Who's up for an open mic reading?"

For a second, there's hesitation. Then, a woman, Miss

Janice, the retired schoolteacher, steps forward, clutching a library book to her chest.

"I'd like to read," she says, adjusting her glasses. "Just a short passage."

Calloway beams. "Go for it."

She flips open the book and clears her throat. "This is from *Anne of Green Gables*, one of my favorites."

As she reads, the crowd quiets, listening. Her voice is gentle, measured, bringing the words to life. And as she speaks, something shifts. People aren't just here for coffee and pastries. They're here for the library itself. For stories, words, the act of coming together in a place that fosters both community and learning. It's exactly what this night was supposed to be.

Over the next hour, a few more people take the mic, some reading poetry, some sharing personal essays, even a teenager nervously reading a passage from a fantasy novel.

Elle leans into me as the next reader steps up. "The board has to see how important this is."

I shake my head. "They won't."

She sighs. "But look at this."

She's right. The crowd is engaged, listening, reacting. Even Tony Holsolm, the owner of Perk Up, is here, standing in the back with his arms crossed, nodding slowly.

I step over to him. "What do you think?"

He glances at me, then looks back out at the crowd. "I think... I might need to keep my café open later."

I smile. "Figured you'd say that."

He chuckles, shaking his head. "This is good, Max. Feels right."

I exhale, nodding. Yeah. It does. And as Elle moves through the crowd, chatting, laughing, slipping seamlessly into this life, I realize this is right. It has to continue.

TWENTY MINUTES LATER, we're in a cramped meeting room, where the air is thick with disapproval.

Mayor Calloway, still riding the high of the event, claps his hands. "Well! I think we can all agree; huge success!"

Silence.

"I vote no," Mulligan says.

Mrs. Thompson folds her hands. "The library isn't a café."

Elle physically recoils. "I—are you kidding me?"

Mulligan sighs, as if he's being incredibly patient. "We must consider the integrity of the library."

I exhale. "So, that's it? No discussion?"

Mrs. Thompson shrugs. "The motion is tabled indefinitely."

Elle gapes at them, furious.

Mayor Calloway sighs, rubbing his temples. "Damn shame."

I lean back in my chair, jaw tight. Elle meets my gaze. And we both know this isn't over.

FIFTEEN
INTERVIEWING US

ELLE

MORNINGS AT PERK UP are sacred. There's a rhythm to them: early risers, regulars, the hum of coffee machines, the occasional sound of Mrs. Thompson's disapproving sigh as she reads the newspaper like it personally offended her.

This morning, though? This morning is for damage control.

Max sits across from me, arms crossed, coffee in one hand, mild rage simmering beneath the surface. "Tell me again," he says, voice deceptively calm, "how an event that was wildly successful, profitable, and had people actively using the library... got rejected?"

I sigh, rubbing my temples. "Because the Library Board is more afraid of joy than taxes."

He mutters something into his coffee.

Before I can continue, Tony Holsolm, the owner of Perk

Up, strolls over. "Heard about last night," Tony says, sitting next to Max. "Damn shame."

Max exhales. "That's one way to put it."

Tony scratches his chin. "People liked it, though. The readings, the atmosphere. Felt... good."

I narrow my eyes. "Tony."

He gives me a look. "Sinclair."

I lean forward. "How much do you like money?"

His expression doesn't change. "That's a trick question."

"She's trying to trick you into hosting open mic nights here."

Tony raises a brow. "Here?"

I nod, sitting up straighter. "Max and I already built the audience. You just have to give them the space."

Tony frowns. "I don't think I can stay open late."

Max leans in. "But what if you did? One night a week. Test the waters."

Tony considers, crossing his arms. "That'd mean hiring more staff."

I wave a hand. "We're talking about one night, Tony. It's low risk, high reward. And I'll even run an ad for you in the *Gazette*, on me."

He exhales, tapping the table. "You really think people would show up?"

Max and I exchange a look. I motion toward the counter, where two women are very clearly discussing last night's event. One of them waves her hand dramatically. "And when that young man read that poem about his truck, I thought, yes, this is literature."

Tony glances at them, then looks back at us. Then he sighs. "Fine," he grumbles. "I'll try it."

I beam. "Excellent."

He holds up a hand. "One night a week. Thursdays. No promises beyond that."

Max nods. "Deal."

Tony squints at Max. "And you're hosting."

Max freezes mid-sip. "Excuse me?"

Tony shrugs. "People like you. They'll show up if you're involved."

I fight every urge to laugh at Max's absolute horror at the idea.

Max clears his throat. "I, uh—"

Tony grins. "Good talk. I'll get the posters made." He walks away. End of story.

Max slowly turns his gaze to me. "Did I just get volunteered?"

I grin. "Oh, absolutely."

He groans. "Sinclair, I swear—"

Before he can finish his threat, my phone buzzes violently on the table. I glance at the screen. Publisher. I frown. "Huh."

Max raises a brow. "Work call?"

"Yeah." I tap to answer. "Elle Sinclair."

"Elle, good morning," my publisher says, all business. "We have an assignment for you."

I blink. "Uh, okay?"

"We want a feature piece for the weekend edition. A personal interest story."

I lean forward, curious. "About...?"

There's a pause. "We'd like you to write about The Man Engaged to the Teen Fantasy Author Liane Cillser."

I choke on my coffee.

Max looks up, alarmed. "Are you okay?"

I hold up a finger. "One second."

The publisher continues, oblivious. "Your last issue on fantasy fiction got a lot of attention. People are fascinated by the mystery fiancé angle. We need to capitalize on that."

I press my forehead to the table.

Max leans in. "What?"

I mouth, *help me*.

He smiles. *No chance.*

The publisher keeps going. "We're picturing something intimate, a behind-the-scenes look at the man behind the author."

I groan.

"You'll have access to him, of course," they add. "Make it personal. Readers love that."

I clear my throat, lifting my head slightly. "So, just to clarify; you want me to write an exclusive piece about a man no one has actually confirmed exists?"

"Exactly."

I stare at the ceiling. "Do we... have any proof this engagement is real?"

The publisher laughs. "Of course not. That's the fun part."

Max leans back, arms crossed, clearly enjoying every second of my suffering.

I sigh, straightening. "Fine. I'll write it."

"Fantastic! Get us the draft by Friday."

We hang up.

I stare at my phone. Then I stare at Max. Then I bang my head on the table.

Max chuckles. "That bad?"

I sit up. "I hate you."

He grins. "No you don't."

I scowl. "I have to write an article about you."

He leans back, arms crossed. "Well, well. Looks like I get an exclusive profile piece."

I glare. "I will make up lies."

"Go ahead. Let's see if you can make me sound more interesting than I already am."

I groan dramatically. "I swear, Donovan."

But he just grabs his coffee, smug as hell. And suddenly, this morning just got a lot more complicated.

I stand in front of my bathroom mirror, arms crossed, scowling at my own reflection. "Alright, Sinclair," I say, pointing at myself. "You are a professional journalist. You have interviewed politicians, investigated corruption, exposed scandals."

I inhale deeply. Then exhale. Then groan and smack my forehead against the mirror.

Because this? This is different.

I have to write an intimate, behind-the-scenes piece on Max Donovan, a man I'm technically engaged to, but also not, while maintaining the illusion that I have no direct knowledge of the very engagement I'm writing about. And I have to sell it. For national syndication.

I stare at myself. "You, Elle Sinclair, are in so much trouble."

I straighten, adjust my stance, and clear my throat. "Alright, let's try this again."

I fold my hands like a proper interviewer, tilting my head slightly, giving my reflection a respectable, journalist-y nod. "So, Max Donovan," I say, affecting a cool, reporter voice, "tell me, how does it feel to be engaged to one of the most elusive fantasy authors of our time?"

My reflection blinks. Then smirks.

I groan. "No, that's exactly how Max would react. Damn it."

I shake out my arms. Focus. I can do this. I just need facts.

I grab my laptop and settle onto my couch. If I'm going to write about Max, I need everything the public record says about him.

I type in his name and start reading. The financial career? Checks out. His nickname was The Red Maestro, for how he orchestrated business deals. He was becoming a bit of a legend.

I pause, trying to claim a vague memory that was surfacing. I think I remember Elliot and Dad speaking about The Red Maestro. I couldn't claim it entirely.

The scandal? Worse than I thought. Not only was he dragged through the mud by that woman who claimed they were fated to be together, but she fabricated entire conversations, sent fake emails, and used photo manipulation to make it look like they were involved. By the time the truth came out, Max had already stepped away from finance.

I exhale, rubbing my forehead. He's never said he regrets leaving that world. But reading this? I can't imagine how it must've felt to be publicly dismantled like that.

I scroll further. Then I see it. His wife's accident. It's a small article. A single column. Then a follow-up months later: Hit-and-run driver who killed local woman—Greenwich, Connecticut—finally apprehended, thanks to traffic cams and video doorbells.

I read it twice. Then a third time.

I close my laptop and press my fingers against my temples. Max told me his story. All of it. And I believed him. But seeing it here, in print, cold and public? It makes my stomach twist.

I stare at my closed laptop for a long moment. Then I grab my notebook, my pen, and my best reporter attitude and head to Max's barn office. Because if I'm going to sell this article, I need to do it properly. And that means Max is getting interviewed.

MAX'S barn office is too small for the entire existential crisis I'm currently experiencing. I sit across from him, my notebook open, my ridiculous journalist hat slightly askew, and a growing awareness that this article is going to change everything. If I do this right, it won't just be a fluff piece about some mystery fiancé. It'll be the first time I truly open up, not just about my relationship, but about why I disappeared from my fans.

I clear my throat, gripping my pen. "Alright, let's do this. Max Donovan, how does it feel to be engaged to one of the most elusive fantasy authors of our time?"

Max smiles, leaning back in his chair. "An honor, obviously. But also? A logistical nightmare."

I blink. "Excuse me?"

He gestures loosely. "Secret identities, stalker fans, elaborate cover stories... It's like living in a spy novel."

I scoff. "I think you mean fairy tale."

Max strokes his chin, pretending to consider. "You know... now that I think about it, I did propose on a beach at sunset..."

I groan. "Not this again."

He grins. "And the seagulls tried to steal our scones."

I roll my eyes. "If you're done rewriting reality, I have actual questions."

"Proceed."

I flip to my notes. "Let's talk about your mysterious past. Former finance guy turned farmer—"

Max nods. "Grew businesses, hated the industry, walked away."

I hesitate. "And... the scandal?"

His jaw tightens, but he nods. "Wasn't fun. But I don't regret leaving."

I tap my pen against my notebook. "And the accident?"

His fingers twitch slightly against the desk. "That's a different kind of past."

I exhale, watching him. "You don't have to—"

"I know." He meets my gaze. "But you already read the article."

I nod slowly.

He leans forward. "It changed me, Elle. Losing her. Raising the kids alone. But it also..." He pauses. "It made me see what mattered. I built something real. For them. For myself."

"And for me." The words slip out before I can stop them.

Max's gaze locks onto mine. "You already know the answer."

Something heavy and warm settles between us. And suddenly, this isn't just an article anymore.

I take a slow breath, then shift in my seat. "Okay. Now, let's talk about the author."

I swap hats, putting on the Liane Cillser persona.

Max watches, clearly amused. "Your author self has a hat now?"

"Of course. She is elusive."

He grins. "Alright, Liane Cillser, tell me, why don't you do fan events?"

I still. The air changes. I grip my pen. "I used to."

Max waits.

I inhale deeply. "Until Indianapolis."

His expression softens.

I clear my throat. "After that, I just... stopped."

He watches me. "And do you miss it?"

I swallow. "Yes."

His voice is quiet, firm. "Then go back."

I stare at him. "It's not that simple."

"Yes, it is."

My fingers tighten around my pen. "Max."

"I'll be there." His voice is steady, certain. "If you go back, I go with you."

I inhale sharply. "You..."

He leans in. "You want to do this again? Then you won't. Do it. Alone."

Something shakes loose in my chest. The truth sharpened. I know what I have to do.

I grab my notebook and write.

Statement from Liane Cillser

For a long time, I believed that stepping into the world meant stepping into danger. That being seen, truly seen, meant exposing myself to the unpredictable, to what I couldn't control. And so, I retreated.

But truth has a way of calling us back to ourselves. *The Veridion Chronicles* has always been about standing in truth, about the power that comes when we strip away fear, deception, and doubt. And yet, I didn't realize until recently that I had been denying myself that very power.

Fear told me to hide. But love? Love showed me that I am safe.

We should never have to question whether someone is worthy of trust. We should expect that they are. Because when a person lives in truth, when they are honest with themselves and the world, there is no doubt; they are worthy of love, the kind of love I have now been so generously shown. Because love is not something to be earned. It is something we are meant to live in, and I am finally learning to do so.

It has taken me time to embrace that for myself. But because of the unwavering love of one extraordinary man, who has shown me a strength in vulnerability I never knew, who has walked beside me, protected me, and reminded me of my own words, I am ready to step forward again.

And I do so with a full heart.

So, to my readers, those who have believed in me, who have carried the stories of Veridion in their hearts, thank you. Because of you, I write. Because of you, I am returning.

This year, I will see you again.

With gratitude,

Liane Cillser

I SIT BACK, breathless. Max reads over my shoulder. Then he nods. "It's perfect."

I glance at him, my heart pounding. "And you're really okay with this?"

His voice is firm, absolute. "I'm all in." He leans forward, presses a kiss to my forehead, and as I exhale I release the weight I've been carrying. I sit with the moment. Then turn and look at Max.

Max smiles. "But wasn't this supposed to be about me?"

I laugh, shaking my head. "Right. Right. Okay." I grab my pen, reset my focus, and turn to him. "So tell me, Max Donovan, how does it feel to be the man who brought Liane Cillser back to her fans?"

His lips curve. "I guess," he says slowly, "it just means I have a hell of a lot more reading to do."

SIXTEEN
WHEN THE PAST COMES TO TOWN

MAX

I'M NOT in my barn office. I specifically choose to wait for Elle somewhere else, because every time we meet there, things seem to get out of hand. And it's about time we start talking through whatever we're doing for the holidays—travel, visiting the Sinclairs, or our romantic beach holiday... with the kids.

So here I am, standing outside Perk Up, coffee in hand, waiting for Elle, and absolutely not expecting to be ambushed by my past.

The warning signs are all there: the click of expensive heels on pavement, the unmistakable scent of designer perfume that costs more than a mortgage payment, and the deliberate pause just behind me, like a hunter savoring the moment before striking.

I take a slow sip of my coffee. "Cindy."

She laughs lightly, stepping around so I can get the full effect of her entrance. Cindy Franklin is the same as always:

a vision of high-end fashion, a smug tilt to her lips, and the expression of a woman who is never told no.

"Red Max," she purrs, tilting her head. "Imagine running into you here."

I glance around. "Yeah, imagine that. In my own backyard."

She grins, unfazed. "I heard the news."

I arch a brow. "That so?"

She hums. "A little birdie told me you're engaged."

I don't react. Which is exactly what Cindy wants, because she steps closer, lowering her voice. "And, of course, I had to see for myself."

I sigh loudly. "Let me guess. You happened to be in the area? A casual detour from your jet-setting lifestyle."

She presses a perfectly manicured hand to her chest. "Max, don't you really think I'd fly all this way just to check in on an old friend?"

I give her a long, unimpressed stare.

"Okay, fine. I heard about the engagement and thought, "No way is Max Donovan actually settling down in Willow Creek."

My jaw tightens, but I say nothing.

Cindy, of course, sees everything. She tilts her head, studying me like a portfolio she's about to acquire. "You used to be someone, Red Max. You used to command boardrooms, make headlines, build empires." She steps closer, voice low, persuasive. "And now? You're... what? Selling organic lettuce at a farmer's market?"

I roll my shoulders. "I own a farm."

She waves a dismissive hand. "Oh, please. You're still The Red Maestro who saw potential where others didn't. The one who could turn ideas into gold. There are people who are missing you, Maestro. This?" She gestures vaguely around. "This isn't you."

I grit my teeth. "It's exactly who I am."

She clicks her tongue. "No. It's who you've had to be."

And that? That lands. Because for one split second, one terrible, treacherous second, I remember. The deals. The strategy. The thrill of taking something small and uncertain and turning it into something powerful. The late nights, the meetings in skyscrapers, the absolute certainty that I was good—damn good—at what I did. "The Red Maestro" they called me, for my skill in orchestrating financial deals.

I hate her for reminding me.

Cindy senses it. She smiles, stepping closer. "See? You feel it too."

I move faster than I mean to, grabbing her by the face, holding her there as I lean in close. She gasps, probably thinking I'm about to kiss her.

I don't. I meet her eyes, my grip firm, my voice low, unshakable. "Cindy," I say, slow and deliberate, "there is nothing between us. There never was. And whatever you thought you could rekindle? It never existed." Her lips part, but I don't let her speak. I keep my grip gentle but final, and I mean every word. "You don't tempt me," I say. "You never did."

And just as I let her go, just as Cindy blinks up at me, trying to regain her footing, I see Elle. Standing at the entrance to Perk Up, watching the whole thing. Her expression is unreadable. Wide eyes, slightly parted lips, frozen in place. And before I can say anything, before I can explain, she turns and walks away.

I feel the loss immediately. It's a cold chill that blows through me.

Cindy, of course, seizes the moment. "Well," she murmurs, smoothing her hands down her coat. "That was intense."

I barely hear her. My entire focus is on Elle. I shove past Cindy without another word, striding after Elle, my heart pounding too hard.

By the time I reach her, she's already halfway down the sidewalk. "Elle."

She doesn't stop.

"Elle!"

Her steps hesitate, just slightly. Then she turns, eyes flashing. "What?"

I stop, too close, too angry, and suddenly I'm not even sure who I'm mad at: Cindy for showing up, Elle for leaving, or myself for letting this entire situation happen.

Elle crosses her arms. "Go back to Cindy, Max."

I exhale sharply. "This isn't about Cindy."

She tilts her head, challenging. "No? Because I just saw you grab her like you meant it."

I grit my teeth. "I was telling her to leave."

Elle's voice drops. "And yet, she still got under your skin."

I look away, frustrated, because she's right. Cindy did get under my skin, not because of her, but because she reminded me of something I've been avoiding for years.

I feel Elle studying me, waiting. And instead of telling her what's actually in my head, instead of admitting the chaos inside me, I do the one thing I shouldn't do. I push her away.

"I don't have time for this, Elle."

She stills, just for a second. "Excuse me?"

I shake my head, still too tangled in my own thoughts. "I just—I need space."

Her expression shifts, tightening. And when she speaks, her voice is quiet, sharp. "You know," she says, "I wasn't going to push. I was going to wait, let you tell me when you were ready." She tilts her head. "But if you want space, Max?"

She takes a step back. "Fine," she says. "Take it." And then she turns and walks away.

This time, I don't stop her. And I hate myself for it.

I drive home in silence, the kind that claws at your skin and makes you feel like you're sitting in the middle of a storm. I should turn on the radio. Should call Oliver to check in. Should do anything other than sit here and think about what just happened.

But thinking is exactly what I can't avoid. Because I was an asshole tonight.

I tighten my grip on the wheel, my knuckles white as Cindy's words loop through my head. "You're still The Red Maestro." "This isn't you." "You used to be someone." "It's who you've had to be."

And the worst part? She wasn't wrong. Not about everything, but about the part that dug its way under my skin like a splinter; the part I can't ignore anymore.

She was right that I miss finance. She was right that I used to be someone else, someone who thrived in that world. And yeah, I walked away. I had to. After the scandal, after Lauren's death, after everything in my life tilted off its axis, I needed something real, simple, grounding. The farm gave me that. The routine, the certainty. A place where no one could touch me, where no one expected me to be the sharp, ruthless strategist I used to be.

But now? Now I'm starting to wonder if I was ever meant to stay hidden forever. And Cindy? She saw it. Exploited it. And I let her.

I exhale sharply, pulling into my driveway and cutting the engine. It's too quiet out here. The stars stretch over the fields, the farmhouse windows glow warm in the dark, and I should feel at peace. Instead, I feel like I'm standing on the edge of something huge, something that's been waiting for me to turn around and face it.

I step out of the truck, slamming the door harder than necessary, my whole body wired with frustration. Not just at Cindy. Not just at my past. But at myself. Because Elle saw it. She saw me with Cindy. And then I pushed her away. And for what?

Because I was too caught up in my own head to deal with what was right in front of me? Because I was so pissed off at Cindy for reminding me of everything I had lost that I transferred that anger to Elle, the one person who's been in my corner without agenda, without manipulation?

I rake a hand through my hair, pacing toward the barn, my steps heavy with regret. Elle didn't deserve that. She didn't deserve me shutting her out. She didn't deserve to stand there, hurt, while I let my own damn resentment get in the way.

I lean against the barn door, inhaling deeply, trying to steady myself. Then, without thinking, I head inside, grab *The Veridion Chronicles* from the desk, and drop onto the futon sofa.

The book is still open to where I left off, a passage that had stuck with me, one I had read twice before but hadn't fully understood until now. "Lumea is fueled by truth.

Power withers when you deny your own. No one can take your strength from you, except you."

I stare at the words, my fingers tightening on the page. Truth. Power withers when you deny your own.

I exhale, rubbing my jaw. Because that's exactly what I did. Yeah, I needed to survive. Needed to heal. My kids needed stability, and I gave it to them. I built something real, tangible, grounding. Something that mattered. But I also took a lesser version of myself. I chose only part of my talents—the part that was safe, the part that wouldn't hurt me again. Organic farming is good work, honest work. It meets some of my values. But it doesn't challenge me. It doesn't let me be who I actually am at my core.

I shut my real talents away—strategy, negotiation, building something from nothing—because I didn't trust myself not to burn again. And what did that get me? A hollow anger. A resentment that made me lash out at the one woman who actually understands me.

I lean back, staring at the ceiling. I get it now. Elle writes this world of power and truth, a world where people lose their strength the moment they lie to themselves. And without realizing it, I did the same damn thing. I took a life that fit part of me, but not all of me. I let fear dictate what came next instead of facing it head-on.

That stops now. I don't know exactly what I'm going to do, but I know this. I want back in. Not Cindy's world. Not the ruthless game of hedge funds and sell-offs. But the part of finance that actually excited me, the part where I helped grow things, build them, make them better. Because I'm damn good at it. And it's time to start acting like it.

I shut the book gently, running a hand over the cover.

Elle would probably laugh her ass off knowing her novel just kicked my ass into an existential awakening.

And speaking of Elle... My stomach twists. I need to fix this. With her. Because now that I see the truth about myself, I need to tell her the truth, too.

Instinctively, I pick up my phone, to call her, to share my revelation. But the time on the screen reminds me—it's too late. It's deadline day tomorrow and we have a town Public Library Meeting in the afternoon.

Then I notice the waiting text message, from Elle.

Elle: *You don't owe me a speech, Max. Just the truth. And for you to walk back in of your own free will.*

My throat and stomach tighten at the evidence of what I did to her. She thought we might be over. I close my eyes, sitting on the sofa we've shared so often, and reach for those memories. The ring I slipped on her finger during our beachside proposal. How easy it was to talk with her brother, Elliot. Our first physical connection, after our exchange of our closely held secrets that seemed so important at the time. Then I hear her voice, "because I want it to last."

My heart pushes me to tap the message app as a tear rolls down, and tap out what is starting to pour from my heart.

Max: *Elle, I'm sorry. I let Cindy poke at something I hadn't healed yet, and I turned that on you. That wasn't fair.*

Max: *Please forgive me.*

Max: *Thank you for walking away. But not leaving.*

Max: *I love you. I love being beside you in every way.*

I wait for a reply, but only get the word "delivered" under the last text. It is late; she is asleep, no doubt.

But my heart isn't done. I tap out one last message.

Max: *Sera, I'm working on living from my truth. Sweet dreams, fiancée.*

SEVENTEEN
FRANKLIN VS. DONOVAN

ELLE

OPEN PUBLIC LIBRARY Board meetings are usually monuments to boredom.

We're talking about hours of budget discussions, policy arguments, and at least one resident complaint about book covers being too suggestive.

But tonight?

Tonight, the tension is thick.

And the reason for that tension?

Cindy Franklin.

She sits prim next to her father, George Franklin, publisher of *The Willow Gazette* and my boss, wearing an expression that barely conceals her smugness. She is dressed in a tweed jacket and navy blue pencil skirt, stilettos, and accented with lots of jewelry. Her fragrance is filling the auditorium.

And I know that look.

It's the look of a woman who has bait on the hook and is waiting for the right moment to reel it in.

I tap my pen against my notebook, jaw tight. I don't know what she's planning, but if she thinks she can just waltz in here and go after Max, she has another think coming.

The public is in attendance, and we start with saying the Pledge of Allegiance and listening to the National Anthem. Singing is optional, but in this town your hand better be over your heart. This is followed by a short non-denominational blessing.

Mayor Calloway clears his throat. "Alright, let's get started. The first item on the agenda—"

Cindy elegantly lifts a hand. "Before we begin, I'd like to raise a matter of transparency."

The room shifts. People glance around, a few murmurs. I don't like where this is going.

The mayor nods. "Go ahead, Ms. Cindy Franklin has the floor."

Cindy smiles, a slow, calculated move. "As many of you know, I'm visiting from New York, and in my short time here, I've heard a great deal about one of your esteemed Library Board members."

She turns her gaze directly on Max, who is sitting stone-still, his expression unreadable.

My stomach twists.

Cindy tilts her head. "And I couldn't help but wonder... does Willow Creek know who Max Donovan really is?"

The room goes still.

Ed Mulligan, the grumpy retired principal who made it his mission to destroy joy, clears his throat. "Miss Franklin, if you have relevant information, I'm sure we'd all like to hear it."

Cindy basks in the attention.

"Well," she says sweetly, "since Mr. Donovan seems so reluctant to share his past, perhaps I should do it for him."

I see Max's shoulders tighten, but he doesn't move.

Cindy pauses for dramatic effect. "He used to be a billionaire. Knowing him as I do, I imagine he still is."

A few people gasp. Others just blink in confusion, like she just announced he was secretly an alien overlord.

Mulligan squints. "I'm sorry... what?"

Cindy crosses her arms. "Max Donovan didn't just work in finance. He was 'one of the youngest rising stars in hedge funds, private equity, and venture capital'. He built businesses. Negotiated billion-dollar deals. He had a fortune, and then..." she gestures dramatically "he disappeared."

More murmurs ripple through the crowd.

I stand up.

Because I am not about to let Cindy Franklin make this about her personal vendetta.

I clear my throat. "I'm sorry," I say smoothly, "I thought this was a Library Board meeting, not a tabloid exposé."

Cindy's eyes flash with satisfaction; she wants a fight. I'll give her one.

"Elle Sinclair, I would think that as a journalist—editor of *The Willow Gazette*—II would think you'd appreciate the importance of truth."

"Oh, absolutely. Which is why I have to ask, what does this have to do with the library?"

Cindy blinks. "Excuse me?"

I tilt my head innocently. "I mean, you seem really interested in billionaires. Which makes sense, of course.

You're the publisher's daughter. Maybe that's why you keep bringing it up?"

I pause, widening my eyes. "Oh! Wait. Are you offering a donation?"

The room shifts again, people perking up at the word donation.

Cindy's lips press together. "That's not what I—"

I cut her off. "But what a beautiful gesture, Cindy." Clasping my hands together dramatically, I continue. "A Franklin-endowed library fund! Maybe even naming rights! Imagine it: The Franklin Community Reading Center."

People nod approvingly. A few even murmur their support.

Cindy looks like she just swallowed a lemon.

"That's not why I brought this up," she says, voice tight.

"Oh?" I blink. "Because if this is just about revealing information on a board member, I have to remind you that personal financial history, as long as it doesn't interfere with civic duties, is private."

Ed Mulligan shifts in his chair. "She's... not wrong."

I turn back to Cindy, all charm. "Unless, of course, you'd like to change the topic back to actual library funding?"

Cindy seethes. "I was simply informing the public."

I shrug. "Well, as someone deeply involved in the library's success, I'd like to inform the public as well."

I place a hand over my heart and turn to the room.

"Max Donovan is one of the most competent, strategic, and hardworking people I have ever worked with. His talents in finance and negotiation have been utterly wasted by a community that refuses to see his value."

Mulligan shifts uncomfortably.

I keep going.

"He has built a successful organic farm, selling to companies nationwide. He provides for this town, for his family, and for the same people questioning him now. Willow Creek is damn lucky to have him."

Silence. A long silence.

Then a few scattered claps.

Then more. More murmurs. And finally a full room round of applause.

The narrative clicked. Cindy realizes it's over.

She huffs, crossing her arms. "Well, I suppose some people are just easily impressed."

Max, who has been silent this whole time, finally leans forward.

His voice is calm, steady, and lethal.

"Cindy."

She tenses.

He meets her gaze. "Whatever you thought this was? It's over."

Cindy flinches.

Then she pivots abruptly, her heels clicking sharply against the floor as she turns to her father.

"Daddy, I'm done here."

George Franklin sighs but stands as well. "Thank you for your time," he says, nodding at the board before following his furious daughter out.

The room settles.

Ed Mulligan coughs. "Well, I think that's enough unexpected theatrics for one evening."

Mayor Calloway smiles, turning to me. "Sinclair, remind me never to get on your bad side."

I just smile sweetly.

Across the room, Max catches my eye.

And I know.

He's grateful.

But more than that?

He's furious.

Because Cindy might be gone, but the past she dragged up?

It's still right here.

And Max?

He has no idea how to resolve it.

THERE ARE two things Willow Creek loves more than a good cinnamon roll: Gossip and a competent man with a clipboard.

And Max Donovan?

He's now the hot topic that no one can shut up about.

I walk into Perk Up, expecting the usual hum of morning coffee chatter, but instead, I get three separate conversations happening at once:

Table One: "Did you hear? Max Donovan is a business growth strategist."

Table Two: "I heard people are going to him for business loans!"

Table Three: "Does he do taxes? Because my accountant just moved to Florida."

I snort into my coffee.

He's been back in finance for approximately twenty-four hours, and he's already being drafted for town economist, business consultant, and possible IRS liaison.

I slide into our usual booth, waiting for Max to arrive, a

cup of black coffee on the table. I have to wait longer than expected.

Because the moment he walks through the door, a group of people immediately swarm him.

I grin behind my peppermint mocha.

Oh, this is going to be fun.

Max glances at me and the coffee on the table waiting for him. He takes a step closer but is stopped by another neighbor inquiring about his assistance.

Mayor Hank Calloway comes through the door. He makes his way through the swarm.

"Max, my boy!" Mayor Calloway claps a hand on Max's shoulder, beaming like a man who just found his new golden goose.

Max sighs, already bracing himself. "Mayor."

Calloway gestures dramatically. "Tell me, how'd you like to fix this town's budget?"

Max blinks. "Excuse me?"

"We need someone like you, sharp mind, finance background, no patience for nonsense."

Max rubs his jaw. "Isn't that your job?"

Calloway waves that away. "Technicalities. The point is, the town council's finance committee is a mess, and we need a three-man oversight team. You'd be perfect."

I snort into my coffee.

Max glances at me, eyes narrowing.

I give him an encouraging nod, all fake sympathy. "Oh no, honey, you must be so overwhelmed by this honor."

He shoots me a dry look. "Help. Me."

I sip my coffee smugly. "Nope."

Calloway claps again. "It's a volunteer position, of course—"

"Of course." Max mutters.

"—but it's prestigious! The people trust you, Max. They need you."

Max exhales long and slow, then mutters something under his breath that sounds suspiciously like "I only declared my intention to return to finance yesterday... Spirit's fast." before saying, "Fine. I'll serve on the committee. I need to leave the Library Committee. Only have time for one."

Calloway beams. "Knew you'd say yes! Of course, consider yourself off the Library Board." He pats Max's shoulder one last time before moving on to his next municipal conquest.

Max slides into the booth across from me, face unimpressed. "Enjoyed that, did you?"

I grin. "Immensely."

Before he can respond, another person approaches.

"Max?" A woman, Mary Beth Hess, owner of the town's antique shop, hesitates, wringing her hands. "I, uh... heard you're helping people with business stuff?"

Max straightens slightly. "That depends."

"Well, I need funding advice. The shop is doing alright, but I want to expand, buy out the space next door and turn it into an artisan market. But I don't know where to start."

Max tilts his head, closing his eyes. Then I see it. That moment I call his 'baton falls'.

His focus locking in, his mind already pulling the pieces together: strategy, potential, risk assessment, all the things that used to make him one of the most sought-after business minds before he walked away.

"Alright," he says, leaning forward. "Let's talk numbers."

I'm curled up on Max's couch, flipping through one of Lily's sketchbooks, when his phone rings.

He glances at the screen, frowning. "It's Elliot."

I perk up. "Oh?"

He answers. "Elliot, hey."

I can't hear Elliot's words, but the moment Max's expression changes, I know this is important.

His back straightens, his eyes sharpen; that same focus I saw earlier, only now, it's even deeper.

"Wait," Max says. "You want me to consult?"

My eyebrows lift.

He listens, nodding slowly. "Yeah, I get that. The off-season would work. My farm is a full-time operation, but winter's slower. Actually, I've been considering hiring a farm manager, with recent developments." He glances at me, "I could structure something around that... "

He trails off, then finally says, "Let's talk details."

I grin, setting down the sketchbook.

Because I already know how this ends.

Max hangs up, staring at his phone like it just rewrote his entire future.

I rest my chin on my hand. "So... consulting?"

He exhales. "Green Agricultural wants help with expansion strategies and independent supplier partnerships. Elliot asked if I'd be interested in consulting in the off-season."

"And?"

Max leans back against the couch, rubbing his jaw. "I said yes."

My smile widens. "You realize what this means, right?"

He nods slowly, as if saying it out loud makes it real.

"I'm back in finance."

"The Red Maestro returns?"

"The better parts of him, yeah. I'm done with soulless transactions and power plays. But if we're talking about growing things, finding new opportunities, building it right, then, yes, that part of The Red Maestro is back."

This is on his terms.

This is his choice.

Max turns to me, his voice quieter now. "This feels... right."

"Because it is. You're starting to live from your truth, so your Lumea is increasing."

He lets out a breath, then looks at me differently, like he's seeing something he hadn't fully grasped before.

His voice is careful, certain. "You know... knowing your background, your family's wealth, your success, it doesn't intimidate me anymore."

I arch a brow. "Oh? And it did?"

He grins. "Not intimidate, exactly. But it made me... question things." He gestures vaguely. "Where I fit. What I wanted. If I could be an equal in a relationship like this."

My chest tightens.

He exhales, shaking his head. "But now? I don't question it."

His fingers brush absently against mine on the couch.

"Because I know exactly who I am again."

The narrative clicked.

EIGHTEEN
PENNY'S PROMISE AND PERSONAL TRUTHS

ELLE

RESIGNING from the Library Board is shockingly easy.

Standing in front of them? Less so.

Thanks to some repairs, we're meeting in the auditorium, though it is just our small committee.

I smooth my hands down my skirt, standing on the stage where our table is set up, aware that every pair of eyes in the space is locked onto me. The tension is thick, but nowhere near as toxic as when Cindy tried to turn this place into an episode of *Exposé Your Local Billionaire*.

This is the first meeting for two new members, Mary Beth Hess, owner of an antique store, and Todd Michaels, an elementary school teacher. They seem like people I'd like to work with, but with Max no longer at the meetings, and other areas of my life realigning, this is the time to go.

I clear my throat. "I'd like to officially resign from the Library Board."

Immediate murmurs. Ed Mulligan, who has never once

looked happy in his life, leans forward, folding his hands. "Miss Sinclair, may I ask why?"

I nod, keeping my voice even. "To avoid a conflict of interest."

Murmurs grow.

Mayor Calloway lifts an eyebrow. "Care to clarify?"

I clasp my hands together. "I doubt any of you know I'm a published author, but I am. I'd prefer to separate my professional life from any decisions regarding town library operations."

Mrs. Thompson, who for a librarian, has the subtlety of a wrecking ball, squints at me. "Author? What do you write?"

Ed adjusts his glasses, suspicious. "And why are we only hearing about this now?"

I smile smoothly, the kind of smile I reserve for high-pressure negotiations; or for when I'm bluffing a plot twist to fans at a Q&A session.

"I've always kept my writing separate from my work in town. But given recent... attention," I avoid Calloway's knowing smile, "I think it's time to step back."

Ed leans forward, too interested. "What kind of books?"

I reach into my bag, pull out a worn paperback, and set it on the table.

Penny's Promise by E.S. Sinclair. A coming-of-age story about an Appalachian teen overcoming hardship to become a leader of men.

Ed eyes the book like he's assessing a suspect. "Never heard of it."

Mrs. Thompson, who has definitely read every book ever written, picks it up, flipping through the pages.

"Huh," she murmurs. "This was well-received when it came out. Some even called it a modern classic."

I shrug. "It had its moment."

Ed narrows his eyes. "Why the secrecy?"

I give him a calm, pleasant look. "I value my privacy, Ed. That's all."

Mrs. Thompson keeps flipping. "Well," she muses, "if it's any good, maybe we should order more copies for the library. I can add the local author tag."

A few people nod in agreement, and I watch as curiosity spreads through the room.

I keep my expression neutral, but inside?

I'm laughing.

Because this distraction works beautifully.

They'll be too busy reading *Penny's Promise* to go digging into anything else.

I'VE ENDED up settling into Max's house without officially moving in.

The kids don't question it. Max doesn't question it. And honestly? Neither do I.

I set up a writing space in his sunroom, tucked between the kitchen and the back porch, where the morning light hits just right.

It's...comfortable.

I glance up from my laptop, catching Lily sprawled on the floor, sketchbook in front of her, feet absentmindedly kicking the air as she draws.

I tilt my head. "What are you working on?"

She flips the sketchpad around. "A warrior. She has magic, but she doesn't know how strong she is yet."

My chest tightens slightly.

I force a light smile. "Sounds like a great story."

She shrugs. "It's your fault. You let me sit here while you write."

I smile. "Oh, so I'm corrupting you?"

She grins, eyes bright. "A little."

I laugh, shaking my head.

Later that evening, I find Oliver at the dining table, headphones in, tapping away on his laptop.

I slide into the chair across from him. "Hey."

He glances up, removing one earbud. "Hey."

I tilt my head. "How's Kim?"

Oliver pauses, then shrugs. "She's... good."

I raise an eyebrow. "Just good?"

He exhales. "It's weird."

I rest my chin on my hand. "Weird how?"

He frowns at the laptop. "I... really like her, Elle. But also? I feel like I'm figuring myself out at the same time."

I nod slowly. "That makes sense. A relationship can reflect back parts of yourself you can't see on your own."

He nods. But I can see there is still something he wants to say.

He tilts his head. "Did you ever feel like that? Like you wanted someone, but you also... didn't know if it was the right time?"

I exhale. "Oliver, I've spent my entire life trying to figure out if things are happening at the right time."

He snorts. "And?"

I grin. "There is no right time. There's just... the moment you decide to go for it."

He considers this, then nods once.

I mess up by getting too comfortable and, without thinking, start to use my unpublished book as an example.

"You know, in *The Veridion Chronicles* Book Three—"

Oliver frowns immediately. "Wait. Book three?"

I clear my throat. "Right. I mean... uh. Book one. Partnerships are sacred. That's one of the society rules, right? Romantic or otherwise. Do you have a concept of 'sacred'?"

"Holy, connected to God, or the Divine." he says.

"Good definition, but do you have a concept, a feeling of what is sacred? What does it really mean, if something is sacred?"

He thinks for a moment. "I guess that if it is sacred, it is a blessing from God, a gift."

"Right. And what does that mean for you, a member of that sacred partnership?"

"It means I don't mess with it. That I need to protect it, like we should our environment, or our loved ones. That makes it important to me." I tilt my head, urging him to continue. "That it is a priority, something that I'm connected to, value."

"Exactly. So do you think that when two people, who are developing and growing on their own, are in a partnership, which is what a romantic relationship actually is, should work off of a timetable, or off their mutual feelings for one another, off their intuition, or gut if you prefer, knowing the next step?"

"Their feelings, and their gut."

"So, though you are trying to learn who you are, and Kim is doing the same, does that mean your partnership should be put on hold? Or do they develop simultaneously? One informing the other."

"But what if your partner isn't developing at the same

rate as you, or suddenly becomes someone they weren't in the beginning? Or we don't go to the same college. What happens to the relationship then?"

"What you want to happen to it. If you both want it enough, you'll find a way. If not, then it might fall away even if only one of you loses interest. But you have to let it go. Don't try to hold on, because that isn't the truth of the relationship any longer, and what happens to Lumea? You can actually become weak, or even physically sick if you hold on to something that isn't right.

"Your dad is changing, he's reclaiming his true self. That affects our relationship, our partnership. When we met, he was just a grumpy farmer, and I was an angry newspaper editor scared of being seen. Our relationship changed all that, but we had to work through some issues. He gently took my hand, got me over the fear, and showed me I was protected in his love. And I nudged, listened, and he returned to his truth. Today, we are so much stronger as people, which makes us stronger in, and dedicated to our partnership. Oliver, I love him a great deal. I feel loved by him. And I love you and Lily. That's my truth, and where my Lumea comes from."

I look at Oliver, waiting for questions or comments.

"If I am hearing you then, I just have to keep working on myself..."

"Always, your whole life. Never stop."

"And Kim should do the same, while we continue to get to know ourselves and each other in this partnership. If we have Lumea, we're doing it right. If that fades, then something needs attention."

"And remember, your gut feeling is important, but so is life experience. At 16, you're still growing into yourself, so what feels right now might evolve. That's okay too." I sit back waiting for questions.

"That's what I have figured out. Now, ask me tomorrow and I might have a different slant, but it seems like you've got it."

"There isn't a right time other than when our guts tell us it is time." He states, confirming.

"Underscore the 'our' and you've got it. The right time isn't just when one of you is ready. It's when both of you feel that clarity and mutual understanding. That's what makes it true."

I look at him. "You know why I say gut, or intuition, don't you? You know about the human energy field, right?" He shakes his head no. "You know all matter is energy, some denser than others, but everything can be measured on the electro-magnetic scale."

Oliver narrows his eyes. "Uh-huh."

"Well, this includes your body. We all have a force or field surrounding our bodies, we call the human energy field. I'm not going to discuss if this is the soul or conscious-ness. But what is important is to know this field seems transactional. Meaning it can communicate with the cells of our body, but also with each other. Researchers are basi-cally telling lay people that this field communicates through our thoughts, which include that gut feeling. So, even when we don't say something, the other person can pick up on that emotion or thought and react to it. Like when you know someone is smiling at you but actually is only tolerating you at that moment. That is one reason knowing yourself, and living your truth is so necessary. Research it, I'm sure you'll find articles on it. Try bioenergy, Valerie V. Hunt, or the human energy field."

I stand up quickly. "Anyway, I'm so glad we talked!"

Oliver smirks. "I am so looking into this later."

I groan and leave the room.

I'm back in the sunroom, laptop open, when Toma's name flashes on my phone screen.

I pick up, bracing myself.

"Tell me," Toma says immediately, "when are we telling the world that Liane Cillser is you?"

I sigh. "Toma."

"Elle." His voice softens, but doesn't lose its urgency. "This engagement with Maxwell? It's put the brand in the spotlight. The interview you wrote? Brilliant. The announcement that you're attending events? Huge. But Elle…"

I close my eyes.

"I know," I whisper.

I hear him exhale. "Then why wait?"

I glance across the room at Lily, still drawing, still completely unaware that her father is engaged to an internationally bestselling fantasy author.

Because once I say it out loud, once I let the world know, there's no going back. I swallow hard.

"Not yet."

Toma is silent for a moment, then sighs. "Alright. But Elle… it's time."

I hang up, staring at my laptop.

It's time.

And yet, I still don't know if I'm ready. Then I remember. This time, Max will be with me.

I feel better.

How about safety in numbers? We should take the whole family. Need to run it past Max. But it feels right.

NINETEEN
AND SO IT IS

MAX

THE RAIN HAMMERS against the barn roof, a relentless downpour drumming a rhythm I've always found oddly soothing. The wind rattles the old wooden structure, testing its resilience. Outside, the world is a hazy blur of silver and shadow, but inside? Inside, it's warm. Dry. Quiet.

Well. Mostly quiet.

The soft hum of jazz plays from the speakers in the corner, and Elle sits curled up in the old leather chair across from me, her feet tucked under my thigh like she owns the place. Which, if I'm being honest? She kind of does.

The barn has always been my retreat, a space to work, to think. A place that's entirely mine. And yet, she's managed to slip into it seamlessly, like she's always belonged here.

She nudges me with her ankle, a small smile playing at her lips. "So... I hear you're officially a civilian again."

I exhale. "You too."

I shake my head, stretching out on the futon, one arm draped along the backrest, the other balancing a water bottle on my knee. "Mayor Calloway's going to have to find two new suckers for the Library Board."

"He has. Mary Beth Hess and Todd Michaels." She shifts slightly, getting more comfortable.

I let out a low whistle. "They seem nice enough. Wonder how long they'll last."

"What with Janine vanishing, then you and me moving on... and Calloway stepping back. The Deputy Mayor is chairing the Library Board now."

I take a slow sip of water. "Calloway has bigger problems. That finance investigation is getting serious."

Elle studies me. "How bad is it?" Thunder rolls in the distance.

I run a hand over my face. "The ledgers are off. Not just a little. Someone's been playing a long game with the town's budget, and the deeper I go, the more holes I find. Fifteen grand a month on 'cleaning supplies'? No way. Either someone's got the shiniest floors in America, or that money's moving somewhere it shouldn't."

She exhales, rubbing her temple. "You think he's regretting pulling you into the Finance Committee?"

"Oh, I think he's thrilled. But he also figured out real quick I don't play politics."

She hums, thoughtful. "Small-town corruption. It never takes a day off."

She sips her tea, letting my words settle. We both know this isn't just about the bakery anymore. This runs deeper.

Outside, the storm rages on. But here? Here, it's steady. Easy.

Elle nudges me with her foot. "So, how's your consulting empire, Maestro?"

I snort. "It's... building itself, apparently."

Her brows lift. "Oh?"

"Mary Beth wants help with expansion funding, Tony cornered me about keeping Perk Up open later, and Moses and Helmut, the hardware store owners, ambushed me when I was picking up your magnets for your thinking board, and stronger bolts for Diesel's gate, about long-term strategy."

"Just don't let them turn into a small version of a big box store. Their yesterday's ways of doing things is part of their charm, attracting customers... and tourists."

"Exactly. That's why they need to really know themselves and their business, not in terms of transactions, but its mission and values. Their charm, their 'yesterday's ways,' that's their differentiator, their competitive edge. The goal isn't to dilute that with a big-box mentality; it's about optimizing their core value proposition. We leverage technology to streamline their back-end, expand their reach digitally, open up new customer segments without sacrificing that high-touch, neighborly feel. It's about smart growth that enhances their core identity, not compromises it, ensuring every strategic move reinforces their authentic brand."

Elle looks at me over the rim of her cup and starts to smile. The smile expands until she is beaming. A chuckle behind her cup brightens her eyes still, and we lock eyes. I'm rewarded with her beautiful laughter.

"What?" I ask, reflecting her amusement.

"Oh, nothing, Red Maestro." She continues to chuckle, sending a warmth throughout my chest. Setting her mug on the side table. "Small-town networking at its finest." She nudges me with her ankle again.

I shake my head, half amused, half exasperated. "I'm basically running a full-fledged consultancy, and I haven't even set one up yet."

"And are you enjoying it?"

I pause, just a beat. "Yeah."

Elle's eyes soften. "Good."

Just like that. No overthinking. No doubt. Just the truth.

I watch her for a moment, then lean back. "You ever think about why we get stuck? Why we end up in places we don't belong?"

She tilts her head. "What do you mean?"

I run a hand through my hair. "When I was in finance, I let myself get swept up in the game. Clients wanted things, I made them happen. Sometimes, I stretched my ethics to keep them happy. It wasn't outright corruption, but it wasn't right, either. In hindsight, I can see how my behavior might have made me look like I was guilty of the rumors. The only secret I was keeping was that I wasn't living my truth, holding to my standards."

"Bet you felt like you were two people? A friend told me that. One for the family, another totally different persona for the business." Elle shares.

"Actually, yes. I was starting to feel like two different people when the rumors started taking over. My handwriting changed. Favorite foods. Habits. It started to scare me. And no, I didn't do drugs. I'd be in Europe for two weeks usually, then two at home. It was very hard on Lauren, I can see that now. But she stayed the course. Hard on all of us. And the whole time, I told myself it was fine because I was providing for my family."

Elle watches me, waiting.

I exhale. "And then I lost them. And looking back? I set myself up for it."

She frowns. "How?"

"I wasn't true to myself." I shake my head. "I forced myself to fit a mold that never felt right. I thought providing money was enough, that my kids didn't really need me around when they were small. I convinced myself my marriage was solid because we liked each other and had a partnership that worked, but I never gave it what I give you." My voice drops. "What I feel for you."

Elle swallows. "And what do you feel?"

I hold her gaze. "Love. The kind that shifts your whole life."

She's silent for a long moment. Then, softly, "That's brave, you know."

"Bravery has nothing to do with it."

She shakes her head. "It does. Love makes you vulnerable. Opening yourself up to an unscripted life? That takes guts."

I let her words settle. Then, "What about you? Any great love before me?"

Her lips twitch. "Just one." She takes a sip of her tea, glancing at me over her mug.

I tense slightly, but she just smiles.

"Storytelling," she says simply. "It's always been my first love."

I chuckle, relieved. "Figures."

She pushes her foot deeper under my thigh, her toes flexing against my leg. "You know, Max... forgiveness heals the past. But once you've done that, you have to let it go. Say, it is done."

I study her, then nod slowly. "It is done."

Her foot presses on my leg. The storm outside rages, but here? Here, I have everything I need. And I'm not letting it go.

She studies me for a moment, then tilts her head. "And the kids? Ollie and Lily doing okay?"

I shift slightly, stretching my legs. "Ollie's... figuring things out. I think he's more serious about Kim than he realizes."

"She's good for him," Elle says softly. "Smart. Focused. Keeps him level."

"Yeah." I run my thumb along the ridges of my water bottle. "And Lily?"

Elle smiles. "She's thriving. Still drawing, still thinking in epic stories and warrior battles."

I let out a slow breath. "Good."

No drama. No dancing around emotions. Just checking in.

This? This is how a relationship works.

The rain beats harder against the windows, and Elle stretches, arms lifting above her head with a content sigh.

Then without thinking, she slides onto the futon next to me, nestling under my arm, fitting against me like she was meant to be there.

I don't even flinch.

My arm automatically tightens around her, my other hand resting lightly on her thigh.

We don't question it. We don't need to.

She rests her head against my chest, exhaling.

"Have you ever had overnight guests before?"

A low chuckle rumbles in my chest. "Once."

She lifts her head slightly, "Oh?"

I smile back. "It was a while ago."

She arches her brow. "And how did the kids react?"

I exhale, rubbing my jaw. "They adjusted. There was a little tension. Some quiet judgment."

Elle snickers. "I bet."

"But as soon as they tasted her pancakes, they got over it."

Her eyes narrow. "Oh, so breakfast was the deciding factor?"

I shrug, completely serious. "Pancakes are a unifying force."

"I can manage edible pancakes."

I chuckle, my voice dropping just a little too low.

"Good."

A pause.

"But just know," I say softly, "there's nothing like your grandmother's cooking."

She mutters something about impossible men, burying her face against my chest. I just laugh, trailing my fingers lightly along her arm.

The rain keeps coming. Hard. Unforgiving.

Elle glances toward the window, frowning. "We're going to have to make a run for it."

I hum. "Clothes will dry."

She sighs. "I don't have clothes here."

I shrug, completely casual. "We'll find you something."

A beat of silence.

Then she tilts her head. "It's probably time you give me a key."

I don't hesitate. Just nod, slow and satisfied. "Yeah. I should."

She smiles. "And I should start leaving things here."

I lean in slightly. "You already do."

She exhales, shaking her head, but there's no hiding the warmth in her eyes.

"My writing space in your house is becoming my favorite place to work."

I grin. "You got that draft done yet?"

She smiles back. "Working on it."

"Am I in it?"

She hums, teasing. "I'll never tell."

But then, softly, "What I've learned about truth leading to an incredible connection of love has influenced my world-building."

I watch her, quiet, steady, waiting.

She runs her fingers across my chest. "I was thinking about the upcoming fan events. You said you'd be there with me. What if we bring the whole family? Lily, Oliver... maybe Kim, if it seems right?"

I say quietly. "I love that idea."

"If we can pull it off, I'd like to wait until then to reveal my author status to them." She offers. I only nod.

"Toma called. He is pushing me to connect Liane Cillser to Elle Sinclair. But I'm not ready, not yet." She sips her tea to mute the hesitancy I hear in her voice.

"I support your decision, Elle, you know that." I tighten my arm around her.

Then she asks, "How do the Donovans celebrate the holidays?"

My heart warms as I tighten my hold on her, settling in.

"We'll figure it out together."

TWENTY

THE FINAL FRONTIER

ELLE

THE HOUSE REMAINS QUIET, punctuated only by the steady tick of the clock in the hallway and the occasional creak of the old farmhouse settling in the night. Max checks on the kids while I stand in the bathroom, brush my teeth, and stare at my reflection as if it might offer some kind of wisdom.

I exhale.

I haven't shared a bed with anyone in well over four years. I haven't let someone into my space, my routine, my body, since I moved to Willow Creek. And now? Tonight?

I glance at the bedroom, where Max gets ready for bed as if this is the most natural thing in the world. He acts like we haven't spent months dancing around this very moment.

Max pulls his shirt over his head and tosses it into the hamper, and I swear my toothbrush pauses mid-stroke.

Lord help me.

I rinse my mouth, straighten my shoulders, and walk into the bedroom. "Kids asleep?"

Max nods, pulling back the covers. "Out like a light."

I hesitate, lingering by the dresser. "So... this is happening."

Max glances at me, a slow smile curving his lips. "This is happening."

I exhale a shaky breath, climbing into bed, nerves buzzing beneath my skin. Max slides in next to me, his warmth immediately radiating into my space. We lie there for a beat, neither of us moving, neither of us speaking.

Then, slowly, he reaches for me.

Fingertips grazing along my arm, tracing the line of my wrist. A slow, quiet touch, not demanding, just... present.

I close my eyes.

I forgot what this feels like. The weight of another person next to me, the comfort of shared space, the way a single touch can ground you in a way nothing else can.

Max shifts, pulling me closer, his arms wrapping around me. I sink into him, breathing him in; warmth, cedar, something undeniably Max.

His lips brush my temple.

"Good night, Elle."

I lie against his chest, the steady rhythm of his heart-beat lulling me under.

The Next Morning

I wake up alone.

The bed is warm, but the spot beside me is empty, and the faint scent of coffee drifts through the air. I groan, stretching, reluctant to leave the cocoon of blankets.

The clock reads 8:45 a.m.

I blink.

Max got up, milked the cows, took the kids to school, and I'm still here, wrapped in a blanket burrito, contributing absolutely nothing to society.

Footsteps.

The door creaks open, and Max walks in, rubbing the back of his neck, his hair slightly damp from the cold. His eyes find me, and something shifts.

Slow. Intentional.

He shuts the door behind him.

Then he disrobes. Completely.

With each layer of clothing removed—and it is now cold so there are a few—I become filled with anticipation, nervous tension, and awe. He's gorgeous. His well-defined abdomen leads to muscular thighs and legs, with a dusting of reddish-brown hair mirroring his chest. He is magnificent, and a surge of sexual desire awakens in my body, radiating out to my fingertips.

This is the man who loves me. Who protects me. Who will blend into my body the same way we have blended into each other's lives. The thought excites me.

As he throws the last layer of clothes on the chair, he moves to the bed, the cold motivating him to move with a little urgency.

"Stop. Hold, for just a moment more. I want to look at you. Please."

"It's rather cool this morning." His voice is husky and deep.

"I think I paused when you wanted to look." I move my hands to cup my bosoms.

He smiles, and stands erect, turning around so I can see all the glorious details of the body sculpted by hard work and an ethical standard few could match.

I sigh, smiling, then raise the covers and invite him into *our* bed. The chilled air rushes in.

"Hurry, it is cold. Get in here."

His chilly body snuggles into my warmth. For a moment we lie together, adjusting.

I slowly move my hand to touch his chest, letting my fingers feel every inch of his hairy skin. My palm radiates an energy that connects us. His hand explores my back and buttock. I feel his touch mirror mine. I take a deep breath, hold it, and surrender my actions to my innate director.

I kiss his chest and his nipples, then move up to his neck. His skin is soft, and I realize he has recently shaved, the scent of musk filling my nose.

His hand claims my jaw as his mouth captures mine. Our breathing quickens, becoming more rapid and shallow, releasing a deeper urgency of desire. I part my lips slightly, and his tongue joins mine as we feel each other, licking our lips and mouths, reaching for a deeper connection.

He slides onto his back, bringing me on top of him.

His hand grabs my breast while the other pushes my buttock into him, kneading the flesh as my crotch rubs against his member.

I tilt my hip and slide my hand between our bodies to cradle his balls, giving a light squeeze. His eyes flash with excitement. My fingers move to the base of his member, feeling it grow and press against my body.

Touching him, he utters my name. I rub his length into my wetness, exploring my excited folds and awakening sensuality that pulsates in my groin. My voice engages as I call his name. He moans at the touch of our bodies.

His hands encompass my breasts, massaging, pinching my nipples, and he licks with his tongue. I bend forward, bringing my breast closer to his mouth, then claim his mouth with mine. His hands move to my buttock, pulling me wider as I feel his strong member rise to tease my groin and ignite my desire. I rise up, arching my back, and let out a guttural moan that fills the room. He joins me, letting out his own sounds of desire as he takes charge of our bodies.

He rolls over, positioning me beneath him. I feel his weight, pressing me into the bed, then he moves his arm to carry much of his weight. The free hand slides between my legs, fingers exploring my heightened folds. His eyes claim mine, connecting us as our focus engages our pleasure.

"Elle, tell me. What do you like? What do you want now?"

I don't know. So, I move my hand down to grab his member, but he moves my hand away.

"You, what do *you* want now?" His voice is low, gentle but firm.

How do I tell him I don't know? That I haven't been in this position but twice before. How do I admit that I've reached my forties but have had very few full sexual encounters?

My eyes start to sting. My throat tightens. My vision blurs as the void of my answer slams my emotions.

He sees this, and pauses.

After a moment, he looks at me, his voice gentle, and asks, "Am I your first? Truth."

My voice is broken with the gut revelation I now send across my lips and to him. My deepest secret. "Truth. Not quite. Second. The other in college, twice. Then we were done."

His face changes as he realizes how little experience I have had.

"But your actions, your..." I cut him off.

"I read. I research. I have an active imagination. I didn't say I haven't often thought about this, especially since meeting you." I have never felt more naked.

His eyes start to smile, then his lips curve upward.

"Well, this is the good part, my dear. Since we're together, then let me teach you." He lowers himself and kisses my lips, gently.

But our 'something' that we have been fighting suddenly explodes, overwhelming us both. His kiss turns passionate, I want him as he wants me. Our mouths merge, my legs wrap around his hips as he moves to connect our bodies. My chest aches with anticipation and want.

The room fills with this electric energy, neither of us willing to fight it anymore.

At first it hurts, and I let out a whimper.

He stops, locking eyes with me. After a breath of adjustment, I urge him to continue.

In a controlled thrust of desire, he starts rhythmic pushes with his hips. His chest brushes my breasts, his mouth kissing mine, then his head raises for a release of sound, and back down to me.

We let out a scream of ecstasy together that fills the house. I feel like I am in him and around him, and he in me and around me, fusing into this two-part being. Separate but one. My body arches against the bed, moving with his body as we leave our earthly bindings and move to another place and time. Together. As One. Complete.

Sweaty, spent, and sensual, our bodies collapse together. Our breath in unison.

We rest, his weight still partially holding me to the

mattress, his arms wrapped around me as my legs wrap around him.

We must have fallen asleep.

I wake up, with him next to me. Our eyes lock.

"I love you so deeply, Elle."

"I love you deeply, Max."

"Are you alright?"

"Better than I've ever been." I pause. "Because you are here."

His eyes start to glisten. Then I see a single tear run down across his nose. My heart is so full.

We help each other leave our warm blanket cocoon love nest.

As we dress, I hear my stomach make a noise. Then his. We look at each other, and then a wild grin that moves into laughter bursts from our lips.

"Late lunch? The Hayloft?"

"Perfect," I agree.

THE HAYLOFT HUMS with the low, steady buzz of small-town lunchtime chatter. The scent of fresh bread and slow-roasted meat drifts through the air, mixing with the occasional burst of laughter from the kitchen.

Chris and Belle Ho are behind the counter when we walk in, their heads snapping up the second they see Max.

Chris stands, crossing his arms. "Well, well. Look who finally decided to bring his girl around."

Max sighs. "You've heard, haven't you?"

Belle grins. "Sweetheart, we own the place. Of course we've heard. Congratulations. We're so happy for you both."

I arch a brow at Max. "Do people have a newsletter for this kind of thing?"

Chris grins. "No, but I wouldn't be surprised if Patty at the salon starts one."

Max groans. "Remind me why I live here."

Belle motions to the booth in the corner. "Because you love it. Now, sit. Eat. Tell us everything."

Max slides into the booth next to me, his hand resting absently on my thigh under the table. The heat of his touch sends a shiver up my spine. Chris and Belle take their seats across from us, leaning in with the air of people who thrive on town gossip.

Chris leans in. "So, what's the latest on the bakery scandal?"

I stir my coffee. "It's unraveling. Fast."

Belle frowns. "You hear anything about Janine?"

Max shakes his head. "Not yet. The ledgers don't match, not all the receipts were deposited in the bakery's bank account. And what's up with the listening devices in the judge's chambers? That's next-level corruption."

Chris exhales. "And people are missing."

Belle nods. "Kitchen staff we hired, recommended by the bakery, vanished. Expected in custody, but no one knows for sure."

Max's jaw tightens. "It's worse than we thought."

Chris glances at me. "And you? You're running the paper, right?"

I nod. "I'm covering the investigation, but there's a lot we don't know yet."

We barely have time to scan the menu before Max's phone buzzes. He glances at the screen, his brows pulling together.

"It's Elliot."

Belle waves him off. "Go, take it. We'll keep Elle company."

Max presses a quick kiss to my temple before sliding out of the booth, heading toward the entrance. I watch him go, something in my chest tightening.

Belle leans in. "So. You're really in this, huh?"

I blink. "I... yes?"

Chris snorts. "That was convincing."

I huff, stirring my coffee. "Look, it's new, but it's not new."

Belle tilts her head. "Meaning?"

I glance toward the door where Max disappeared, then back at them. "Meaning we've been building this for months. Slowly. The right way."

Belle nudges Chris's arm, "See, I knew they were using the engagement as a cover so they could date in peace." She turns to me, "You're not the only one who says something is true before it really is. The way this town gossips, it is the only way to keep the interrogations quiet."

Chris nods. "We do that too. Hey, Elle, we just wanted to... you know, test the waters before we talk to Max about something."

I pause, my curiosity piqued. "Go on."

Chris folds his hands on the table. "Donovan Organics is a major supplier for us. And now that Max is taking on more consulting work, well... should we be preparing for the possibility that he won't have time for the farm?"

Belle adds, "We don't want to pressure him. Just trying to be proactive."

I shake my head. "Don't worry. If Max needs to hire help, he will. He's already been considering it."

Chris exhales, visibly relieved. "Good. We'd rather talk to you first before throwing it at him over dinner one night."

Belle smiles warmly. "You know, you are good for him."

I blink, caught off guard. "I... thank you."

Belle's gaze softens. "And how's Oliver?"

I smile. "Good. Navigating young love. Kim's been a steady presence for him." Max slides into the booth next to me.

Chris chuckles. "Ah, young love. They're handling it well."

Max grins. "Better than some adults I know."

Belle laughs. "He's getting his driver's license soon, right?"

I nod. "Which means he'll be driving Kim on actual dates."

Chris raises a brow. "You ready for that, Max?"

Max sighs. "Not even a little."

Belle pats his arm. "You'll survive."

I shake my head, laughing, but something settles in my chest. I *am* good for him.

I sip my coffee, watching Max, the way he relaxes in this space, the way his hand never leaves me. The way this feels... right.

A FEW HOURS LATER, I'm standing in the driveway, watching Oliver scowl at his phone.

"Nothing?" I ask.

He sighs, shoving it into his pocket. "Nope. Nothing. Guess Dad's lost in the numbers."

There's a weight in his voice, disappointment curling around the edges.

I tap the car keys against my palm. "Well, *I'm* still here."

Oliver lifts a brow. "You offering?"

I grin. "If you think you can handle my excellent coaching skills."

He snorts. "Fine. But if we die, I'm haunting you."

"That's fair."

"Lily, will you be okay here by yourself? I'm giving Oliver some driving time." She nods yes, lost in a drawing. In that way, she is definitely Max's daughter.

Oliver climbs in, gripping the wheel like it might suddenly take off on its own. "Okay. What now?"

I gesture ahead. "Foot on the brake. Start the car, eh, push the button. And put it in gear, D for drive."

The engine rumbles to life, and Oliver inches forward like he's tiptoeing on ice. We ease onto the main road, his knuckles white on the wheel.

"You're doing great," I say, watching his posture. "Try not to hold the wheel like it owes you money."

He exhales, relaxing his grip. "Sorry."

"Totally normal. First time I drove, I was convinced I'd take out a mailbox."

He chuckles. "Did you?"

I shrug. "That's classified."

He laughs, tension loosening in his shoulders.

I direct him toward the cemetery.

Oliver frowns. "The cemetery? Really?"

"Less traffic. Plenty of stop signs. Good curbs to practice turns."

He exhales. "Morbid."

But he turns in, maneuvering down the narrow road. His grip on the wheel steadies, his confidence building; until his eyes flick to a familiar row of headstones.

I see it the moment recognition hits. His shoulders stiffen. His jaw tightens. And then, without thinking, he drives past his mother's grave.

The silence is thick, heavy.

I place a hand over his. "Oliver."

His throat bobs. "I, I didn't mean to."

"I know."

He swallows, his grip tightening again. "I was nine when she died."

I nod, waiting.

"She was on her way home from picking up takeout. It was supposed to be a normal night." His voice wavers. "Dad didn't cry in front of us. But I heard him. At night."

My chest aches. "Ollie..."

He shakes his head, eyes locked on the road. "I don't know why I'm telling you this."

"Because it's okay to remember. And it's okay to miss her."

He exhales sharply, fingers twitching on the wheel.

I place my hand on top of his, squeeze it, and hold for just a moment. "You're doing really well, Oliver."

He finally looks at me, his eyes glassy, but a small, grateful smile tugs at his lips.

"Thanks."

"We can leave when you're ready." He nods, then maneuvers the car to return the way we came in. We pull out of the cemetery, the air lighter, like something unspoken has settled. We drive for a while, making slow loops around town.

"And by the way?"

He glances at me. "What?"

"You nailed that three-point turn."

He lets out a surprised laugh. "You're ridiculous."

"Welcome to the Elle Sinclair School of Defensive Driving. Our motto? 'If we don't die, you pass.'"

He groans. "You're actually the worst."

I grin. "Dinner?"

He sighs. "Yeah. Let's pick up something."

DINNER IS QUIET.

Because Max is missing.

And not just missing, silent.

No texts. No calls.

I poke at my food, watching Oliver and Lily chat, but my mind is elsewhere.

This is new, I remind myself. A shift. We're adjusting.

But our relationship isn't new. And he didn't even text me. Doubt creeps in, uninvited.

Did he want me to move in because our partnership is sacred, built on mutual love and respect? Or because it fills a need? A practical solution? Someone to help with the kids, the house, while he builds his career?

I hate that my brain is going there. But also, where is he?

I pull out my phone. Call Max? Voicemail. Text Max? No response.

Something unsettles in my chest.

I grab a piece of paper and scribble down a note.

"In *Veridion*, partnerships are sacred. Just tell me if ours is."

I leave it on the table, exhale, and head upstairs.
I don't want to leave the kids alone overnight. So I stay.
And wonder if he will.

TWENTY-ONE
MISSING MAX AND MILKING COWS

ELLE

Morning comes, and Max is still missing.

I stare at the empty spot in the bed, frown at zero unread messages on my phone, and let out a slow, measured exhale.

Okay. Fine. I'm fine.

It's not like I expect to wake up to a text that says, "Hey, babe, sorry I ghosted. Totally fine, just casually thought I'd leave all night. Be home for dinner."

I groan and shove the blankets off.

Downstairs, I shuffle into the kitchen and start opening cabinets, determined to make breakfast like a competent adult.

Unfortunately, Max is one of those organized humans who actually knows where things go, which means I do not.

I squint at a tin labeled **WHEAT FLOUR**, shake it, and make an executive decision that it's probably pancake mix.

Oliver walks in, sees me holding the tin, and immediately pivots to the fridge.

Lily trudges in behind him, rubbing her eyes. "Where's Dad?"

I glance at them, at their sleepy faces, and then at the empty doorway where Max should be walking in, smelling like cows and coffee.

I exhale. "We don't know yet."

Oliver crosses his arms. "Should we be worried?"

I close the tin (definitely not pancake mix) and lean against the counter. "Here's what I do know: when things feel uncertain, the best thing we can do is hold to the truth."

Lily frowns. "What truth?"

I wave them over, pulling out the chairs at the kitchen table. "Sit."

They exchange a glance but obey.

I take a breath. "Now, close your eyes."

Oliver groans. "Elle—"

"Just do it," I say, nudging his knee under the table.

They sigh but humor me.

"Okay," I continue, voice soft. "Get quiet. Ask yourself, deep down: is Dad okay?"

Silence. For a long moment, we just breathe.

Lily cracks an eye open. "He's fine. He's just... stuck somewhere."

Oliver nods, eyes still shut. "Yeah. Detained."

Lily perks up. "It's the town scandal, isn't it? The one he's investigating?"

I meet Oliver's gaze, something like realization flickering in his expression.

Lily is *thirteen*. Thirteen-year-olds shouldn't be casually guessing that their dad is tangled in a government investigation before finishing their orange juice.

I inhale through my nose. "Yeah, sweetheart. I think you're right."

Oliver suddenly sits up straighter. "Wait. If Dad's not home... who milked the cows?"

We all freeze.

Then, at the same time, "Oh, crap."

I STAND in the milking parlor, hands on my hips, staring at a row of twenty-four cows like they might offer some wisdom.

"Okay," I say slowly, turning to Oliver. "I assume there's a system to this."

Oliver sighs, tugging on a pair of gloves. "Yes. There's a system, Elle."

Lily beams. "We'll show you!"

I stare at her. "Have you done this before?"

She giggles. "Nope."

I shoot Oliver a look. "Is she messing with me?"

He snorts. "Yes. She helps sometimes."

I exhale. "Okay. Fine. Teach me."

What follows is a crash course in Cows & You: A Beginner's Guide to Not Dying in a Barn.

The cows line up, shuffling in like seasoned professionals, and Oliver walks me through the process:

✓ Clean the udders (yes, that is a sentence I just lived through).

✓ Attach the milking machine (*it makes a weird suction noise that I hate*).

✓ Each cow takes about eight minutes.

✓ Don't stand behind them unless I want to regret my life choices.

Two and a half hours later, my boots are wet, my hair smells interesting, and I have what I can only describe as a spiritual respect for dairy farmers.

"Not bad," Oliver says as we finish up.

I wipe my hands on my jeans. "So, does this mean I pass Farm School?"

Lily beams. "We'll see how you do on the goat test."

I stare at her. "There's a goat test?"

Oliver grins. "Oh yeah."

Lily nods solemnly. "And chickens."

I groan. "I'm leaving."

After dropping the kids off at school, late but there (Oliver still smelling slightly of cows), I do what any reasonable, mature adult would do.

I call my contacts in law enforcement.

And by "call," I mean I badger until someone slips up and confirms that Max Donovan is currently sitting in an FBI office outside town.

I hang up, grip the steering wheel, and mutter, "Oh, hell no."

Fifteen minutes later, I storm into a small, beige-walled office, past an unimpressed receptionist, and slap my hands on the counter.

"I want to see Max Donovan."

The man behind the desk doesn't even blink. "And you are?"

I narrow my eyes. "The person who's going to make your life very annoying if you don't let him out."

He sighs. "Ma'am—"

"Don't ma'am me." I cross my arms. "He's a civilian. A Finance Committee member, not a criminal. You either let me see him or get ready for the Willow Creek Chronicle's front page to have a very interesting headline tomorrow."

A door opens.

A tired-looking agent steps out. "She's with him."

Desk Guy grumbles but waves me through.

The moment I step into the room, Max looks up.

And damn, he looks exhausted.

His hair is mussed, his shirt slightly wrinkled, but it's his eyes that get me: intense, wary, and carrying something I don't like.

I march over. "You okay?"

He exhales. "Yeah."

I cross my arms. "That was very convincing."

He huffs a tired laugh. "Elle."

I turn to the agent. "You are releasing him, right?"

The agent shrugs. "He's free to go."

I point at Max. "Move."

He sighs but stands, rolling his shoulders like he's shaking off the past eighteen hours.

We walk outside, the cold air biting, and Max rubs a hand down his face. "That was fun."

I nudge him. "You gonna tell me what's going on?"

He exhales. "They wanted details on the town finances. What I found when I followed the money."

I study him. "And?"

"And they want me to help."

"And do you want to help?"

He hesitates.

I step closer. "Max."

His jaw tightens. "It's... a lot. This is deeper than we thought. If I get involved, I'm in it. And I don't know how dangerous that is yet."

I hold his gaze. "So what's your truth?"

He looks at me.

Long. Searching.

"My truth is standing against corruption," he says, voice steady. "Being honest. Ethical."

I smile. "Then there's your answer."

His lips twitch. "You make things sound simple."

I grin. "That's just good writing."

He exhales, running a hand through his hair, then pulls me in for a quick, hard kiss. It feels good having him back again.

"You hungry?"

He groans. "I've been detained since yesterday. Of course I'm hungry."

I grab his hand. "Then let's get you home."

By the time we pull into the driveway, the weight of the morning settles deep in my bones. The relief of having Max back is real. So is the lingering unease that I can't quite shake.

I park the truck, kill the motor, and we sit for a moment.

He exhales and runs a hand down his face. "Well. That was an experience."

Watching him carefully, I unbuckle. "Welcome back to civilian life."

I help him into the house, using my key to unlock the door.

His lips twitch, but there's something in his posture, something hesitant. He glances at me, like he's about to say something, but then his gaze shifts toward the room.

And lands on the note.

It's still on the table, right where I left it. The words stare up at him like a quiet accusation.

"In Veridion, partnerships are sacred. Just tell me if ours is."

Max picks it up, his jaw tightening. He reads it twice, fingers flexing against the paper.

Then he turns to me, his voice quiet. "You really thought I wouldn't come back?"

I exhale. "No. But I did think... maybe you didn't tell me because I wasn't someone you needed to tell."

His brows pull together, his face unreadable. "Elle."

I cross my arms. "I mean, I get it now. You didn't just disappear. You weren't ignoring me. But last night? I didn't know that. And when you don't know something, your brain fills in the gaps with worst-case scenarios."

Max sets the note down, his eyes locked on mine. "Then let me be clear."

I hold my breath.

He steps closer. "Our partnership is sacred. You aren't here for convenience. You aren't here because it's easy. You're here because this is real."

Something inside me softens, but that small, stubborn voice in my head still whispers, *Then why didn't you call?*

Max must see it in my face because he exhales, rubbing a hand over his jaw. "Elle, I'm sorry. I should have found a way to contact you."

I nod, accepting the apology, but the tension in my chest doesn't fully fade. "We need to plan for this. In case it happens again."

He nods. "Agreed."

The lead emerged. So, we move into problem-solving mode.

Because this is what we do.

We face problems together.

Max grabs a notepad, flipping to a clean page. "Okay. First, if something happens and we need to leave quickly, where do we meet?"

I think for a second. "Somewhere we can get to without being tracked. Nothing obvious."

Max taps the pen against the page, then nods. "The old hunting cabin in Pine Hollow. No cameras. No neighbors."

I blink. "You have a hunting cabin?"

He smiles. "I have a run-down hunting cabin. You'll hate it."

"Perfect."

He scribbles it down. "Okay. Next, contacts."

I grab my phone. "I'll send you my emergency numbers."

We exchange lists, adding each other's contacts, making sure we have mutual connections who can be trusted.

Then Max hesitates. "I want to do something else."

I tilt my head. "What?"

His expression turns serious. "I want to make you my emergency contact."

Something in my chest tightens. "Max..."

"And my power of attorney," he adds, voice firm. "If something happens to me, you need to be able to act fast."

I swallow. "Max, that's—"

"Necessary." His eyes don't waver. "I won't move forward with the FBI until I know you and the kids are taken care of."

I let out a slow breath. "Okay."

We each call our lawyers, updating our emergency contact and POA details. The conversations are quick, professional, and efficient.

By the time we hang up, Max looks at me, his gaze steady. "That's everything."

I nod. "Now you just have to decide if you're really doing this."

He exhales, leaning against the counter. "I already decided."

I arch a brow.

He huffs a quiet laugh. "I have to do this, Elle. You were right this morning; standing against corruption is who I am."

I smile softly. "Glad you're finally listening to me."

He shakes his head, amused, then picks up his phone, dialing the agent's number.

I watch as he lifts it to his ear, his voice steady. "This is Max Donovan. I'm in."

TWENTY-TWO

FOLLOWING THE MONEY

MAX

I NEVER THINK I'll miss the simplicity of worrying about cattle feed and fence repairs.

But sitting here, staring at the financial ledgers of Willow Creek, I realize I'd take shoveling cow manure over this any day.

Because this? This is a mess. A deep, tangled, rotten-to-the-core kind of mess.

I run a hand over my face, then rub the tension at the back of my neck. The numbers don't just not add up, they're deliberately designed not to add up. Someone's been laundering money through town projects for years, and the deeper I go, the more I realize Willow Creek's quaint, small-town charm is just a very well-polished lie.

And I think I'll just be handling local corruption. How naïve. Turns out, some of these transactions are connected to out-of-town business interests, which means this thing isn't just a local scandal anymore. It's bigger. Riskier.

I lean back in my chair, exhaling. The FBI already suspects this, but now I have proof. The question is, how far do I go with it?

Because the truth? The actual truth?

I don't know if I want to know what happens next.

I step out of my office and into the brisk November morning air, rolling my shoulders. My mind is still tangled in numbers, but there's real, tangible work to do.

Cows don't care about corruption.

Chickens don't embezzle funds.

Goats, well, they might if they have the opportunity.

I grab my work gloves and head to the hayloft, where Oliver is already loading hay. He glances at me, eyes narrowing. "You look like you've been staring at numbers too long."

I grunt. "That obvious?"

"Yeah." He grins. "You have 'finance face'."

"Finance face?"

"Yeah. It's like resting grump face but with more existential dread."

I chuckle, shoving a bale of hay into place. "Good to know."

Lily trots in, dramatically waving her arms. "Dad, can we get a baby goat?"

I blink. "A what?"

"A baby goat," she repeats. "They're cute, they hop, and they'd be my best friend forever."

I shake my head. "No goats."

She pouts. "You never let me have anything."

"You have a pony."

"Yeah, but he's so serious all the time. I need something unhinged."

Oliver snorts. "Get a gremlin."

Lily gasps. "Can I?!"

I sigh. "No gremlins. No goats. We have enough chaos."

Lily crosses her arms, muttering, "We'll see."

Which is never a good sign.

By mid-morning, I'm at Perk Up, nursing a black coffee while Elle works on something at our usual corner table.

She looks focused, brow furrowed, her fingers flying over her laptop keyboard.

I lean in slightly. "Writing your next great novel or taking down a corrupt government?"

"Both," she says, not looking up.

"Multitasking. Impressive."

She finally glances at me, her eyes searching. "You okay?"

I shrug. "Just... processing."

Elle sets her laptop aside. "Talk to me."

I hesitate, then sigh. "This whole investigation. It's making me question how people see the truth. I mean, we have facts. Numbers don't lie. But when people interpret those numbers, suddenly there's spin, emotion, personal bias. Everyone thinks they know the truth, but what they actually know is just their version of it."

Elle tilts her head. "You're talking about perception versus reality."

I nod. "Exactly."

She leans forward, resting her chin on her hand. "That's the difference between facts and truth. Facts are just data points. You can arrange them in a thousand ways to support whatever narrative you want. But truth, real truth, is deeper than that. It's who you are, what you stand for.

The thing inside you that doesn't change, no matter how the facts shift."

I stare at her, something in my chest tightening. She just puts into words what I've been wrestling with for weeks.

"Veridion truth," I murmur.

She nods. "Exactly. In Veridion, truth isn't just about what happened, it's about who you are in the face of it. Living your truth gives you power, confidence, strength. That's why the magic in my books is tied to authenticity. When you deny your truth, when you let fear, lies, or perception dictate your actions, you lose your power."

I tap my fingers against my coffee cup, thinking. "So what does that mean for me?"

She holds my gaze. "It means you already know what to do. You just have to decide if you're willing to do it."

Silence settles between us, warm and heavy.

Then I sigh. "That's annoyingly profound."

"It's what I do."

I shake my head, chuckling. "And you're sure you're not secretly a philosopher?"

She lifts her coffee. "Writers are just philosophers with deadlines."

As I walk back to the truck, Elle's words sit heavy in my mind.

She's right.

I know the truth. I know what needs to be done.

I'm ready to put everything on the line to do it. And that?

That's the hardest truth of all.

. . .

THE SCENT of coffee lingers in the barn office. My farmhands' break table is cluttered with financial reports, spreadsheets, and case notes; evidence that my life has, once again, become about tracking numbers and uncovering deception. Not the part of my past that feeds my soul.

After nearly a full day mired in these ledgers, my body is starting to revolt. But I agree to meet with agents here, to keep from returning to their interrogation room.

Across from me, Special Agent Grayson studies the town's financial records, his brow furrowed as he flips through the highlighted discrepancies I've mapped out. His partner, Special Agent Rivera, leans against the doorway, arms crossed, waiting.

"You've been busy, Donovan," Grayson mutters, tapping a page. "This is some impressive forensic accounting."

"Old habits die hard."

"Do you ever sleep, Red Maestro?" Rivera asks dryly.

"I've not been called that in a long time, so what are you implying?" I feel defensive.

"We know your history. You're not a stranger to scandal, are you? So, I'm just saying, if you think you'll pull a fast one on us, think again."

"Excuse my partner, Max. She doesn't trust anyone. Even me. Hazard of the job."

"Well, that scandal is bogus. But it is why I can spot corruption quickly. I have firsthand experience with what it looks like, like you, Agent Rivera."

"I suppose you use your girlfriend to come up with some of this research, she being a writer. Actually, I like her fantasy books, though they are fantasy. Truth isn't something you live by." Rivera comes closer, leaning over me.

"Elle Sinclair isn't part of this..." I'm interrupted.

"You mean, Liane Cillser, don't you."

"Elle Sinclair and I build a Chinese wall since she has to report on this for the paper. Odd as it may seem, but some people still believe in integrity to go with their truth, Agent Rivera." I stand and face her, looking her in the eye.

"Some wall. The Willow Gazette has been less than a step behind us ever since Janine Moore comes forward. We've got Moore locked down, so where else could she be getting her intel? You are all on the Library Board together, you two hire Moore for your event. I'm not so sure you're really as upstanding as you appear to be, either of you." Agent Rivera holds herself inches from my face.

Max, not a time for your temper. Get a grip. She wants a reason to arrest you so you can sit in that interrogation again, this time with reason. I hold my breath. Then sit back down while I exhale.

"Grayson, you want to see what I find?" Grayson nods his head. Rivera steps away.

"Janine apparently takes out the loan about three years ago. The strings attached include switching to this accounting firm, as you know. After she hires them, I find very few transactions that Janine has direct knowledge of, actually a few she tries to adjust for townspeople or city hall. That's when the bakery starts hiring the fake ID people, giving them credibility, some of them moving on to jobs at other merchants, looking for businesses that the boss can arm-twist, I assume.

"In order to make these adjustments in the town books, they have to have someone in the accounting office of Willow Creek, or a back door to the new software accounting package installed two years ago. See, that is when we start to see these monthly 'write-offs' and 'discretionary' entries. Mayor Calloway signs these purchase orders, but I don't see anything that says he initiates them. So good luck on making him involved directly."

"I'm really impressed by the causational train you have here, Donovan." Special Agent Grayson scans the report I pull together.

"Yeah, well, I think I've given you a map for what you're looking for in the other town finance records. This is a list of twenty-five questionable vendors that might be the receiving end of the laundered money. These guys are good. They choose small items, everyday items, like hand soap and cleaning supplies as the bogus invoices that are actually cleaning their funds. It takes a moment to recognize that a small town won't use that much hand soap, not at the price they're charging." I sit back and watch Grayson review the papers.

"You really don't sleep, do you, Red Maestro." Agent Rivera moves back to the table.

"Not when there's work to do."

Grayson exhales sharply, shaking his head. "Willow Creek isn't the only town showing these patterns. You're right. The same types of financial misallocations are popping up in at least six other small towns across the state."

I suspect as much. "Calloway might not be the mastermind. He is aware of the inconsistencies. In hindsight, I think that is why he taps me for his finance committee. The two city councilmen on the committee with me either don't want to see what I point out, or don't understand.

Calloway's shaping up to be the right politician at the right time."

Grayson chuckles. "That he is. He urges Moore to call us—"

Rivera sits down, shooting a look at Grayson. "We'll keep looking. If there's a bigger player moving money, someone's going to notice. And we'll be watching."

Grayson sighs, closing the folder. "You know, if you ever want a full-time job in financial crimes, I can put in a word."

I snort. "Tempting. But I have two businesses to run."

Rivera raises a brow. "The farm?"

I shake my head. "Consulting. Helping small businesses, setting them up for success. Growing things, not just tearing down corruption."

Agent Rivera offers her hand. "Sounds like Red Maestro rides again."

I shake her hand. "Only if I can do it on my terms, keep to my truth."

Before they leave, Grayson hands me a card. "We'll be in touch. Keep your eyes open."

I watch them go, exhaling a breath I don't realize I'm holding. The work isn't over, not by a long shot.

My phone buzzes. A text from Elle.

Elle: *Hey. Oliver is setting up for Open Mic Night. Are you coming?*

Elle: *Or are you still lost in numbers?*

I smile and type back.

Max: *Just finishing up. Be there soon.*

Elle: *Good. You need a break. Try acting like a human for a few hours.*

I chuckle, shaking my head. Maybe a break isn't a bad idea.

I shut the laptop, stretch my stiff limbs, and head out into the cold, knowing this battle isn't over.

But at least for tonight, I can be with the people who matter.

I SHOULD KNOW tonight will get out of hand the second I step into Perk Up and see Tony Holsolm standing on a chair, brandishing a tambourine like he's leading a revolution.

"Welcome to Open Mic Night: Holiday Edition!" Tony bellows, rattling the tambourine so violently a nearby college kid flinches and spills his coffee all over himself.

Elle snorts beside me, slipping her hand into mine as we navigate through the overcrowded café. "Is it just me, or is Tony getting more dramatic with age?"

"Not just you," I murmur, eyeing a three-piece folk band setting up in the corner, already arguing over whether they can legally perform a Mariah Carey song without summoning her lawyers.

Tony hops down from his chair, landing in front of us with the grace of a man who definitely sprains an ankle doing this before.

He grins. "Look who finally decides to grace us with their presence."

I smile. "We hear there'll be free entertainment."

Tony waves an arm toward the chaos around us. "Oh, it's entertainment, alright."

Then his eyes flick to Elle, and the grin shifts into something softer. "And I especially can't believe you're here, Miss Rebel Journalist."

Elle sighs, but there's amusement in her expression. "Is that my new title now?"

"Oh, absolutely," Tony says.

I squeeze Elle's hand, watching as her lips twitch; not quite a full smile, but something close.

And then, from behind us, a voice chimes in.

"For what it's worth, I think your article is spot on."

We turn to see Martha Elderman, one of Willow Creek's longtime residents, clutching a steaming cup of tea.

Elle blinks. "Then why don't you say anything?"

Martha shrugs. "Because it's common sense. I don't think it needs defending."

Elle exhales, a mix of frustration and understanding flashing across her face. "Yeah, well... apparently, it does."

Martha frowns. "People can be ridiculous. But I won't let it get to you, honey. The town will come around. They always do."

Elle nods, but I can see it: the way she absorbs those words but doesn't quite believe them yet.

Tony claps his hands together, cutting through the tension. "Alright, enough emotional depth. Time for caffeine and regret!"

Elle snorts, shaking her head as we make our way toward the counter.

We grab our drinks and settle near the back, Elle perched on the arm of my chair, her fingers tracing idle circles on my sleeve as she sips her mocha.

"You look good in this sweater," she murmurs, voice just low enough that only I can hear.

I grin, glancing up at her. "Yeah?"

"Yeah," she says, her eyes appraising. "Very respectable farm-owner meets sexy undercover agent."

I chuckle. "That's a very specific aesthetic."

Elle leans in, brushing her lips just below my ear. "It's working for you."

My hand tightens around her thigh, but before I can respond, there's a loud crash from the front of the café.

We both turn to see Oliver, standing next to a tripod-mounted camera, looking like a man who just loses an argument with gravity.

"Oliver?" I call.

He waves us off, wild-eyed but determined. "It's fine! Everything is fine! Just setting up for Perk Up's social media."

I narrow my eyes. "Since when do you run Perk Up's social media?"

Oliver, now furiously adjusting the camera, mutters, "Since Tony says he'll pay me in both cash and unlimited coffee."

Elle winces. "So basically, we'll never see you sleep again."

Oliver just grins, thrilled by this fact. "Exactly."

The night rolls on, full of bad poetry, acoustic guitar solos, and a particularly confident performance of "Jingle Bell Rock" that should come with a warning label.

Elle and I sit close, our conversations weaving effortlessly between playful teasing, quiet check-ins, and those unspoken moments where nothing needs to be said at all.

At some point, I slide my arm around her waist, pulling her in until her head rests against my shoulder. She hums in contentment, fingers tracing absentminded patterns along the fabric of my shirt.

Elle leans into me, her voice soft but sure. "You good?"

I glance at her, at the way the light catches in her eyes, at the warmth in her expression. "Yeah," I murmur. "I'm great."

She tilts her head. "You sure?"

I reach out, tucking a strand of hair behind her ear. "You are the best thing that ever happens to me."

I don't realize how quiet the room gets, or that Oliver's camera is still rolling.

Elle breathes in, "If thou must love me, let it be for naught except for love's sake only. Do not say, 'I love her for her smile—her look—her way of speaking gently—for a trick of thought that falls in well with mine, and so forth.' These are all things that might change or cease to be, and love so built on such a thing as this built upon sand. O Love, I love thee!" She pauses, "Elizabeth Barrett Browning."

She recites it like she says it a thousand times, like the words live in her bones.

I blink at her, thrown for a second. "You just have that ready?"

Elle smiles, sipping her coffee. "You don't?"

Oliver, still behind the camera, stares at the screen like he just discovers the meaning of life.

Kim grins, nudging him. "Told you," she whispers.

Oliver mutters, "Huh."

Later, after the event winds down and people start trickling out, Oliver stays behind, reviewing footage.

When he gets to the part where Elle and I aren't paying attention, he freezes. Rewinds. Listens.

Max: "You are the best thing that ever happens to me."

Elle: "O Love, I love thee."

Oliver watches the screen, watching the way we look at each other.

Kim leans in, studying his expression. "What?"

Oliver swallows. "That's... what it's supposed to be, isn't it?"

Kim tilts her head. "What do you mean?"

He keeps staring at the footage, at the unguarded truth in our faces, the way we just fit.

Oliver exhales. "That's what love looks like."

Kim watches him for a moment, then bumps her shoulder against his. "Took you long enough."

Oliver doesn't respond. But later, when he walks Kim home, he reaches for her hand. And this time, he doesn't let go.

By the time we get home, Elle is kicking off her boots in the doorway, stretching in a way that makes all rational thought temporarily leave my head.

She glances at me, lips twitching. "So. You really think I'm the best thing that ever happens to you?"

I smile, stepping closer. "Caught that, do you?"

"Oh, I catch it." She places a hand on my chest, tilting her head. "You planning on making that a habit? Saying sweet things when you think I'm not listening?"

I slide my arms around her waist, tugging her flush against me. "I don't think you aren't listening. I just don't care who else hears."

Her breath catches, just for a second, before she exhales softly.

"Good answer."

And then she kisses me, slow and deep and absolutely certain.

Love isn't just words.

It's showing up, every day, even when it's hard.

It's fighting for each other, even when the world pushes back.

It's two parts of a whole, choosing to be stronger together than apart.

And I know, without a doubt, I choose her every time.

TWENTY-THREE
THE BREAKING POINT

ELLE

TUESDAY MORNING, I wake up to chaos.

Not the usual, pleasant kind where Max and I linger over coffee while Oliver and Lily bicker about who used the last of the milk. No, this is a different beast entirely.

My phone vibrates against the nightstand, buzzing non-stop with notifications. A glance at the screen tells me everything I need to know.

Social media has exploded.

I take a slow breath and open the first message.

"Fake news hack."

Charming.

The next one:

"Hope you enjoy destroying innocent people's lives."

I let out a breath. Here we go.

Sliding out of bed, I throw on a sweatshirt and head to the kitchen, my bare feet padding across the hardwood.

The smell of coffee greets me before I see Max, already dressed, sipping from his mug at the counter.

He glances up. "You read it yet?"

I rub my temple. "Define 'read.' If you mean have I waded through an ocean of hate speech, then yes."

His jaw tightens, his protective streak kicking in. "Ignore it."

I let out a sharp laugh. "Oh, sure. That'll work great. I'll just pretend the town isn't imploding because I dared to point out that using crime as entertainment is bad for a community."

Max sets his mug down and pulls me into his arms, pressing a kiss to my temple. "People will get over it."

I close my eyes against his chest. "Will they?"

He doesn't answer. And that silence? That tells me exactly what I already know.

By the time I pull up to Willow Creek High School, I've convinced myself that maybe, just maybe, I'm overreacting.

Then I step out of the car.

The sharp-eyed PTA dad, Greg Thompson, makes a beeline for me before I even reach the front doors. His expression is tight, his stance rigid.

"Elle," he says, voice clipped. "We need to talk."

Oh, fantastic.

I cross my arms. "Good afternoon to you, too, Greg."

He doesn't waste time on pleasantries. "Your editorial. It was completely out of line. You think it's okay to drag our town through the mud like that?"

I exhale through my nose, keeping my tone even. "I didn't drag the town through anything, Greg. I pointed out that we have an issue."

"Yeah? Well, the issue now is you. People are upset. You're making us look bad."

I bite back a dozen responses, settling on, "I'm allowed to have a position. Even if you don't agree with it."

Greg scoffs. "Sure. Just don't be surprised if people stop reading your paper."

I smile tightly. "Greg, I'll lose exactly zero sleep over people choosing willful ignorance. Have a nice day."

He opens his mouth, but Lily appears at my side, slipping her backpack over her shoulder.

"Hey, sweetie," I murmur, shifting my attention. "Ready to go?"

She nods, but as we walk to the car, I feel her hesitate beside me.

"Elle?" she asks quietly. "Why was he so mad?"

I take a breath. "Some people don't like when others challenge the way things have always been. Even when change is necessary."

She frowns. "That's dumb."

I huff a small laugh. "Yeah. It is."

WEDNESDAY MORNING, I stop at Miller's Market for milk and bread and something for dinner. I brace for impact.

The first few shoppers avoid eye contact. One or two couples appear split, one partner offers me a slight tilt of their head while their mate won't look at me.

Then, Maggie Ross, the owner, slides a fresh loaf of sourdough into my basket.

"On the house," she says, then lowers her voice. "For

what it's worth, I think you're right. And I'm sorry people are acting like this."

Relief floods through me. "Thanks, Maggie."

Maybe not everyone in town wants my head on a pike.

THURSDAY MORNING, I walk into Perk Up, the shift is impossible to ignore.

Some people nod politely. Others stare, whispering behind their coffee cups. A few read today's weekend edition, looking at me as if my retraction is missing.

Tony waves me over, grinning. "Well, if it isn't Willow Creek's most controversial woman."

I slide into the seat across from him. "You're enjoying this way too much."

"Absolutely." He sips his latte. "But for real, you struck a nerve."

"Yeah, no kidding."

Tony leans forward. "Look, as a small business owner, corruption is expensive. If crime gets worse, it could drive businesses under. You were right to say something."

The weight in my chest eases slightly. "Thanks, Tony."

Across the room, someone glares at me over their mug.

Right. Not everyone agrees.

IT'S FRIDAY MORNING.

I freeze when I see it.

Scrawled in red paint across the Willow Gazette's front door:

FAKE NEWS.

My stomach drops.

I should be angry. But mostly? I'm just tired.

I step inside, heading straight to George Franklin's office.

He looks up, already knowing why I'm here. "Elle."

I don't sit. "I'm done."

George sits down, nodding slowly. "I figured."

I exhale, running a hand through my hair. "I didn't sign up to fight a town that doesn't want to be saved."

He sighs. "I wish you'd stay. But I get it. And for what it's worth? I agree with you."

I smile, genuine this time. "Thank you."

George leans back in his chair, rubbing a hand over his face. "You know, Elle... I used to think my job was just to keep the paper running. Make sure it sells. Give people what they want to read. Now, I see that maybe that was the problem."

I tilt my head. "What do you mean?"

He lets out a tired sigh, shaking his head. "I raised a daughter who never learned to hear 'no.' If she wanted something, I smoothed the road. I wanted her to be happy. Thought that was what a good father did. But now, she stands up in a public meeting, trying to humiliate a man; not because he's done wrong, but because he wouldn't rewrite his truth to fit her story."

I watch him carefully. "And you think the town is doing the same thing?"

George nods, rubbing his temple. "Yeah. I think we've raised a generation that never learned to separate truth from what feels true. They think real life is just another story to be shaped, another episode to be consumed. And people like us? We fed into it."

I fold my arms. "You're talking about the paper."

He nods, a quiet admission. "For years, I told myself we were just giving people what they wanted. But what if what they wanted was to be distracted instead of informed? To be entertained instead of challenged? To laugh at corruption instead of fixing it? That wasn't our journalistic role. Our role was to inform, so they could make good decisions."

I exhale. "So what now?"

George surveys the newsroom, like he's seeing it for the first time in years. "Now? I start saying 'no.'"

George pauses, then asks. "Are you... leaving Willow Creek?"

I shake my head. "No plans to. Not with me marrying Max."

He smiles. "Good. The town would be worse off without you."

I stand. "Take care, Geo."

He watches me for a moment, then says, softly: "You too, Elle. Happy Christmas."

I may not know what comes next.

But I know what I'm *leaving behind*.

Outside, I inhale the crisp air, letting it settle in my lungs.

No more spinning stories for ad revenue. No more battles I can't win.

Instead, I start thinking about what would make me happy.

And suddenly, the answer is clear as day.

THAT NIGHT, curled up on Max's couch, I look at him and smile.

"Let's set a date."

He blinks. "For?"

"The wedding. Christmas. In Willow Creek."

Max's lips curl into a slow grin. "You sure?"

I lace my fingers through his. "Absolutely."

Because I know exactly where I belong.

TWENTY-FOUR

THE DONOVAN-SINCLAIR CHRISTMAS

ELLE

THERE ARE few things more formidable than the Sinclair family descending for the holidays.

It's a flurry of designer luggage, polished greetings, and the distinct aroma of old money meeting small-town living.

As I look out the window for the dozenth time, I see Elliot's SUV arrive at the house. They're here. The ice on the window distorts the white rental car that arrives next. I grab my coat, yell for the Donovans to come help greet our guests.

I barely step onto the porch before my twin brother, Elliot, sweeps me into a hug, murmuring, "We've arrived, Sis. Prepare yourself."

Behind him, his wife, Patricia, elegant in an emerald cashmere coat, smiles warmly. "Elle, darling. We've missed you."

Trailing behind them are their three children, Charles, 15; Peter, 12; and Cece, 8, who immediately take stock of their surroundings, as if calculating exactly how far Willow Creek is from the luxuries of their life in eastern Pennsylvania.

Then, as if the chaos wasn't enough, my parents, Howard and Rita Sinclair, step out of their white rental car.

Dad takes in the farmhouse with a contemplative nod. "Rustic."

Mom adjusts her pearl earrings. "Charming."

Translation? They're processing.

Max steps onto the porch, his posture relaxed but his blue eyes sharp, reading my family the way he reads financial reports.

"Welcome to Willow Creek," he says, shaking Elliot's hand. "Hope the drive was smooth."

Elliot smiles. "Smooth enough. Though Charles complained about the lack of an in-flight meal."

"I was joking," Charles mutters, but his grin says otherwise.

Max chuckles, motioning toward the house. "Come on in. Make yourselves at home."

Once inside, the controlled dance of Sinclair diplomacy begins.

My mother inspects the kitchen with an appraising glance, making approving sounds at the handcrafted wooden countertops.

Patricia, ever the diplomat, leans in. "It's lovely, Elle. And it suits you."

But I have a more urgent mission.

"Kids, who wants to see the barn?" I announce, summoning a distraction.

Lily perks up. "Can I show Cece the horses?"

Max nods. "Go for it. Oliver, you mind giving the boys a tour?"

Oliver shrugs, but Peter looks genuinely intrigued. "You have a real barn?"

Elliot claps his son's shoulder. "Careful, Peter. You might actually touch nature."

Peter rolls his eyes, but follows Oliver out.

Once the kids are safely out of earshot, I turn to my family and lower my voice. "Listen carefully."

They all pause, sensing Sinclair-level importance.

"Oliver, Lily, and Kim do not know I'm Liane Cillser." I pause for impact. "They're huge fans of *The Veridion Chronicles*. If they find out, I will never have a moment's peace again."

Elliot bursts out laughing. "Oh, this is delicious."

I shoot him a glare. "Not. A. Word."

My father rubs his chin, amused. "So, let me get this straight. Your future stepchildren adore your books, but they have no idea you wrote them?"

"Exactly. So, no slip-ups."

Patricia smiles knowingly. "I assume you've prepared a cover story for when they inevitably start asking questions?"

I groan. "I am hoping to delay that until the fan event in April. I'm returning. Max has agreed to be by my side, so I'm going to be with my fans again." My voice starts to reveal the impact of sharing this with the people who know me best.

"Oh, jolly good, Sis." Elliot says. Turning to Max, "Well done, mate."

"So, please, try to keep this little secret a bit longer.

Please?" I put my hands together like a prayer and point to each one.

My mother, with a suspicious twinkle in her eye, simply hums. "We'll do our best, darling."

I don't love the tone.

That evening, just as I think I've survived the first wave of family inspections, Max clears his throat.

Everyone turns toward him.

He stands, taking my hand. "Elle, I had planned something more... private. But since your family is here," he glances at my father and Elliot "and since I believe in doing things properly..."

My stomach flutters.

He takes my left hand, removes the simple diamond solitaire off my finger, and drops it into his pocket.

Max reaches into his other pocket and pulls out a ring box, flipping it open.

I suck in a breath.

A deep sapphire, encased by diamonds, catching the firelight.

I can't move. Can't breathe.

He takes my left hand again, his voice steady but thick with emotion. "How do I love thee? Let me count the ways."

My breath catches.

He continues, looking at me. "I love thee to the depth and breadth and height my soul can reach, when feeling out of sight for the ends of being and ideal grace. I love thee to the level of everyday's most quiet need, by sun and candlelight." His voice builds with depth and emotion.

"I love thee freely, as men strive for right. I love thee purely, as they turn from praise. I love thee with the passion put to use in my old griefs, and with my childhood's faith. I love thee with a love I seemed to lose with my lost saints. I love thee with the breath, smiles, tears, of all my life—and, if God choose, I shall but love thee better after death."

By the time he reaches the final lines, tears are threatening to spill. In a low voice that only he could hear, "You remembered. My favorite."

He slides the ring onto my finger. It feels like it was always meant to be there. Then we kiss.

My father clears his throat, and Elliot mutters, "Alright, that's bloody impressive."

I laugh through the tears. "Yes. Yes, a thousand times, yes."

Patricia bumps Elliot's arm, a tear running down her cheek. "You'd better be taking notes. Max just raised the bar, darling."

"Right. Thanks, mate." Elliot kisses Patricia on the cheek.

Max smiles. "Figured I should prove myself properly. And... I may have consulted with both of you before choosing the ring."

Elliot raises an eyebrow. "So, you do understand business negotiations."

Max grins. "Of course. This is the most important contract of my life."

Rita takes my hand, looking at the ring. "Well, that's more like it. I was so curious when I saw that other one. This is better. Congratulations, Elle. He does seem to be the right one."

I give my mother a hug, grateful she and Dad decided to join us for this special holiday.

SLAM.

Lily, Peter, and Cece yell at Storm to stop. But paws click

across the kitchen floor, heading for the fireplace where we were all gathered. A wet, muddy golden retriever shakes cold water all over everyone. Then he starts jumping up on me and Max, nuzzles Howard and Patricia, looking for a friendly hand for a stroke or two.

"STORM!" Lily yells, running after him. "He got out again!"

Max sighs, wiping wet dog off his sweater. "Well, that was a short-lived romantic moment."

I laugh. "Welcome to our future, Donovan."

He pulls me close, water be damned. "Wouldn't have it any other way."

Later, once everyone has changed into dry clothes, we gather in the living room.

Oliver clears his throat. "I have news." Everyone pauses. "I got hired by Perk Up to record Open Mic Nights. And I'm running their podcast."

There's a beat of silence before my father claps. "Impressive initiative."

Elliot nods. "Sounds like you're building a real brand."

Oliver glows. "Thanks."

I glance around the room, at the warmth, the easy conversation, the respect. This is what wealth truly is. It is good to be able to get whatever we need when we need it, don't get me wrong. But we can't buy this moment of a newly blended family feeling like we've been at this for years. My parents are looking at Oliver and Lily, my soon-to-be stepchildren, just the same as Elliot and Patricia's three. And I know at that moment, if Max and I expand our family, however that might happen, the Sinclairs will welcome them as well. It isn't just blood. It is love, respect, and joy for each other's life expression. My heart fills with gratitude.

THE STORM WARNINGS are coming in faster and louder.

My phone buzzes with another update as I sit at the kitchen table, staring at the weather radar. Dark clouds creeping toward Willow Creek.

"More alerts?" Max asks, setting a fresh cup of coffee in front of me.

I sigh. "The weather service just upgraded the advisory. Could be snow, could be ice. Either way, it's making a mess of travel plans."

Across the room, my father, Howard, clears his throat. "Marriages in churches are blessed," he states firmly. "We keep the church."

Elliot, leaning against the counter, raises an eyebrow. "Is that a rule, or just something you decided?"

Dad gives him a pointed look. "Both."

Max, ever the voice of reason, nods. "Keeping it at the church makes sense, especially if the power goes out here. Better to have backup."

I exhale. "Fine. Church it is."

Elliot, Max, and my father settle onto the sofa, discussing bachelor party plans like they're orchestrating a royal affair.

"Nothing too wild," Max warns. "I have kids."

"Oh, so no international travel? No helicopters?"

"No headlines," I interject. "Or bail money."

Peter, Elliot's twelve-year-old son, perks up from across the room. "Can we come?"

Charles, his fifteen-year-old brother, leans in. "Yeah, we should be included. We're old enough."

Elliot snorts. "Absolutely not."

Peter scowls. "That's age discrimination."

Howard sips his tea. "It's called common sense."

Max smiles, glancing at Elliot. "See? I told you your kids would be trouble."

Elliot shrugs. "They take after me. You should be concerned. She's my twin."

"Oh, I know. She certainly is." Max chuckles.

They continue their brainstorming until Max suggests dinner out at a local pub, considering the weather reports. Together, they decide to plan a big trip in early summer.

Patricia is thrilled when I suggest picking up dresses and having lunch in the county seat.

"Oh, fabulous! A proper bachelorette outing. A bit of indulgence before you walk down the aisle."

Mom, already slipping on her tailored wool coat, smiles. "We could all use a bit of luxury."

Patricia hums. "And champagne. Definitely champagne."

We pile into the car, heading toward an upscale boutique that Patricia had "coincidentally researched." As we sift through gowns, she studies me over the rack. "How are you holding up, darling?"

I pause, adjusting the delicate beading on a dress. "Honestly? A bit overwhelmed."

Mom gives me a knowing look. "You always did manage under pressure. Just like your father."

"High praise," I mutter.

Patricia grins. "And marrying someone equally formidable."

I smile. "Yes. Yes, I am."

That evening, as snow clouds hover, Max takes over the kitchen.

The dining table is set with an exquisite spread: roasted vegetables, herb-crusted lamb, freshly baked bread.

Dad lifts a fork, intrigued. "Impressive, son."

Elliot, cutting into his meal, raises an eyebrow. "Wait. Max, since when do you cook like this?"

Max, plating another dish, shrugs. "I started in culinary school. Then went into finance. Then farming. And back to finance."

Elliot blinks. "You just casually left that out?"

"You didn't ask."

I lean in, grinning. "I love this part of him."

Elliot turns to our father. "Did you know Max is consulting with *Green Agricultural*?"

Dad pauses, then nods. "Yes. And I approve."

Patricia lifts her wine glass. "So, when's Max running the company?"

Max laughs. "Let's not get ahead of ourselves."

"Elle, I almost forgot. The attorneys called just before we left, and the foundation is all sorted. It will actually help Green Agricultural, and you can transfer funds before the end of the year, if you still want. Brilliant idea, sis, thanks for pushing."

"Green Agricultural is forming a foundation? I've been thinking about forming one as an asset catch basin. Maybe focused on micro-loans or low-interest loans to small businesses, like the ones I've started consulting with. Many small businesses just need a bridge loan to help them position themselves for bigger profits," Max informs us.

Howard sets his wine glass down with a thoughtful

smile. "You know," he says, voice warming, "your idea for small loans through the foundation reminded me of something my dad, Willard, used to tell me. It's a story about his father, your great-grandfather Elias."

I look at Elliot, who shrugs his shoulders. "Elias? Dad, you never talk about him. He founded Green Agricultural, didn't he?"

Howard nods. "That's right. Elias came back from the Great War with nothing but the clothes on his back and a dream of owning land. But he was broke, no credit, no connections, couldn't buy a cemetery plot, let alone a homestead. So he started with what he had—the seeds from the apples he bought for his meals that week."

"He sold them, then bought more apples with the proceeds. He was able to eat, and made money from the seeds," Elliot adds.

"So you did read the corporation history I left for you." Howard looks at Elliot, impatient for the interruption. Elliot just puts up his palms and motions for Howard to continue.

"He had started an apple seed business. Worked out good, too. Then one day the local market was out of apples, which meant he didn't eat nor have any products to sell."

My eyes brighten. "That's when he started to try to convince people to let him plant on their land, right?"

Howard nods. "Exactly. That's how he met your great-grandmother, Maxine Morehouse. She was an artist, full of wild ideas, and curly reddish hair. She had lots of artistic talents, mostly creating printed fabrics, some going to the local seamstress, others picked up by the co-op for feed sacks."

Rita explains. "In those days, ladies would repurpose

the sack the chicken feed came in into clothes for the family. It was either cotton muslin or poplin, in colors or prints."

Seamlessly, Howard continues, "He convinced her to let him plant apple seeds on her family's small plot. He stayed in the shed, helping out around the place. Her father had died, and her mother was sick, so she was glad for the help. It takes a while for an apple tree to grow and bear fruit. By the first harvest, they didn't just have apples, they had each other."

Max smiles softly, as if he's picturing it.

Rita continues, "She was the one who saw the star hidden inside the apple. She'd cut them in half and use the shape as a stamp to decorate the walls of their first little home. That's why Green Agricultural's logo is a star—it's not just a design, it's her apple star. She also gave art lessons to the children of prosperous families."

Elliot blinks. "I had no idea."

Howard's smile turns reflective. "When Willard, my dad, was about five, Elias was running a thriving apple farm. Then they had a bumper crop. Seeing the opportunity, he tried to get a loan. But he was turned down."

"Maxine was teaching the children of a wealthy businessman, who loved Elias's apples and apple products," Rita nods to Howard.

"They needed to expand, but money was tight. Then, that businessman gave Elias the short-term, low-interest loan he needed to buy extra baskets and packaging for that year's bumper crop. The extra profits didn't just help the family, they launched Green Agricultural as a proper seed and fertilizer company."

I tilt my head. "What kind of fertilizer?"

Howard grins. "Homemade brilliance. Apple pomace from the cider press, mixed with aged manure and layered in a special composting process. It made the soil sing. Just like we do today, right, Elliot?"

"Yes, Dad."

He pauses, voice softening. "But here's the part I love. Elias realized something as the farm grew. He wasn't meant to just raise apples. He was meant to help things grow— other farmers, neighboring businesses, the whole community. Just like that businessman helped him. That's what Green Agricultural was founded on. That was his truth, and by keeping to it, we've been able to weather many storms and shifts in business. 'Your power is in your truth,' I heard my father say that all his life."

Max leans forward slightly, heart pulling tight. "That's what I believe too. The people I've been consulting with, they don't need handouts. They need tools. Access. Small, intentional loans they can use to build something real. It's not charity. It's helping them invest in their own worth."

Howard lifts his glass. "That's a vision I can stand behind."

I ask, "Maybe we should name the foundation Green Seeds. Or, Green Vision Seeds?" I look around the family. "Anyone mind if we invite Max to join this foundation, instead of starting his own?"

"Of course, yes, mate, that would be perfect. We don't want every board member named Sinclair."

Then Elliot looks at me, as Patricia says, "Elle, darling, what name are you using after the wedding? Hyphenating? Another pseudonym?"

I laugh. "I hadn't considered." I look at Max. "We

haven't talked about this. Donovan. Sinclair-Donovan." I pause. "We need a follow-up on that one."

"By any other name, you're still the one I love and choose every day," Max says. He grabs my hand from across the table and squeezes it.

Then he turns back to Elliot, just as Patricia pokes him in his arm. "Yes, I would like to be part of the Vision Green Seedlings Foundation. We can figure out the details after dinner."

Patricia smiles. "I just want to know if we can put apple stars on the foundation's letterhead. They'd be quite trendy."

"Can I help?" Lily speaks up.

Elliot smiles. "If you pitch me before we leave."

"Pitch you?" Lily queries.

"He means tell him your ideas, just like you do me all the time. I'll explain more later," Oliver tells Lily.

"Max, the dinner is delicious. Thank you. Perfect." Patricia raises her wine glass to Max.

"Second that. To Max, with gratitude for a lovely, productive family dinner." Dad raises his glass, then we all follow, toasting the amazing, multi-talented man I'm about to marry.

Over dessert, the conversation turns to books.

Peter, ever enthusiastic, says, "*The Veridion Chronicles* is the best fantasy series."

Kim nods. "The world-building is insane."

Elliot, who knows exactly who wrote it. "Elle, didn't you say you were planning on taking the kids to the next fan event?"

I stiffen slightly. "Yes."

Patricia tilts her head. "Oh, what a lovely experience for you all."

Kim perks up. "Wait, you are? I gotta go then."

Lily brightens. "Really? To like the real one, Veridion Kingdom?"

Oliver narrows his eyes at me, suspicious. "You never seem that interested in fan events."

Max smoothly intervenes. "I think Elle just wants to experience it with you all."

Elliot bites back a laugh. "Yes. That's exactly why."

"Of course," Patricia adds, sipping her wine, "I hear Liane Cillser might be making an appearance at this one."

Howard turns slowly to look at me. "Is that right, Elle?"

I hold my wine glass carefully. "That's what I've heard."

Max, thoroughly enjoying himself, simply sits back and watches.

The kids, completely oblivious to the tension, start debating what costumes to wear.

As the evening winds down, snowflakes begin to drift past the windows.

Dad pats Max on the shoulder. "You've built something real here. That's more valuable than anything."

Max meets his gaze. "I intend to keep it that way."

I glance around, at my parents, at my brother, at Max and the kids, feeling something I've never quite felt before.

Total. Absolute. Belonging.

The wind howls as we bundle up, preparing to leave for *Perk Up's Open Mic Night*.

"This is utter madness," Patricia declares, fastening her cream wool coat with the kind of dignity only a lifelong Brit could manage while stepping into a rented fifteen-passenger van.

"It's tradition," Elliot counters, adjusting his cashmere scarf. "Can't let a little Arctic blast ruin the boy's big night."

"Besides," Max says, closing the hatch with a grin, "this is the good kind of chaos — the kind you don't want to miss."

I glance at the kids, all practically vibrating with excitement, and smile. "Everyone ready?"

A resounding "Yes!" from the back rows.

Patricia sighs, sliding into her seat beside Elliot. "I suppose we'll see if this quaint little café can handle all of us."

Max starts the engine, and immediately, the bickering begins.

Lily, wedged between Peter and Cece, bounces excitedly. "Road trip rules: no complaining, no boring talk, and no one is allowed to play 'I Spy' because Uncle Elliot cheats."

Elliot scoffs. "I do not cheat."

Patricia adjusts her gloves with pointed elegance. "You absolutely do, darling."

"I enhance the game," Elliot corrects. "A touch of strategy never hurt anyone."

Peter leans forward from the back row. "Oh, I fully intend to cheat. Let's not pretend otherwise."

Cece giggles. "This is going to be the longest twenty-minute drive of our lives."

Peter smiles. "Or the most entertaining."

Howard, sitting in the far back with Rita, clears his throat. "Does anyone have a map? Just in case Max decides to take an 'alternate route' again?"

Max glances at me in the rearview mirror, grinning. "Still glad I didn't take two cars?"

"No, this is already worth the entertainment value."

Patricia shakes her head. "I can't believe I let myself be talked into this."

Elliot grins. "Trish, admit it, you love the chaos."

She scoffs, adjusting her seatbelt. "I tolerate it."

Lily gasps dramatically. "Oh! Can we play 'Guess That Sound' instead?"

Peter perks up. "Excellent idea. I'll start." He lets out a high-pitched screeching noise.

Elliot groans. "Max, I'll triple your consulting fee if you turn this van around."

Patricia sips her tea, because of course she brought tea, and shakes her head. "Too late, love. We're committed."

Max shoots me a look.

I pat his thigh reassuringly. "You've survived worse, Donovan."

He shifts the van into drive. "Pray for me."

The ride to Perk Up is a mix of heated debates over song choices, questionable road trip games, and Elliot vowing never to travel with us again.

Lily and Cece start a ridiculously off-key rendition of a song from the *Beauty and the Beast* soundtrack, while Charles tries to convince Peter to beatbox.

Patricia, ever composed, silently judges all of us.

Howard and Rita exchange knowing glances, as if they've seen decades of this madness and have simply learned to endure.

Max? He just drives, grinning the whole time.

I lean against him, feeling the warmth of family, of laughter, of belonging.

"Full speed ahead, Donovan."

Perk Up is packed when we arrive, the air rich with

espresso, conversation, and nervous performers clutching crumpled notes.

At the front, Oliver and Kim are in full production mode, adjusting their camera angles.

"Everything set?" Max asks, as Oliver waves at us, beaming.

"Yeah, just a few final tweaks," he says, focused and confident. "Kim's getting the last few release forms signed. Charles is helping with the mic checks."

Patricia blinks. "Wait, Charles is helping?"

Elliot smiles. "Darlings, you knew he was, that's why he wasn't in the van with us."

From across the café, Charles leans against the counter, casually handing Kim a clipboard.

"Thought you might need this," he says smoothly.

Kim takes it, raising a brow. "Thanks. But I do have an extra pair of hands already."

Oliver, standing just behind them, frowns. "What's going on here?"

Kim smiles. "Nothing. Just that your cousin thinks he's charming."

Charles grins. "I am charming."

Kim tilts her head. "And yet, I have a boyfriend."

Charles looks at Oliver, then back at Kim. "Tragic for me. Great for him."

Oliver stiffens slightly, his jaw tightening, but Kim just laughs, handing him the clipboard. "You're cute, Sinclair, but Oliver's my guy."

Charles holds up his hands. "Fair enough. Just saying, if you ever develop a thing for British aristocracy—"

Kim snorts. "Yeah, I'll call Buckingham Palace. But you're American."

Oliver relaxes slightly, but his gaze lingers on Charles for a moment longer.

I nudge Max. "Should we step in?"

Max sips his coffee. "Absolutely not. This is too good."

Tony takes the stage, shaking his tambourine aggressively. "Ladies and gentlemen, welcome to Open Mic Night! The storm may be coming, but art shall prevail!"

The audience cheers, and Oliver presses the record.

I lean back, watching as he focuses completely on his work, adjusting the audio levels, nodding to Kim when it's time for the next act.

Max nudges me. "Proud?"

I watch Oliver, so dedicated and serious, and smile. "More than I can say."

Two days later, Oliver bursts into the living room, waving his phone.

"Guys! The Open Mic Night video went viral!"

I sit up. "What? How viral?"

He grins. "Perk Up's page got over ten thousand views in one day. They're hiring me to record all future events!"

Max claps his shoulder. "First paying gig. Nice work, Ollie."

Oliver glows.

I ruffle his hair. "You'll be famous soon. Better get a manager."

"Already hired myself one."

Charles, from the couch, raises a hand. "You should've hired me. I could've tripled your rates."

Kim rolls her eyes. "Because that's what Oliver needs."

Oliver grins. "Actually, I did hire someone."

I raise a brow. "Who?"

He throws an arm around Charles. "I drafted him to help record the wedding."

Patricia chokes on her tea. "You what?"

Charles grins. "I get paid, I get cake, and I get to capture all the embarrassing family moments. It's a win-win."

Max smiles. "Kid might be onto something."

Oliver shrugs, grinning. "Might as well put his charm to good use."

Charles laughs. "I am nothing if not resourceful."

I shake my head, smiling. This family is a force of nature.

And Oliver? He's found his path.

And we're all right here, cheering him on.

TWENTY-FIVE
I DO, DESPITE THE ICE

MAX

I'VE DRIVEN blind through a sandstorm in the Nevada desert with nothing but instinct and a barely working GPS. I've closed a multimillion-dollar deal in a sheikh's palace while protestors pound the gates, chanting loud enough to rattle the marble columns. Once, I tackle a man trying to break into the cockpit mid-flight, just to keep a planeload of strangers safe.

But nothing, nothing, has quite prepared me for the chaos of a wedding day mixed with an ice storm.

The air outside is thick with frost, the wind howling like it has personal objections to this wedding. The roads are barely navigable, the sky a swirling gray-white void of impending doom.

And yet, here we all are. At the church.

Against all odds, family and friends have arrived, wrapped in layers of wool, cashmere, and a stubborn refusal to let bad weather ruin a perfectly good love story.

Patricia, wrapped in an elegant winter coat that probably costs more than my entire barn, sighs dramatically. "Honestly, I can't believe we made it. It's practically the Arctic out there."

Elliot grins, brushing ice off his immaculate lapel. "Yes, well, this is what happens when you insist on Christmas weddings, darling sister."

Elle, standing next to Patricia in her winter-white coat, narrows her eyes at him. "We are not relitigating the wedding date right now, Elliot."

I chuckle, reaching for Elle's gloved hand. "Too late. We're here now. No backing out."

She exhales, smiling up at me, the candlelight from the church flickering in her hazel eyes. "Not a chance, Donovan."

Then, just as I'm about to revel in the fact that I get to marry this stunning, brilliant woman in just a few minutes, it hits me.

I forgot the rings.

"Mate, you're joking."

Elliot stares at me like I've just declared I've decided to elope instead.

I run a hand through my hair, my pulse hammering. "Elliot, I swear to God, I put them on the nightstand last night. I had them."

He exhales sharply. "And yet, here we are. Ringless."

Elle, thankfully, is still in the bridal suite, oblivious to my sheer incompetence.

I grab Elliot's coat and shove it at him. "We need to go. Now."

He blinks. "We?"

"You think I'm driving alone in this weather? Let's go, Sinclair."

Elliot grumbles but follows, pulling on his leather gloves. "Bloody hell, it's like an action film, but instead of saving the world, we're retrieving jewelry."

The truck rumbles down the icy road, the windshield wipers barely keeping up with the freezing sleet.

Elliot leans back, watching me maneuver the road like I'm piloting a fighter jet. "So. While we're on this idiotic mission, you might as well tell me."

I flick him a glance. "Tell you what?"

He gestures vaguely. "How you managed to make my sister fall for you."

"Oh, I just wore her down."

Elliot laughs. "Ah, a man of strategy." Then, more seriously, he studies me. "You do know she was never going to get married, right?"

I nod, gripping the wheel. "I figured."

"She had plans, a life structured, controlled. After Indianapolis, after everything that happened, she swore off—"

"—Being vulnerable," I finish for him, eyes on the road. "I know."

Silence stretches, the weight of Elle's past pressing between us.

"She didn't even tell us everything," Elliot murmurs, watching the snow outside. "She wanted to handle it alone. Thought she had to."

I exhale. "She doesn't have to anymore."

Elliot watches me for a moment, then nods. "No. She doesn't."

A pause. Then he clears his throat. "I hope you know, if you ever hurt her—"

I cut him a look. "I won't."

He studies me, then nods once, satisfied. "Good."

The weather whips into a total whiteout, ice pinging against the truck windows and doors. I slow to almost a crawl.

"Bugger, this is about as bad as trying to drive in Davos in January." Elliot braces a hand on the dashboard, his other gripping the overhead handle.

"Davos in January? Switzerland? You go to the World Economic Forum? Haven't thought about that unpredictable mountain weather in a long time." I glance quickly at Elliot. "Now that was tricky."

"You've been? I'm scheduled to attend next month."

"Of course. In fact, SVG sponsored an event for five years. Oh, Strategic Vision Group. That was the name of the consulting firm I started."

Elliot suddenly turns, eyes widening. "*You're The Red Maestro!* Oh my mate, you're a legend."

I chuckle. "I wouldn't go that far."

"Well, it all makes sense now." He shakes his head. "I've got *The Red Maestro* consulting for *Green Agricultural*. I'm either bloody lucky or brilliant."

I grin. "Go with brilliant. It looks better on paper."

We fall into easy conversation, discussing business, strategic partners, and growth. Talking shop at this level again, with someone who understands the finer details, feels natural.

"So, are you relaunching SVG or creating a new entity?" Elliot asks.

"I'm not sure. Right now, most of my clients are small businesses. Green Agricultural is the only corporate client."

Elliot shakes his head. "Once it gets out The Red

Maestro is returning, I'll be lucky to have ten minutes of your time."

I chuckle. "No, you're family. Or you will be in about half an hour. But you know, Elliot, this time, I want to build it better. Only take on deals or businesses that are focused on helping instead of just making a profit. Your sister has had a real effect on me; live my truth. It makes a difference. Stress levels. How well things work. You know what I mean."

Elliot nods slowly. "I do. We didn't know Grandad long, but living your truth was what he lived and taught us. It's rather a Sinclair motto now."

"I think the Donovans will be adopting it too."

By the time we make it back, we're both covered in snow, the rings secure in my pocket.

The storm howls outside, battering against the church windows, but inside? Inside, it's warm, glowing, alive.

Candles flicker along the aisle, casting golden light over the gathered friends and family, their breath still visible in the chill of the air. The church is intimate, almost other-worldly, the kind of place where time slows, where things matter.

Elliot and I head to our place with the minister.

Patricia helps Rita to their seats.

The processional music begins, reminiscent of Handel or Bach. It lends an air of timeless elegance to the Christmas Eve ceremony. All eyes turn to see where the bride and her father will enter.

The doors open, and Howard appears with an angelic vision beside him. I stop breathing. For a moment. Elle wears a winter-white dress covered in pearls and crystals, the bodice creating a heart shape with a sheer lace over-jacket trimmed in white fur. The fabric of the dress drapes down, accenting her slender frame. Her hair is up, with a fur-trimmed pill hat that has a short veil. Her lips are red, matching the red roses sprinkled among the white roses in her bouquet.

Howard stands tall, obviously proud to be standing next to this beautiful woman.

An honor he is passing to me in moments.

My mouth is dry. They proceed down the aisle. My chest is pounding. They step, then pause, now halfway to my future. I can see Elle's face now. Her whole face is smiling, I swear a light is radiating around her. If there are still people in the church, I do not hear them. The music elevates the moment and the emotions of this never again moment. It is complete.

Elle's eyes lock onto mine, and everything else fades.

Not the storm outside.

Not the whispers in the pews.

Just her.

Howard reaches me, and for a moment, we stand there, the weight of tradition heavy but right.

"She is yours now," he says, voice gruff but warm. "Take care of her."

"I will," I promise, meeting his gaze. "Always."

He nods once, then steps back, giving Elle's hand to me.

Her fingers curl around mine, cool, but steady.

"Hey," she whispers, just for me.

I grin. "Hey yourself."

The music stops. The minister starts his service. I can't take my eyes off Elle Sinclair.

Now it is our turn to speak our vows to one another.

Elle's voice is clear, strong, but her fingers tremble slightly in mine as she speaks.

"Max, before you, I had my life carefully planned. Structured. Controlled." She exhales, soft laughter threading through her words. "And then you happened."

Laughter ripples through the pews.

I smile. "That does sound like me."

She rolls her eyes but continues. "You challenged me, frustrated me, and most of all, you saw me. Not the image, not the polished version, but the real me. And somehow, you decided that was enough."

Her eyes shine, and for the first time since this whole thing started, I feel a sting behind my own.

She squeezes my hands. "You are my sacred partner. My balance. My home. And I promise, for the rest of our lives, to walk beside you. To trust you. To love you."

I swallow hard. Damn.

Then it's my turn.

"Elle, I don't plan for this either," I admit, voice gruff. "Hell, I don't think I plan for you any more than you plan for me. But from the moment you crash into my world, I know one thing; you belong in it."

She inhales sharply, eyes brighter now.

I keep going. "You are the most infuriatingly stubborn, brilliant, gorgeous woman I have ever met, and I wouldn't change a damn thing. You are my equal. My greatest joy. My sacred partner. And I promise, no matter where life takes us, no matter how messy it gets." I shoot her a grin and she laughs through a sniffle. "I will always choose you. In every way, in every moment, for the rest of our lives."

Her bottom lip trembles, but her smile is radiant.

I slide the ring on her finger.

Then the moment comes. "You may kiss the bride."

I look at her with a heart that is bursting with a myriad of emotions. Steady, Donovan. Then I move in and lightly touch her lips with mine.

But she has other ideas.

Before I know it, we are in a kiss that feeds my soul.

We are married.

We are now joined in the sacred partnership that feels so right, that the only way to explain it is to give homage to the truth of the Divine, to God is Love.

Elle and I move back down the aisle, greeting friends and accepting wishes as we progress.

The wind outside screams through the trees, rattling the farmhouse windows like an impatient guest demanding entry. Snow blankets the landscape, the storm having buried any plans for an elaborate reception at the lodge.

So instead? We've crammed into the warm, fire-lit chaos of home.

And honestly? It's better this way.

Patricia, wrapped in what I'm convinced is the most expensive cashmere shawl on Earth, surveys the scene with a sigh. "Well, this isn't The Ritz, but I suppose it has its charm."

"Admit it, Trish, this is the best wedding reception you've ever attended."

She takes a delicate sip of wine. "It's intimate. That much, I'll give you."

Elle leans into me, still glowing from the ceremony. "I like intimate."

I press a kiss to her temple. "Me too."

Just as we turn toward our family, Oliver clears his throat.

Everyone pauses.

Oliver, standing by the fireplace with Kim and Lily beside him, looks somewhat nervous, somewhat proud.

"I wasn't asked to do this," he says, rubbing the back of his neck. "But I wanted to."

Elle tilts her head, smiling. "Oh?"

Oliver nods. "Yeah. Because, Elle, you're not just marrying my dad today. You're marrying us."

The entire room softens.

I see Elle exhale, blinking fast.

"I've spent my whole life watching my dad take care of people," Oliver continues. "He's strong, and tough, and ridiculously stubborn,"

Laughter ripples through the room.

"but he's never let anyone take care of him. Not like you do." Oliver clears his throat. "So, I just wanted to say: welcome to the family. And also, good luck. Because you're married to Max Donovan now, and that is going to be an experience."

The entire room laughs, and Elle pulls Oliver into a hug.

"Thanks, kid," she whispers. "I wouldn't have it any other way."

Chris and Belle Ho, Kim's parents, make it despite the storm, now standing near the fire, sipping steaming mugs of mulled cider.

Chris Ho shakes his head, smiling. "I don't know how you two pulled this off with the storm, but you did. And the ceremony was beautiful."

Belle nods in agreement. "It was so moving. And Kim has been absolutely gushing about how wonderful everything was."

Kim, who is sitting with Oliver near the fireplace, smiles. "I have not been gushing, I've been making professional observations."

Oliver grins, adjusting the camera equipment. "Right. That's why you made me replay Elle's vows twice while we were editing."

Kim huffs. "I was ensuring quality."

Elliot chuckles. "Ah, young love. Watching this dynamic unfold is fascinating."

Charles, sitting beside them, snaps his fingers. "Right, before I forget, I'm officially claiming credit for half of this recording masterpiece. I mean, I handle at least 40% of the operation."

Oliver tilts his head. "More like 15%."

Charles scoffs. "Outrageous. This is why I should have negotiated a contract."

Kim grins. "You were paid in wedding cake."

Charles sighs dramatically. "Fine. But next time, I'm drafting an agreement."

Howard chuckles, sipping his drink. "You'll make a ruthless businessman one day, Charles."

Patricia laughs. "Oh, he already is."

Chris Ho shakes his head at them. "And here I was hoping my daughter would be around sensible influences."

I laugh, squeezing Elle's hand. "I think she's holding her own just fine."

The farmhouse isn't a ballroom, but we make do.

Elliot takes Patricia's hand, leading her in a slow waltz across the wooden floors, his movements practiced and smooth.

Howard surprises everyone by dancing with Rita, the

two moving together in the easy rhythm of decades spent side by side.

Chris and Belle join in, swaying together, their joy radiating through every step, every turn.

Then Oliver and Kim move to the dance floor; though self-conscious and a bit awkward, they move together, swaying. Oliver manages a turn, pulling her back to him, their eyes meeting.

And me?

I pull Elle into my arms, swaying with her as the firelight casts a golden glow over her soft smile.

She rests her head against my shoulder, and for a moment, I forget about the storm, the cold, the chaos.

It's just us.

Just this.

She sighs, content. "This turned out perfect, didn't it?"

I chuckle, kissing her forehead. "It did. But you knew it would."

She tilts her head, grinning. "Oh, absolutely. I always know what I'm doing."

I shake my head, pulling her closer. "Good thing, because I just married you."

She laughs softly, her hands tightening over mine. "Best decision you've ever made, Donovan."

I smile. "You have no idea."

Oliver clears his throat behind us. "I hate to break up the newlywed moment, but someone has to cut the cake."

Elle laughs, not letting go, we move to the wedding cake.

Two tiers of white chocolate icing, with decorative patches of shiny fondant icing, accented by silver sugar beads hiding among white chocolate roses and dark chocolate leaves. On top, old-fashioned typewriter keys of various heights support the sitting bride and groom, each on their own key, but holding hands. I marvel at the sugar work, the design. Truly a work of art.

Elle gasps when she sees it. "Chris and Belle, thank you so much. It is stunning, really." She turns to me, "This is our gift from Chris and Belle, they made it, at The Hayloft."

"Oh, Chris, Belle, thank you so much. It is exquisite. Your sugar work. I never get that right. Really, thank you." I move to shake Chris's hand, share a quick hug with Belle.

We gather, slicing into the cake as champagne glasses are filled, toasts are made, and laughter rings through the room.

Elliot lifts his glass. "To Elle and Max, may your life together be as adventurous as your beginning."

Patricia nods approvingly. "And may Max always remember the rings from now on."

The room erupts in laughter, and I groan, shaking my head as Elle leans in, whispering, "You will never live that down."

I kiss her quickly, just to shut her up.

The music plays on, the snow falls outside. Inside this house, our home now, everything feels right.

TWENTY-SIX
SUNRISE SURPRISES

ELLE

THE FARMHOUSE FEELS DIFFERENT NOW. Not physically; Max hasn't renovated, nor hired an interior designer; but the energy has shifted.

It's not just his house anymore. It's ours.

My writing desk now has a permanent home in the sunlit corner of the library. My books, once confined to boxes and temporary shelves, have migrated into the main living space.

And my coffee cups? They've taken over the kitchen.

Max notices.

He stares at the overflowing cabinet. "You own approximately fifty mugs," he observes one morning.

I sip from my newest one, a sleek white ceramic with Write. Edit. Caffeinate. scrawled in gold script. "I like options."

"You have an entire collection."

I smile. "And you, my dear husband, have an entire fleet of tractors. We all have our things."

"Fine. But if you start collecting matching saucers, I'm intervening."

With the wedding behind us and the new year stretching ahead, Max has finally done what I knew he would: stepped away from the daily grind of the farm.

"I'm still involved," he assures me, watching from the porch as the new farm manager, Brady Walsh, checks in with the hired farmhands.

"I know," I say, leaning into him. "But you're letting them run it."

Max exhales, adjusting his stance. "It's weird."

I smile. "It's growth."

He glances down at me. "You think everything is about personal growth."

"Because it is."

He kisses my temple, sighing dramatically. "Married a philosopher."

"Actually, you married a multi-genre bestselling author."

"Ah yes, that's right." He smiles. "You do love having the last word."

I grin. "And yet, you still argue."

The biggest change? Our late-night check-ins now happen at home, not in his barn office.

The first time we settle into the couch with our coffee instead of trekking across the snowy yard, I glance at him and say, "Symbolic, don't you think?"

Max raises a brow. "Of?"

"Us. No more hiding in your barn office to have the important conversations."

He leans back, stretching his arm over the back of the couch. "Guess that means you're stuck with me now."

I sip my coffee. "Guess so."

Max nudges my knee with his own. "Still time to run, Sinclair."

"Nah. I like my coffee mug shelf too much."

IT HAPPENS on a Friday night in late-January.

Max, Lily, and I are having dinner at The Hayloft, seated near the fire as the snow falls steadily outside.

Chris and Belle Ho join us, a quiet but noticeable tension hovering over the table as we all wait for Oliver to arrive and pick up Kim after her shift.

Max checks his watch. "He should be here any minute."

Belle smiles, though there's a trace of motherly worry in her eyes. "I'm sure they'll have a lovely evening. It's just... first dates are a big moment."

Chris nods. "And you taught him to open doors? Pay for the meal?"

Max sighs. "Yes, Chris."

Belle tilts her head. "Where is he taking her?"

Lily, ever the informant, pipes up. "They're going to that new café in town with the live acoustic set."

Belle smiles. "That's a lovely choice."

Max still doesn't look fully convinced.

A few moments later, Oliver walks in, brushing snow off his jacket, exuding a calm he clearly does not feel.

Kim finishes untying her apron behind the counter, spots him, and grins.

Chris leans toward Max. "This is the part where we let them leave without interrogation."

Max mutters something under his breath. Then, louder, he says, "Oliver, a word."

Oliver sighs, clearly expecting this. "Dad. No."

Max forges ahead anyway. "I expect check-ins. If your location drops off the map for more than ten minutes, I'm sending a SWAT team."

Oliver groans. "Dad."

"I'm just saying, I have connections."

Elle covers her mouth, laughing.

Kim arrives at Oliver's side, raising an eyebrow. "Mr. Donovan, I will personally text you updates if it means we can leave now."

Belle hides a smile. "They'll be fine, Max."

Max nods at Oliver. "Be a gentleman."

Oliver straightens. "Always."

Kim rolls her eyes. "*We've* trained him well, Mr. Donovan."

Oliver grabs Kim's hand and leads her toward the door.

Lily waves dramatically. "Have fun! Don't do anything I wouldn't do."

Chris snorts. "That's not as comforting as you think."

Max watches them go, his expression a mix of approval and barely suppressed nerves.

I lean against him. "You barely survived your teenage years, and you know it."

Max grumbles. "That's why I'm worried."

I laugh, wrapping my arms around him. "Relax, Max. You raised a good kid. He's got this."

Max exhales, pulling me close. "Yeah. But I reserve the right to worry."

I press a soft kiss to his jaw. "That, I'll allow."

We stand there, watching through the frosted window as Oliver opens Kim's car door for her.

Chris sighs. "Well. At least he's been raised right."

Max grumbles something unintelligible.

Belle pats his arm. "Welcome to parenting a teenager in love."

He groans. "I hate it."

I just smile, knowing this is only the beginning.

I wake up alone. The room is dark. The digital clock shows 6:43 a.m. The bathroom is dark, door open. Where's Max?

Throwing the covers back, I hurry to slide into my robe and slippers. Coming down the stairs, I become concerned that the house is only illuminated by what light the security utility lights offer. Once downstairs, I move through the lower level towards the kitchen.

I see the blue light on the coffee pot. Moving over to it, I feel the machine. Hot, half-full carafe. Turning around, I notice the silhouette of someone at the kitchen table. Max. I move to him, placing my hand on his shoulder. The touch jerks him out of the reverie or sleep.

"Oh, Elle. Ollie home yet?" Max asks, his voice rough.

"Oliver's not home and you didn't wake me?" I am surprised.

"I didn't see a need. I couldn't sleep, then I discovered he still isn't home. Just thought I'd stay up and wait a bit. In case he wanted to talk."

"Good." I sit in a chair next to him. "In the dark? Is this support or ambush?" I chuckle.

I look out across the driveway. It is a clear night crowned with a hundred stars and illuminated by moonlight. New snow dusts the ground, bouncing the light to make odd shadows. The utility light by the barn plays hide-and-seek with the branches of the Charter Oak tree. The dairy barn is aglow with our farm manager and crew milking. I catch a glimpse of taillights of a truck on the main road.

"Hey Donovan, let's seize the moment. Let's go on an adventure. Game?"

"What do you have in mind?"

"You told me once the sunrise over your fields is mandatory viewing. Show me. The sun rises, what, around seven forty this time of year, so we can make it. Let's go, come on, please." I nudge his arm.

"Elle, it's cold, are you sure you want to?"

"Are we walking or driving? It won't be that bad, I'll have you to keep me warm."

Max stands up and wraps me in his arms. "Always." We kiss. "Okay, let's do this."

After putting on layers, we step outside. Max's truck isn't in its usual parking space, so we take my Range Rover Sport SUV.

The best spot to see the sunrise unobstructed is on a small hill near the cow pasture. From there, you can see the horizon without trees or buildings obstructing the view. Max pulls up just as the world is getting dark again. He maneuvers the Range Rover so we can raise the tailgate and sit to watch the show.

Bundled in his arms and a fleece blanket, hot coffee in our insulated mugs, I'm already rating this adventure five stars. Birds go silent as it gets very dark, and the breeze stops shaking the tree branches. It's eerily still and quiet.

Max whispers in my ear, "Wait for it, just over there, southeast." His finger points the way.

I release the breath I hadn't realized I'd been holding. The anticipation is palpable.

The sky at the horizon starts to lighten, then light reflects off some clouds that float nearby. The breeze stirs, a sweet, fresh smell of the fields mixing with the birthing day. More colors light up the horizon and spread across the sky, driving back the dark blue night. Just as the first ray of light peaks above the horizon, the birds start singing, the breeze whipping up to spread their music. There's an energy pulling on me, as if awakening my soul, emotions surfacing.

Another ray of light joins the party, helping to push the night away. The southeastern horizon displays streaks of gold, yellow, red, and blues, one dissolving into the next. Anticipation seems to call the birds' songs and the breeze and the colors of the sky to intensify, just as the first white-yellow glow of the sun breaks over the horizon.

"Oh, it's coming," I whisper in expectation and joy. Max just nods his head.

Rapidly, the white-yellow globe rises above the horizon as the day now extinguishes all traces of the night. The clouds are painted in a dissolving array of colors. Snow-dusted fields mimic the show of colors. The breeze sends the trees into a clapping kind of sound, as if Mother Nature herself is celebrating this new day.

I don't expect it to be such an emotional, even spiritual, experience. As the full orb displays above the horizon, I become aware again of Max's arms around me, his chest to my back, both of us bundled in the warm blanket.

He kisses the side of my head, then softly says, "Thank you. I needed that."

Now that he's no longer working the farm, he rarely has

reason to catch the sunrise. I know he misses this, a trade-off for staying warm in bed with me and working for his financial consultancy.

"Oliver isn't the reason you couldn't sleep, not directly anyway. You know that, don't you?"

He takes a deep breath, holds it, and then exhales.

"Yeah, I know. We're on the cusp of a major change," he admits.

"Yes, we are. We've been in a major change for some time now—with our marriage, now Oliver's first love, the freedom of driving, the success of their podcast business. But change is inevitable, you know that. We wouldn't want it any other way." I twist around so I can meet his eyes and see his face. "You raised him right. So trust him."

"I do trust him." The redness in his eyes turns brighter as they start to glisten. "What does it say about me? I'm aging, Elle. In April, I'm forty-five. The clock doesn't stop." The look in his eyes is concerning.

"Is this some kind of midlife crisis? Did reading the Chronicles and all these life changes trigger some kind of midlife crisis? Or are you telling me your health is waning and I should start planning your funeral?"

"Elle! No. I guess I'm just aware that Oliver, and Lily, are growing up and moving on, and if you hadn't accepted me, I'd be here alone."

"Max, I did accept you. Lily is very much still in our house—actually, speaking as a creative person, we might have her here for some time yet. Oliver has been very clear about his focus, and he still has another full year of high school." I place my hands on either side of his face and turn him to look directly at me. "I'm going wherever you go.

Kind of what I meant when I said I chose you on Christmas Eve." I plant kisses on his cheeks and forehead as I speak.

"Really, Sinclair. Anywhere I go?" The sunrise colors now bathe his face.

"That's my truth, and I'm sticking to it. And as I recall, it has been a couple of days since I had direct knowledge, but your body is one... very fine... powerful... incredibly desirable..." I slide my hands under the bottom of his jacket. "... and sexy, oh so sexy... healthy, young adult male..." My finger traces his waistband. "...and mine, all mine." I kiss his neck just under his ear. "So, don't... you go criticizing... that body, because... it is... the source... of unimaginable... pleasure."

Max firmly grabs my arms to stop my movement. "Be careful or you'll start something you might not want to finish." Our eyes lock.

"With you? I'll always want to finish it with you, Donovan."

Max brings my mouth to his and kisses me deep and long, until our heat is no match for the cold morning air. I break from his embrace and move to unlatch the rear seat and turn on the heating system. His face reflects his surprise and more curiosity, though he doesn't say anything. I motion for him to close the tailgate, and I crawl back to him, scrambling to get to his body warmth.

"Elle, we're not teenagers. Why aren't we moving toward our warm, comfortable bed?" His hand strokes my hair, then wraps along my neck, before resting on my breast.

"Oh, don't worry, I know the owner. It's Saturday morning, after a very moving sunrise, and I want to make out with my boyfriend. Is that all right?"

Max looks at me, a smile blossoming on his lips. "Yeah, yeah, that is very all right."

The spark of mischief in his eyes lights something deep in me—a daring, a thrill I haven't felt in years. I want him to know: I'm his partner, his lover, his equal in passion.

Kissing each other, I unzip my jacket and move his hand onto my breast. That's when Max takes charge. He knows my body and how to get it to respond to his lightest touch. We pull on each other's cloth layers until our bare bodies mingle, sliding under the blanket until our passion takes over. Being so exposed in the back of the Range Rover heightens every touch, every kiss with a new level of risk and danger.

The danger triggers something in Max, and he makes love to me with new energy, a youthful arrogance that even brightens his face and eyes. I can see a glimpse of what he was like in his younger days, when he was fully in his power. Confidence supports his every movement, the way he teases my hard nipples, fingers my wet folds, and takes charge of my pleasure and his. It's a new level of stimulation, this dominant version of the multi-layered man I've come to know and love. God, what a turn on.

I didn't know my body could crave so deeply, as if it wanted to fuse with him just as our emotions and energy merge. My hands pull his body closer, feeling the fire from the touch. I can't control myself, calling for more, wanting to give myself to him, so I start kissing his body: nipples, chest, navel, and cock. The taste of his skin is warm and salty, increasing my desire to know him, taste him, suck in his manhood, exploring his member with my tongue. He gasps. Then his voice starts to pulse with every movement of my mouth on his cock. I echo his sounds with my own, expressing the overwhelming sensation of having him in my mouth. I start alternating breathing deep-throated hot air on him, then the gentle blow of cooler air. The sensation causes him to become very vocal, until he calls for me to stop; he wants to control his climax. Being able to get such a reaction from him feels leveling, stimulating, and I return to join my lips with his.

"Elle, Elle, you've never..." he says between heavy breaths. I place my finger to his lips. He takes back control and pins me under him, sliding himself into my wet, slippery core. And I admit, it feels good. Electric-like synapses start shooting throughout my groin, my body, my mind. The suspension on the Range Rover allows us to thrust together, moving our whole bodies. With every electric impulse, I become vocal, and Max opens his throat fully to join me. I laugh in delight as our bodies pulse together, pulling his voice to fully join me. The climax is multi-layered and I feel it throughout my body, nay, throughout my soul. What overwhelms me most is how completely he gives himself, how every touch carries a silent promise: this is where he belongs, where I belong, where we choose each other, again and again.

Sweaty and exhausted, we collapse together. Max pulls the cover over us, only falling slightly to the side, but still on top of me. It gives me a sense of safety, of deep protection like I've never felt. I relax, feeling like I can't move, satisfied, and loved.

We lie together, our nakedness a source of stimulation, until we fall asleep.

Until we're awakened by a cow pushing on the vehicle as if we're over its favorite spot. Then I'm aware of a dog's bark.

"Huh? What are the cows doing out?" Max queries. "Get dressed, I think we need to go."

We both start layering on our clothes. Soon we are bouncing over the field back to the access road and back to the house. As we approach, Max's truck is in its usual parking spot. Oliver's back.

"Max, hear him out before you say anything. Please."

"I'll try, that's all I can offer."

When we walk through the back door, Lily is sitting at the kitchen table finishing her breakfast. Oliver is pacing behind her. Then he sees us.

"Where have you been? I've been so worried. It seems so unlike you to leave Lily here by herself," Oliver demands.

I bite down to stop myself from laughing. Max turns his head away from Oliver to control his smirk, which is trying to join the laugh I am attempting to squelch. Under control, we turn back to face his concern.

"Lily can take care of herself for a bit. We had our phones with us. The question is where were you? When did you get home?" Max stands confidently before his son.

"He got home less than a half hour ago," Lily informs us.

"Thank you, Lily. But your brother needs to answer me," Max says calmly.

"You won't believe me."

"How can you know that unless you tell us your truth?"

Oliver takes a couple of steps, his hands flexing. He takes a deep breath. "Kim and I fell asleep. We wanted to talk after dinner, so we went to the barn office and talked for hours. Brady Walsh woke us around six-thirty when he came in to get more sanitizer for the cows. I took Kim home, and have been driving around trying to come up with what to tell you. Lily is right. I just got home, a few minutes before you did. The truck needs gas."

"Thank you. I believe your story. I have fallen asleep more than once in the barn office. You need to call Kim's parents, if you haven't. Offer a sincere apology for the late return and explain the situation honestly. Be ready to address any concerns they might have. I'll follow-up with them afterwards. Let me know once you've spoken with Mr. and Mrs. Ho."

"Yes, sir. Thank you. I'll call them now."

"Oh, and Ollie, thanks for taking the truck down and filling it up, on your dime." Oliver just nods.

After apologies are offered and accepted, I join Max on the living room sofa. Oliver is taking a nap in his room, and Lily is working her way through Book Three of *The Veridion Chronicles.*

"Oliver's explanation reminded me of our first date, and the hours we spent on the sofa in the barn office." Max draws in a breath, holds it a moment, then nods his head as he exhales a very heavy breath.

I kick off my shoes and curl up under Max's outstretched arm. Twenty minutes later we both are enjoying a Saturday afternoon nap.

TWENTY-SEVEN
THE INSTIGATOR

MAX

I KNEW this would be big, but I wasn't prepared for the sheer magnitude of it.

The convention center is packed; thousands of people, dressed as characters I don't recognize, filling every available inch of space. Posters of *The Veridion Chronicles* hang like banners in a medieval great hall, and the energy?

Chaotic. Loud. Frenzied.

"Dad," Lily breathes, eyes huge as saucers. "This is... amazing."

Oliver nods slowly, adjusting his camera bag. "Yeah. It's insane."

Kim is already grinning, clearly in her element. "Told you. Welcome to Veridion Kingdom, people."

I glance at Elle, who's smiling behind her sunglasses. She's been too calm about this whole thing.

"You enjoying yourself?" I ask, bumping my shoulder against hers.

She tilts her head. "Oh, immensely."

I narrow my eyes. What aren't you telling me, Sinclair?

Somewhere between navigating the crowd and dodging an overly enthusiastic fan dressed as a warlord, we make it to a small café inside the venue.

Kim sets a cupcake in front of me, the single candle flickering mockingly. "Happy birthday, Mr. Donovan."

I stare at it. "Seriously?"

Oliver grins. "We're doing this. Just accept it."

Elle leans in, grinning. "Make a wish."

I exhale. "Fine." I blow out the candle, and Kim cheers like we just won a championship.

"I hope you wished for patience," Oliver mutters, watching as Lily gleefully smears icing on his sleeve.

"I wished for peace and quiet," I mutter back. "Not that I'll ever get it."

Elle kisses my cheek. "Not a chance, Donovan."

We walk through the convention center, taking in the elaborate vendor booths and fan exhibits. I've traveled extensively for finance, but this? This is another world entirely.

Broadswords are everywhere, strapped to backs, belts, or proudly displayed across chests. Eric Harris wouldn't have stood out here. The thought makes my shoulders tighten.

The costumes are fascinating. Some wear long, flowing gowns, cinched at the waist with intricate bindings, reminiscent of ancient Greece. Others favor warrior tunics, draped over bare shoulders, sometimes baring a little more than necessary. The footwear choices? Everything from sandals to combat boots.

There doesn't seem to be a pattern: age, gender, or body

type dictating who wears what. Just pure freedom of expression.

Kim and Oliver blend seamlessly, wearing simple tunics over street clothes. Lily, with her usual scarves and flowing fabrics, fits right in. Elle, though? She keeps it simple, off-white pleated trousers, a silk shell, and low-heeled shoes. Easy to slip into her author's robe when the time comes.

Me? Just my usual jeans and Henley. Though, for the occasion, I dug out an old silk scarf I wore back in culinary school when I thought I'd be the next big celebrity chef.

Wham, baby.

Oliver checks his phone alarm. It's time.

We make our way to the auditorium, finding seats among thousands of eager fans, all waiting for Liane Cillser. Our tickets are for the front section, near the stage.

The house lights dim.

The stage lights up.

A low, rhythmic drumbeat, a heartbeat, echoes through the massive room. Fog creeps onto the stage.

A platform rises from the back, and there she is.

A woman in a white robe, holding a book, and her reading glasses, emerging from the mist like something divine. The moment the fans see her, the roar is deafening.

My chest tightens with pride and love.

Lily tilts her head. "I can't believe we actually get to see her." She joins in the screams.

Oliver's brows furrow. "I... I"

Then Elle starts to read from the just-released *Book Three*. The crowd goes silent.

Her voice echoes through the speakers, rhythmic, familiar, powerful. The words ripple through the auditorium.

Then it happens.

Lily's mouth drops open. Oliver? Completely freezes.

His voice cuts through the reverent silence.

"Wait. WAIT. WAIT. You mean I've been living with my favorite author this whole time?!"

The crowd laughs, but my kids? They are spiraling.

Lily grabs my arm. "Dad. Dad. Are we in a dream?"

Oliver just stares at the stage, short-circuiting.

Kim? Kim smiles. "I knew it."

And me? I just cross my arms, lean back, and smile.

"Yup," I say, watching my wife own the stage. "That's your stepmother."

Lily squeals. Oliver? Still buffering.

Elle glances down at us, grinning like the troublemaker she is.

I mouth, you're unbelievable.

She winks. *And you love it.*

Damn right, I do.

After the presentation, Elle is scheduled to sign books.

I make my way toward her table, but before I can get close, a security guard steps in my path, holding up a hand.

Toma strides over, arms full, one hand gripping a case of water bottles, the other stacked with boxes of pens.

I nod toward Elle's table. "Toma, help me out here. I'm Liane Cillser's husband, Max Donovan. I need to be with Elle, eh, Liane, while she signs."

Toma doesn't hesitate. He waves to security. "Let him through."

As I step closer, Toma studies me, his expression thoughtful. "I want to thank you for helping Liane find her way back to her fans. It's a love affair that shouldn't be denied." He pauses, then tilts his head. "But tell me, Maxwell, why won't she let me reveal her whole self?"

I frown. "Eric Harris came to her in Willow Creek. As Maldric. To claim her as Sera." I keep my voice even, but just saying his name makes my muscles tense. "It was fortunate I was there. He was intense. The sheriff finally took him away. She has every right to be wary."

Toma lets out a slow breath, shaking his head. "She didn't tell me that."

I go rigid. "That's why I'm staying close now. You hired her security, but we're not taking any chances. You understand?"

Toma meets my gaze and nods, serious now. "Oh, I understand. Some of these fans can be a bit much."

I spot Oliver, Kim, and Lily standing near the security boundary, waiting for a cue. I wave them over.

"Toma, I'd like you to meet our kids, Oliver and Lily Donovan, and Oliver's girlfriend, Kim Ho."

Oliver extends his hand. "Nice to meet you, Mr. Hector. We're so grateful for how you support, ah, Liane." He glances at Kim, who gives him a subtle nod of encouragement.

Oliver straightens. "I don't know if Liane has told you, but I run a podcast for a local open mic night back home." He hesitates, then squares his shoulders. "Kim and I have an idea about launching a fantasy fiction-focused podcast with Liane. Maybe other authors, too. Would you have time to talk?"

Toma arches a brow, intrigued. "Oh, how very Elle of you."

He shifts his gaze between Oliver and Kim. "We have another day here, so certainly, we can chat. But is Liane on board with this?"

Kim steps in smoothly. "Not yet. But she will be."

There's no hesitation in her tone. "There's a growing market for spoken word and video podcasts. Even if it's audio only, it'll find an audience." She glances at Oliver before continuing. "Maybe she reads a passage from the books or something original. Of course, a podcast is a promotion tool, marketing, branding, and self-sustaining through ad revenue. Sounds like something worth considering?"

Toma's expression shifts, calculating. "After this signing, yes. Find me then." He turns, stacking copies of *Book Three* behind the table.

I check my watch, then tell the kids when we'll meet up and set a time schedule.

Toma suddenly brightens, his sharp gaze locking onto me. "You're the new storyline in *Book Three*, aren't you?"

I blink. "What?"

Toma grins. "Oh, haven't you read it? *Book Three*: at the end, Sera meets the man of her truth, and his love protects her. Together, their Lumea is the greatest of any, all-powerful, bringing peace to all the regions."

I huff a laugh. "Guess I have some reading to finish. I admit, I just cracked *Book Two*."

At that moment, Elle arrives, slipping behind the table. Her security escort positions themselves at either end of the signing area.

She leans in, pressing a soft kiss to my lips. "Thank you for being with me."

I squeeze her hand. "Always."

She turns to Toma. "Alright, let's get this started."

For the next two hours and twenty-five minutes, Elle signs books, meets fans, listens to their stories, and laughs at their excitement.

I sit close enough to hear the comments fans are making; stories of what her books mean to them, how their lives have changed because they now try to live the Veridion way.

Almost every fan thanks her.

Some of them glance at me, putting pieces together. I see the recognition bloom in their eyes as they realize I'm the man whose love offers her protection. Some even thank me, too.

I'm struck by the dedication; how many stand in line for more than an hour just for a moment with her. How they see her books not just as fiction, but as a guide. A framework for how to live with truth, integrity, and self-awareness.

My wife has affected so many lives by creating this world where each person's power, even life force, grows or declines not based on economics, or physical traits or any external value, but on how true he or she is with themselves and others.

And I realize something: they're mirroring her world in real life.

Between fans, Elle glances at me. Just checking. Just reassuring herself that I'm still there.

Each time, I give her a small nod.

You're stuck with me, Sinclair.

And she knows it.

After the signing, we're escorted to the VIP suite where Elle slips out of her robe and refreshes. She looks energized; flushed cheeks, eyes bright. Meeting her fans does that to her.

As we step back into the swarm of people, she reaches

for my hand, lacing her fingers through mine. I give hers a light squeeze, grounding her.

And that's it.

It's official. I'm the man who brought Liane Cillser back to her fans. The face of her sacred partner, her protector, her truth.

As we move through the crowd, people look at us differently now. Some smile knowingly. Others nod in quiet acknowledgment.

Much like *Book Three*, I hear.

Turns out, being Elle's family comes with baggage, too.

People stop us for photos, ask how long we've known each other, if I knew she was Liane Cillser before we got together.

And then there's Oliver and Lily.

Lily's thriving with the attention, eating up every bit of it.

Oliver? Not so much.

People keep calling him Liane Cillser's stepson. He stiffens every time he hears it.

Later, back in the hotel suite, he throws himself onto the couch, rubbing his temples.

"I get it now," he mutters. "Why you don't talk about it back home."

Elle nods, unsurprised. "Exactly."

Kim, ever the instigator, grins. "But you love it."

Elle smiles, tilting her head. "Maybe."

The next morning, we decide to let the kids have two more hours at the convention before heading to the private airport where our charter jet is waiting.

That's when I sense him before I see him.

Eric Harris.

Dressed as Maldric, the villain of Elle's books.

His expression is sharp, intent, the same eerie focus as that night in Willow Creek; our first date, the night he tried to claim Elle as his.

I should probably thank him. If not for that, Elle and I wouldn't be here now.

"You don't belong here," he says, his voice low, weighted.

I keep my stance easy, controlled, but my body is coiled tight.

"And why's that?" My tone is even. Measured.

Eric's jaw flexes. "Because Maldric belongs with Sera."

Ah. So we're doing this again.

I've dealt with him before. I know how this game works.

I tilt my head. "Maldric, you haven't been true." My voice is calm but firm. "I am Sera's man of her truth. We are joined in sacred partnership. We do belong together."

Elle steps beside me, slipping her hand into mine, her wedding rings catching the light.

"Eric," she says, her voice steady, unwavering. "This is my husband. We belong together."

His eyes twitch. The fantasy is fracturing.

His gaze shifts between me and Elle, then back to me.

"You are her sacred partner." His voice sounds different now. Like he's convincing himself. His hands twitch slightly before he stills them.

Lily and Oliver are watching from a few feet away, taking it all in. They're understanding, in real time, exactly why Elle keeps her private life private.

Eric shifts, moving forward slightly. My muscles coil, ready.

Security closes in.

Eric sees them too. He freezes, then slowly extends his hand.

"Thank you," he murmurs. "Sera must be protected. Your love protects her, bringing her back to us. She is our leader. The power is your truth."

I hesitate, then shake his hand. Firm. Steady.

After a long, tense beat, Eric mutters something under his breath and walks away.

I exhale, muscles finally relaxing.

"That was... different," I mutter.

I glance at Elle. "I think he might be getting over you."

Lily nods slowly. "Yeah. And that's why we don't tell people who Mom really is unless we have to."

Oliver rubs his temples. "This trip has been insane."

Kim smiles. "Welcome to Elle's world."

As we make our way out, Toma appears like he's been waiting for this moment.

Elle's ever-dramatic manager sweeps his gaze over me, Oliver, and Lily, his expression full of knowing amusement.

"So," he says, clasping his hands together. "The famous Donovan family. Did you enjoy yourselves?"

I nod, keeping my tone even but amused. "Yeah. Very much."

Toma beams like I just confirmed some long-held theory of his. "Well, Elle, I must say, I haven't seen you this happy in a long time."

Then he glances at Oliver and Kim, eyes twinkling. "And I must tell you, your fans, darling, will be thrilled with the podcast. So brilliant. My most brilliant client." He sighs dramatically. "Ciao."

Then, before Elle can even respond, he spins on his heel and vanishes into the crowd.

Elle turns to Oliver and Kim. They exchange a look, silently celebrating whatever deal they just managed to pull off.

Then they grab as many bags as they can and head toward our waiting limo.

On the flight home, the kids crash almost immediately, exhausted from the whirlwind of the convention.

Elle and I, though? We have our regular check-in.

She raises the armrest between us, then slides her feet under my thighs, seeking warmth. She curls into me, her body fitting against mine like it belongs there. My arm wraps around her, my hand settling on her hip.

It's quiet; just the hum of the jet, the occasional shift of turbulence.

"I think I figured out what bothers me when I look at Oliver with Kim," I murmur.

Elle, already half-drowsy, hums. "Oh? Tell me more."

"At their age, I hadn't read *The Veridion Chronicles*." I pause, exhaling. "I didn't have a granddad who taught me to live from my truth, that my real power was in being true."

She smiles softly, urging me to go on with a tilt of her head.

"They do," I say simply. "They have your books. They grew up with them. And now, their lives are different because of that simple philosophy. Like all your fans. You're raising a better generation, Elle." I pause, thinking. "I just don't know if that's intentional or a by-product."

She exhales, something shifting in her expression.

"Yeah," she says quietly. "Let's see if their generation continues to use crime and corruption as entertainment."

The words are light, but the weight behind them isn't.

I see it, the flash of hurt in her eyes, a brief flicker of

something raw. An echo of that flour-and-dough moment, the first time she let this anger slip.

She closes her eyes tight, as if trying to hold something back.

And in that moment, I see her completely.

Her capacity for love and caring stretches far beyond one relationship.

No wonder she never married until now. She was too busy trying to shift the world. Trying to save us from ourselves.

She saw what was happening; as a journalist, witnessing firsthand how we'd gone off course, blind to the shift.

And when she couldn't fix it that way?

She built a world where people could see the truth. Feel the truth. Where power had nothing to do with wealth or status, and everything to do with how honest you were with yourself.

Truth is power.

And now, my life has proven it.

In helping small businesses grow, in guiding people through financial pitfalls, I've learned that my job isn't just about numbers, it's about helping people create the life they actually want.

I ask my clients to get quiet, to ask themselves what they truly want.

I'm really asking them to live from their truth.

I glance down at Elle.

Her head rests on my arm, her breathing even, slow. Sleep has finally claimed her.

I reach down, adjusting her lap belt slightly, making sure she's secure.

Then I smile, murmuring just for her, even though she won't hear it.

"My darling instigator."

TWENTY-EIGHT
LIVING IN TRUTH

ELLE

THE SCANDAL that once rattled Willow Creek is now nothing more than a story people tell over coffee at Perk Up. Janine Moore disappeared into witness protection as a whistleblower. Hank Calloway resigned as mayor and is currently on an extended hiatus. When he noticed the town's accounts seemed off, and the town council was unable or unwilling to clear it up, he knew he needed to do something. That's when Cindy Franklin tried to out Max in front of the whole town. Hank saw his answer, which is why he moved quickly to pull Max in to help uncover the rot that had taken over our town coffers. Good people in bad situations do the best they can. An age-old story.

The town, resilient as ever, has moved forward, settling back into its familiar rhythm. The whispers of corruption have faded, replaced by the kind of small-town concerns that feel almost quaint in comparison.

Max's work with the FBI wrapped up weeks ago. No

more late-night calls, no more tense meetings at Town Hall. He stepped away without regret, ready to reclaim his time, his focus, his peace. In some ways, it was good for Max. Helping the authorities uncover the rot helped heal any residual hurt about losing his first career. But when we live from our truth, the old and unneeded will find a way to fall away.

These days, he divides his time between the farm, which remains his grounding place, and his growing financial consulting business. He's doing what he loves, on his terms. Vision Green Seedlings Foundation has helped several Willow Creek residents secure the bridge financing that they need, lessening any effect of the town corruption on the local economy. We don't talk about our connection to the foundation; Max just includes it on a list of possible funding options.

I've never seen him more at ease.

The house is quiet but alive.

The rhythmic tap of my keyboard fills the library, mingling with the soft hum of the summer breeze drifting through the open window. No more hiding. No more secrets. Just me, my words, and the story waiting to be told.

This book feels different.

Because for the first time in years, I am fully myself, not a woman balancing a thousand masks, not someone calculating every move. Just Elle. Just a novelist creating something real.

And Max? He lets me be.

Sometimes, he'll lean in the doorway, coffee in hand, watching me work before stealing a kiss and disappearing back to his world. No interruptions. No questions. Just quiet support, the kind that roots you in place and reminds you that you're loved and supported.

The summer sun dips toward the horizon, spilling gold and crimson across the sky, painting the farmland in hues of warmth and fire.

Max and I sit on the wraparound porch, the wooden boards warm beneath our bare feet. His hand rests over mine, thumb tracing slow, lazy circles against my skin.

"Feels different, doesn't it?" he murmurs, eyes fixed on the endless stretch of farmland ahead.

I nod, inhaling the crisp air, scented with earth and the distant hint of rain. "Like we made it through the fire and came out... clearer."

He turns toward me, blue eyes steady, filled with something deep and knowing. "Because we did."

We sit in the easy stillness of knowing.

We've fought, we've struggled, we've lost pieces of ourselves and found them again, in each other, in truth, in love. And now, in the quiet glow of the evening, there's nothing left to prove. Just what comes next.

Max exhales, a slow, content breath. "Love isn't just passion, is it?"

I shake my head. "It's a sacred partnership. It's choosing each other every day."

He presses a kiss to my knuckles, his voice a low promise against the fading light.

"Love is truth."

I smile, leaning into him, letting the words settle deep.

"And truth," I whisper back, "is home."

Max pulls out his phone and checks the weather. I hear a 'hum' then he puts it back in his pocket.

"Sunny all weekend, no rain until next Thursday. The

fields could use the rain." I hear the unasked question in Max's voice under his small talk.

"Maybe this heat will back off a bit. I'm not complaining, I just would feel better with a bit more moisture in the air."

"Since the sky will be clear, it's a great morning to watch the sunrise. You interested?" Max's voice is hopeful.

There it is.

"The sun rises at five thirty this time of year. I don't until at least eight."

"Yeah, but the kids are home all day, it's Saturday. We'll take the Range Rover. You can make whatever noise you want. Summer sunrises are different from winter or spring sunrises."

A smile rises to my lips, then my eyes. Amused, I fake my outrage, "Maxwell Declan Donovan, are you asking me for what I think you're asking me?"

"Yes, wife. We go watch the sunrise. Take coffee and some of the scones we baked today. Enjoy nature." His hand moves under my chin. "Best Saturdays ever." He pushes my chin up, meeting my lips with his, a meaningful connection that sparks my heart.

"I'll follow you wherever you go, Donovan."

THE HEADPHONES STILL FEEL WEIRD, as does hearing Ollie's or Kim's voice over the electronic signal. I'm in the sound booth of the small recording studio Max built for Oliver and Kim here on the farm. It's intimidating. No echo when I speak, only the feed piped into my headset. My fan persona is thrown by this dead room, as they call it. It's like the lack of echo of my own voice shuts down my thinking mind.

This studio is half of a new building we built to house Oliver's recording business and Lily's art studio. Max designed it to easily convert into a produce farm stand for Donovan Organics, which he's expanding once the kids have moved on. It's located in front of the house, near the road. This way, should Oliver and Kim 'fall asleep' working late, we can know where they are and easily check in with them. "Enough distance to be smart about it," Max said.

Lily is using her space to learn sculpting. Her paintings sold at her first showing in May, part of a student show at Jane Reed's art school. The sale reinforces her confidence and self-view of being an artist. Her work has always had a maturity about it, but now it's blooming. She's exploring. Working in different styles, mediums, and techniques, she's finding several that appeal to her and what she wants to capture. We discuss art and life weekly when I have a girls' night out with her.

I'm recording our first fantasy fiction podcast today. For this one, I lay the premise of our show, and I will be my own guest. Eventually, we hope to host virtual or in-person authors and fantasy storytellers. The show has five minutes of advice for unpublished authors, and the rest of the forty-three minutes will include readings, interviews, and genre publishing news from around the world.

"Elle, could you speak and keep speaking? Oliver is setting your mic profile."

The best way to make me speechless is to tell me to speak continuously. I try to think about what to say, being self-conscious in this dead room. Good name for it—it kills my brain.

"Can you practice the opening? Just keep reading your opening until we tell you to stop." Click. Then another click. "Thanks," Kim adds.

"I'm Liane Cillser, and you are listening to The Story Weaver's Den. In each episode of The Story Weaver's Den, we'll embark on a journey through the realms of fantasy. We'll feature author interviews, dramatic readings, and discussions on the craft of storytelling. Plus, we'll dedicate time to helping new writers find their voice and keep you up-to-date on the hottest fantasy news."

Click. "Great. I'm ready, are you, Mom?" I can hear some nerves in Oliver's voice.

"As ready as I'll ever be."

He gives me the signal to start.

"I'm Liane Selzer, ah, okay. I'm Liane Cillser, and you are listening to The Story Weaver's Den." Oliver is waving to stop.

"I'm getting a clicking noise. Is your bracelet hitting something?"

"We can fix that." I take my bracelet off. "Better? Still hear it?"

"No. Thanks. Go again."

"I'm Liane Cillser, and you are listening to The Story Weaver's Den. In each episode of The Story Weaver's Den, we will embark on a journey through the realms of fantasy fiction. We feature author interviews, dramatic readings, and discussions on the craft... What now?" The room is getting hot, and I'm noticing the lack of circulating air.

"You're doing great, Elle. It's just for this part, I'm not sure, it doesn't sound right. There is no energy. Maybe we just get a professional announcer," Kim says almost apologetically.

Max appears behind them. My stress decreases at just seeing him. He says something to Oliver and Kim; they nod, and then he comes into the booth with me.

"So, how's it going?" He says, leaning in to get a quick kiss.

"Glad you're here. We're all learning, let's just say that." His hand is on my shoulder. Tension starts to release, lowering my shoulders, which are even with my ears. He gives them a little squeeze.

"What are you reading? How far have you gotten?" Pointing to the script before me, he leans in and reads. My nose picks up his fragrance, and I start to smile.

"My voice gets squeaky with nerves. I try, but I guess I'm still too high-pitched."

He glances at me, clears his throat, then, using his so-sexy deep voice, he reads, taking his time, adding emphasis in the right places. I feel my body respond as if on cue.

"You are listening to The Story Weaver's Den." He pauses, "In each episode of The Story Weaver's Den, we will embark on a journey through the realms of fantasy fiction. Featuring author interviews, dramatic readings, and discussions on the craft of storytelling. Plus, new authors finding their voice, we'll keep you updated on genre news and events." He turns to me. "A couple sticky places for the tongue to trip."

I look up, and Oliver and Kim are frozen, watching us in the booth.

Oliver comes over and pulls open the door. "That was great. Dad, your voice records really well. Please, record the open and close."

Max glances at me. I nod, silently adding my support.

I take a break while Max is in the dead room, recording

several versions of the open and close. His voice does record well and will be the perfect contrast to mine.

After some more adjustments, it's decided that for this first show, for now, Max will interview me. Max sits feet away, behind his own mic and wearing his own head-phones. When we speak, his voice comes through my head-set, which still disorients me. Oliver gives me the signal to standby and starts his finger count. I swallow, smooth the papers in front of me, and glance across at him through the booth window. I clear my throat. "My fans are ever so important to me, and I'm glad I've decided to return to doing appearances." I flick a look toward Max, then back to the mic. "Thank you."

I pause, steadying myself.

"For those who don't know, I stepped back from public appearances, well, media of any kind, after an incident in Indianapolis about five years ago. If you saw my statement earlier this year, you know I'm returning to you because of the love of one incredible man, my new husband, Max." I smile softly. "And you're listening to him here today, joining me on this inaugural episode of The Story Weaver's Den. So fans, say hello."

Max leans into his mic, his voice smooth and deep—the voice that still makes my toes curl when I'm not expecting it. "It is I who should be saying thank you. It was empow-ering meeting so many of you in April, and I look forward to meeting more of you yet this summer."

I grin. "Check the socials or website for fan details."

Max smiles slightly, playful now. "In your statement to the fans—and in *Book Three*—you wrote about how the love of someone can be protective. That was a new idea for me, so maybe we should expand on it."

I nod, settling into my rhythm. "When we live from a place of truth—our truth, which connects to the greater truth—we let falsehoods fall away, including our fears."

Max arches a brow. "That sounds scary. All fears leave?"

"Not the fear of an empty coffee pot, let's stay real."

"I just made a fresh pot. But you won't taste it in those atrociously sweet concoctions you drink. I like mine–"

I join him. "--Black. No sugar. No nonsense."

"Yes, I know. And I still say you're missing out."

"We were talking about how scary it would be to be without fear," Max redirects.

I can't help the small smile curling at my lips. "Well, that's the paradox, isn't it? Living from truth doesn't erase fear like magic dust. It transforms it. We stop being controlled by the little fears—the daily anxieties, the fear of not being enough, or the fear of being too much. But big feelings like grief, loss, or facing our limits? Those still visit. It's part of being human."

Max leans in, his voice thoughtful. "So even if we trust the Divine or the Universe, we still feel those things?"

"Yes," I say softly. "Trusting the Divine doesn't mean we're numb. It means we can feel the wave and know we are held by something greater as it passes. Living from truth gives us the grounding to face fear, not be ruled by it."

Max's eyes crinkle with warmth. "In place of the fear is a new freedom, real freedom that comes from being self-directed in what you do, say, how you respond. You no longer live dancing to someone else's tune. Not to say you don't dance, but you dance when and if you want to. You live in your personal power, your confidence, which leads to the security you wrote about. Real freedom."

I beam. "Absolutely. And then the magic begins. Our

vibration rises, attracting what's right for us, supplying our needs and desires, and our vision on all levels expands and intensifies."

Max chuckles softly. "You've just described what happens to Sera in *Book Three*. Can we assume you write what you know, or is much of your world-building from your imagination?"

I start shaking my head in agreement. "Both, really. But yes, the frame is from what I know and was raised on. I can't take credit for 'Your power is in your truth'—it was a family motto for generations."

Max leans back, mock-stern. "So you got a head start on this living-your-truth thing."

"I don't have a magic sword, or glowing Lumea."

Max looks at me. "You glow when you write. Or when we are just enjoying being together."

I say softly, "I'm just reflecting your light."

Max clears his throat. "Or it is I who is reflecting yours."

My breath catches. I look at him, unable to speak, my throat full of emotion.

"Since this is audio only, I will share that Liane has a pretty intimidating author glare, which I just got to witness." He is chuckling. I stick my tongue out at him.

"Living from your truth is not a static state," I say, lifting my chin, "but an ongoing dance. It's holding both the grand cosmic truths— love, connection, oneness—and the quirky, personal truths, like..." I grin, "I've learned to bake. I really enjoy it. My hands in the dough, kneading it: push, turn, push. I light up when I bake. I'm a happy baker. Everyone has something that brings them total joy; they just have to find it."

Max points a finger, grinning. "Fans, you heard it first

here, that Liane bakes up more than just fantasy tomes, but fruit-filled scones."

I blurt out a laugh, then the laugh takes over, and I can't stop, adding between chuckles, "Is this plot twisting or are we headed for a roll... like a nut twist?"

Max responds, "That depends, can we rise to the occasion?"

"Only if you don't get all puff pastry on me," I say, amused.

"Me? Never. I'm definitely more Pâte à Choux. Real dough has stature and air pockets."

"And yet our wordplay is as thin as phyllo."

Through the glass, Oliver groans, burying his face in his hands, while Kim dissolves into silent laughter.

"Are you saying our yeast needs to rest?"

"Quickly, before it falls like a bad joke soufflé."

"That was brave, fun, and totally self-aware. Like opening yourself up to being true," Max brings us back on topic.

"Really opening yourself up and being true to yourself and others takes living brave, aware, and authentic—not fearless, but trusting. Trusting that even when fear, loss, or grief appear, you're held. You're still aligned. That's the truth we stand on."

Max grins. "Well, our time is up. On behalf of your fans, let me thank you, Liane Cillser, for your stories, your wisdom, and for urging us all to live from our truth."

I glance across at him, heart full, and lean into the mic one last time. "And to you, Max Donovan, thank you for helping me find my way home."

Oliver gives us the all-clear wave. I lift off my headset, as Max does the same. He takes my hand and squeezes it. "For the first show, I think that was really good. We were honest."

The door to the dead room opens, and a rush of cool air rushes in, followed by Oliver. "Good job, thanks so much. I can clean up the rough spots in post. But it was good, really. The Story Weaver's Den is now officially launched."

"I caught you and Kim laughing, were we really that funny or embarrassing?" I ask.

"Uh, I can handle it in post. No problems, all good." Then he adds, "It is almost four. Kim's shift starts soon. I'm going to go ahead and take her, so she isn't late. You and Lily can come on at your own speed. See you soon. And really, it was good, thanks to both of you."

We're all heading over to The Hayloft to join Chris and Belle for an early dinner. Kim starts her shift at four. Tonight's trivia is on romance fiction. I've been studying since I'm considering writing a romance now that the fantasy series is concluding. I've certainly had the right teacher to write a really good one. But some things should remain hidden in plain sight.

It has been a year since that blackout at Perk Up. It seems like yesterday, and last decade all at the same time. The presence of gratitude is always underpinning the love that surrounds us.

Max has something planned. I can feel it. There's a glint in his eyes, something unspoken, something just for us.

A reminder that love isn't just found once. It's something you wake up and choose, day after day.

And we will. Always. Because that is our truth.

THANK YOU

Thank You for Reading

If this story made you laugh, smile, swoon—or maybe even believe in love a little more—I hope you'll share it. Stories don't live in silence. They come alive when we pass them on, say, "This one mattered to me," and let our truth echo out into the world.

And today, one of the most powerful ways to speak up is through a review.

For a long time, people were taught to only speak up when something was wrong. But the world shifted—and our habits didn't. Reviews might feel like you're asking for attention, or trying to be an influencer, but that's not what they really are. **They're signals. Votes. Nudges to the algorithm that say, "More of this, please."**

And those nudges? They matter.

Not just to authors like me (though they do!)

But to the shape of the shelves, the stories we amplify, the kind of world we keep creating.

So if you liked this book, click the stars. Write even one sentence.

Say, *"Thanks, I enjoyed that."*

Say, *"More of this."*

Say something that helps shape *your* world.

In a time when so many people feel powerless to make a difference, this is one small but mighty way to start:

Live your truth—and leave a review.

With gratitude and a wink,

Sable Burns

A NOTE FROM SABLE

When I first published this story under the title *Brewing Truth*, I poured my heart into every scene—love, grief, laughter, and the quiet magic of finding your truth. But I've grown since then—as a writer, and as a person. And something in me whispered: "It's okay to laugh a little louder."

So I rebranded this book with a title that reflects what it truly is: a love story with sass, sweetness, emotional depth... and a whole lot of coffee-fueled banter.

Sunshine Wakes Up Grumpy isn't just a better name—it's a better mirror of where I am now as a storyteller. I still believe in soul-deep connection, found family, and the power of telling the truth. But I also believe in joy. In whimsy. In second chances that come with side-eye and stolen muffins.

Years ago, I bought a sign from an Amish store that read:

"Anything that makes you giggle, smile, or laugh... buy it or marry it."

That pretty much sums up my writing goals these days.

Thank you for joining me on this journey. For every reader who read this book when it was *Brewing Truth*, and for those discovering it now under a sunnier title—I'm so glad you're here. I hope it made you smile.

With love and a wink,

Sable Burns

COMING

He's Shirtless ...with Kids

She moved to start over. She didn't expect a shirtless single dad—and his wise, adorable kids—to rewrite her idea of home.

A standalone romantic comedy full of heart, heat, and healing.

Releasing on Amazon in August 2025.

Want to read it early and help shape its success?

Join **Sable's Sassy Street Team** for sneak peeks, early access, and fun behind-the-scenes extras.

It's free, it's low-key, and your voice makes a difference.

Sign up now at **SassyStreet.SableBurns.com**

ABOUT THE AUTHOR

SABLE BURNS

Sable Burns writes romantic comedies with soul, sass, and a side of spiritual swagger. Her stories flirt with tropes —but don't stop there. Expect heart, heat, and the kind of truth that sneaks up on you between stolen muffins and shirtless farmers.

She grew up with inspiring parents. Together, they proved that real love is both sacred and practical—best served with good coffee, working brakes, and a healthy dose of laughter.

Sable's characters don't just fall in love. They evolve, stumble, wake up, laugh, burn casseroles, and rewrite the rules—usually in that order.

She currently lives wherever the Wi-Fi works, writing stories for readers who want romance with meaning, mischief, and the occasional awkward open mic night.

Say hello at **SableBurns.com** or on social media **@SableBurnsWrites.**

Her books are available on Amazon and wherever books with feelings and punchlines are sold.